THE CALL OF THE TOAD

Other books by Günter Grass

The Tin Drum
Cat and Mouse
Dog Years
The Plebeians Rehearse the Uprising
Four Plays
Speak Out!
Local Anaesthetic
Max: A Play
From the Diary of a Snail
Inmarypraise
In the Egg and Other Poems
The Flounder
The Meeting at Telgte
Headbirths
Drawings and Words 1954–1977
On Writing and Politics 1967–1983
Etchings and Words 1972–1982
The Rat
Show Your Tongue
Two States – One Nation?

GÜNTER GRASS

The Call
of the Toad

Translated from the German by
RALPH MANHEIM

Secker & Warburg
London

First published in Great Britain in 1992
by Martin Secker & Warburg Limited
an imprint of Reed Consumer Books Ltd
Michelin House, 81 Fulham Road, London SW3 6RB
and Auckland, Melbourne, Singapore and Toronto

Translated from the German *Unkenrufe*

A CIP catalogue record for this book
is available at the British Library

ISBN 0 436 20064 3

Printed in England by Clays Ltd, St Ives plc

For Helen Wolff

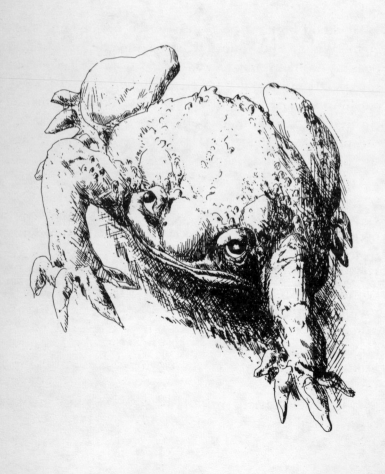

1

Chance put the widower next to the widow. Or maybe chance had nothing to do with it, for the story began on All Souls'. Be that as it may, the widow was already there when the widower tripped, stumbled, but did not fall.

He stood beside her. Shoe size ten beside shoe size eight. Widow and widower met facing the wares of a peasant woman: mushrooms heaped in a basket or spread out on newsprint, and three buckets filled with cut flowers. The woman was sitting to one side of the covered market in the midst of other truck farmers and the produce of their small plots: celery, rutabaga the size of a child's head, leeks and beets.

His diary confirms "All Souls' " and makes no mystery of the shoe sizes. What made him stumble was the edge of the curbstone. But the word chance does not occur in his diary. "It may have been fate that brought us together that day on the stroke of ten o'clock . . ." His attempt to give body to the third person, the silent intermediary, remains vague, as does his bumbling attempt to pin down the color of her head scarf: "Not exactly umber, more earth-brown than peat-black . . ." He has better luck with the brickwork of the monastery wall: "Infested with scab . . ." I have to imagine the rest.

Only a few varieties of cut flowers were left in the buckets: dahlias, asters, chrysanthemums. The basket was full of chestnuts. Four or five boletus mushrooms with slight slug damage were lined up on the title page of an ancient issue of the local paper *Głos Wybrzeża*. Also a bunch of parsley and a roll of wrapping paper. The cut flowers looked bedraggled: leftovers.

"No wonder," writes the widower, "that this and other stands in St. Dominic's Market seemed so poorly supplied. Flowers are much in demand on All Souls'. Even on All Saints', the day before, the demand often exceeds the supply . . ."

Though dahlias and chrysanthemums are showier, the widow decided in favor of asters. The widower was hesitant: Even if "the surprisingly late mushrooms" and chestnuts may have lured him to this particular stand, "I'm certain that after a moment's dismay—or could it have been the ringing of the bells?—I gave in to a special sort of seduction—no, call it magnetism . . ."

When from the three or four buckets the widow took a first, a second, then hesitantly a third aster, exchanged this last for another, and pulled out a fourth, which also had to be put back and replaced, the widower began to take asters from buckets and, no less picky-and-choosy than the widow, to exchange them; he chose rust-red asters just as she had chosen rust-red asters, though white and pale-violet ones were still available. The color harmony went to his head: "What gentle consonance. Like her, I am especially fond of the rust-red, how quietly they smolder . . ." Be that as it may, they both concentrated on rust-red asters until there were no more left in the buckets.

Neither widow nor widower had enough for a bouquet. She was ready to shove her meager selection back into one of the buckets when the so-called plot set in:

The widower handed the widow his rust-red spoils. He held them out, she took them. A wordless surrender. Never to be reversed. Inextinguishably burning asters. That made for a bond between them.

Stroke of ten: that was St. Catherine's. What I know about the place where they met is a combination of somewhat blurred but also ultradistinct knowledge about the locality through the widower's assiduous research, the product of which he has confided to his notes in dribs and drabs, for instance the fact that the octagonal seven-story-high fortress tower constitutes the northwest corner of the great town wall. It was nicknamed "Kiek in de Köck" (Peek in the Kitchen) after a smaller tower, which had been so called because it was next door to the Dominican monastery and offered an unobstructed view of the pots and pans in the monastery kitchen, which toward the end of the nineteenth century had fallen into such disrepair that trees and shrubs took root in its roofless interior (for which reason it was known for a time as "the flowerpot") and was torn down along with the rest of the monastery. Beginning in 1895, a covered market in the neo-Gothic style was built on the site. Named St. Dominic's Market, it survived the First and Second World wars and under its broad vaulted roof it still offers sometimes abundant, more often scant wares in six rows of stands: darning wool and smoked fish, American cigarettes and Polish mustard pickles, poppy-seed cake and pork that is much too fat, plastic toys from Hong Kong, cigarette lighters from all over the world, caraway seed and poppy seed in little bags, cheese spread and Perlon stockings.

Of the Dominican monastery nothing remains but the gloomy Church of St. Nikolai, its interior splendor resting entirely on black and gold: an afterglow of past atrocities. But the memory of the black-robed monastic order lives on only in the name of the market, as it does in that of a summer holiday named St. Dominic's Day, which since the late Middle Ages has survived all manner of political change and today attracts natives and tourists with street musicians, sausage stands, and all kinds of baubles and trumpery.

There between St. Dominic's Market and the Church of St. Nikolai, diagonally across from Peek in the Kitchen, widower and widow met at a time when the name "Kantor" on a hand-written sign identified the street floor of what was the former fortress tower as an exchange office. Teeming with customers spilling out through the wide open door; a blackboard at the entrance, brought up to date every hour, bore witness to the deplorable situation by indicating the steadily increasing number of zlotys obtainable for one American dollar.

The conversation began with "May I?" Wishing to pay not only for his own asters but for the whole now unified bouquet, and somewhat bewildered by the look of a currency so rich in zeroes, he drew banknotes from his wallet. The widow said with an accent, "You may nothing."

Her use of the foreign language may have lent additional sharpness to her negative reply, and if her next remark—"Is now pretty bouquet, yes?"—hadn't opened the door to conversation, the chance encounter between widower and widow might have begged comparison with the diminishing rate of the zloty.

He writes that while the widow was still paying, a conversation had started up about mushrooms, especially the late, belated boletus. The summer that had seemed endless and the mild autumn were cited as reasons. "But when I said something about global warming, she just laughed."

On a sunny to partly cloudy November day the two of them stood face to face. It seemed as though nothing could separate them from the flowers and the mushrooms. He had fallen for her, she for him. The widow laughed frequently. Her accented sentences were preceded and followed by laughter that seemed groundless, just a little prelude and postlude. The widower liked this almost-shrill laugh, for it says in his papers: "Like a bellbird, sometimes frightening, I have to admit, but I enjoy the sound of her laughter and never ask what seems to amuse her. Maybe she's laughing at me. But even that, even for her to think me laughable, gives me pleasure."

So they stood there. Or rather: they stand there a while and another little while, posing for me, to give me a chance to get used to them. If she was fashionably dressed—he thought her "too modishly done up," his tweed jacket and corduroy trousers gave him the look of shabby elegance that went with his camera case—a traveler for educational purposes, the better type of tourist. "If you won't accept the flowers, suppose we go back to the subject of the conversation we had just started, namely, mushrooms; will you permit me to select this one and perhaps this one, and make you a present of them? They look inviting."

She would. And she watched carefully to make sure that he wouldn't peel off too many bills for the marketwoman. "Here is all so crazy expensive," she cried. "But cheap perhaps for a gentleman with deutschmarks."

I wonder if he succeeded by mental arithmetic in interpreting the multidigital figures on the zloty bills, and whether he seriously, without fear of her laughter, thought of mentioning the reference to Chernobyl and global warming in his diary. It is certain that before buying the mushrooms he photographed them with a camera identified in his diary as a Japanese make. Because his snapshot is taken from above at a sharp angle, so sharp that it takes in the tips of the squatting marketwoman's shoes, this photo bears witness to the astonishing size of the boletus mushrooms. The stems of the two younger ones are wider than their high-arching hats; the wide brims of the older ones, now curled inward, now rolled outward, shade their fleshy, convoluted bodies. Lying together, the four of them turn their tall wide hats toward one another, but are so placed by the photographer that there is little overlap. Thus they form a still life. The widower may have made a remark to that effect. Or was it she who said, "Pretty, like still life"? In any case, the widow reached into her shoulder bag and found a string bag for the mushrooms, which the marketwoman wrapped in newspaper, throwing in a small bunch of parsley.

He wanted to carry the string bag. She held on tight. He said please. She said no, "Pay then carry is too much." A slight battle, a tussle, taking care, however, not to harm the contents of the string bag, kept the two of them in place, as if they were unwilling to leave the spot where they had met. Back and forth they pulled the string bag. Nor was he allowed to carry the asters. A well-rehearsed battle—they might have known each other for years. They might have done a duet in any opera; to whose music I can already guess.

They didn't lack an audience. The marketwoman looked on in silence, and there were witnesses all around: the octagonal fortress tower, with its latest subtenant, the overcrowded exchange bureau, and next to it the broad-beamed covered market that seemed bloated with mist, and the gloomy Dominican Church of St. Nikolai. And the peasant women in the adjoining stands, and finally the potential customers, all making up an impoverished crowd, driven only by their day-to-day needs, their scant funds diminishing in value by the hour, while widow and widower looked upon each other as money in the bank and showed no desire to separate.

"Now I go to different place."

"May I come with you, please?"

"Well, it's far."

"It would be a pleasure, really . . ."

"But it's cemetery where I go."

"I'll try not to bother you."

"All right, come."

She carried the bunch of asters. He carried the string bag. He gaunt and stooped. She with short percussive steps. He inclined to stumble, dragging his feet a little, a good head taller than she. She with pale blue eyes, he far-sighted. Her hair tinted Titian-red. His mustache salt-and-pepper. She took the scent of her aggressive perfume with her, he the mild counterpoint of his after-shave lotion.

They merged into the crowd outside the market. Now the widower's beret was gone. Shortly before the stroke of eleven from the top of St. Catherine's. And what about me? I have to follow the two of them.

When did he first collect reasons for sending bundles of his junk to my address? Couldn't he have sent them to some archive? Or if not an archive, why not some obliging journalist? What made the fool take me for an obliging fool?

This pile of letters, these canceled bills and dated photos. His scrapbook, now resembling a diary and now a time capsule stuffed with newspaper clippings and audio tapes—wouldn't it have been better to store all that with an archivist than with me? He should have known how easily I tell stories. Why did he nevertheless choose to bury me under his junk? And what made me run after him, no, after the two of them?

All because half a century ago, according to him, he and I sat ass by ass on the same school bench. He records: "The row of benches on the window side." I don't remember having him next to me. At St. Peter's High School. It's impossible. But I was in and out of that school in less than two years. I was always having to change schools. Different flavors of schoolboy sweat. Playgrounds with different kinds of bushes. I really don't know who doodled stick figures next to me where or when.

When I opened the package, his covering letter was on top. "I'm sure you'll be able to do something with this, precisely because it all borders on the incredible." The familiarity of his tone—did he think we were still in school? "I know you were no shining light in other subjects, but your essays soon made it clear . . ." I should have sent his junk back to him, but where to? "Actually you could have made up the whole story, but we did live through it, we did share an experience of more than ten years."

He dated his letter ahead: June 19, 1999. And toward the end, while otherwise expressing himself clearly, he writes about worldwide preparations to celebrate the millennium: "What useless expense! To think that a century dedicated to wars of annihilation, mass expulsions, and countless deaths by violence, is drawing to an end. But now, with the dawn of a new era, life will again . . ."

And so on. Enough of that. Only this much is true: They met on November 2, All Souls' Day, in sunny weather, a few days before the Wall came down. A cheap novel might have begun like this: The world, or at least a part of this immutable world, suddenly changed, no ceremony, in a total free-for-all. Everywhere monuments were overturned. My former classmate noted these often simultaneous acts of heroism in his diary, but he treated them as mere statements of fact. Reluctantly he made room, in parentheses, for events that demanded to be termed historic but irritated him because, as he wrote, "they distract attention from the essential, the idea, our great nation-reconciling idea . . ."

With this I am already in his, in her, story. Already I am talking as if I had been there, talking about his tweed jacket and her string bag; I put a beret on him because berets stand out—as do his corduroy trousers and her stiletto-heeled shoes—in the photographs in my possession, both black and white and color. Like their shoe sizes, her perfume as well as his after-shave he considered worth noting. The string bag is not an invention. Later, he describes lovingly, almost obsessively, every mesh of this useful object as if wishing to make it the basis of a cult. But the early introduction of the crocheted heirloom—the widow had inherited it from her mother—appearing with the purchase of the mushrooms, is my contribution, as is the anticipated beret.

As an art historian and a professor to boot, he could not have done otherwise: Just as he had made memorial slabs and tombstones, sarcophagi and epitaphs, ossuaries and crypts legible by rubbing, and had identified motheaten funeral banners—which traditionally furnish brick Gothic churches in the Baltic area—by their heraldry and rendered them eloquent by condensed histories of once eminent patrician families, so did he make the widow's string bags (there wasn't just this one, there were half a dozen) witnesses of a past culture superseded by ugly oilcloth carry-alls and radically devalued by plastic bags.

"Four of the string bags are crocheted," he writes, "two knotted by hand as fishnets used to be. Of the crocheted ones, one is solid moss-green . . ."

And just as, in his doctoral dissertation, he had interpreted the three thistles and five roses in the bushlike coat-of-arms of seventeenth-century theologian Aegidius Strauch—taken from the bas-relief of a tombstone in the Church of the Holy Trinity, whose priest Strauch had been—and related them to the vicissitudes of an embattled life (Strauch had spent years in prison), so he quibbled and fussed over the widow's inherited string bags. Learning that she always carried two of her six in her calfskin shoulder bag, he attributed this precaution to the shortages prevailing in all East Bloc countries: "Suddenly there's cauliflower or cucumbers to be had somewhere, or a peddler produces bananas from the trunk of his Polski Fiat. That's when a string bag comes in handy, for plastic bags are still a rarity in the East."

He then goes on, for two pages, to deplore the demise of handmade products and the triumph of the Western synthetic bag as a further symptom of human self-abasement. It is only toward the end of his plaint that he remembers his affection for the widow's string bags, which he finds loaded with significance. And when mushrooms were being bought, I anticipated the presence of one of these string bags, to wit, the solid-color crocheted one.

I let the widower carry the heirloom and must admit that as he shuffles along slightly stooped beside the widow, not only his beret but the string bag as well is most becoming to him, as though he and not she had inherited it, as though the Japanese camera had been only borrowed and from now on he would carry his specialized literature, his thick tomes on Baroque iconology, in a crocheted or knotted string bag, on his way, for instance, to Ruhr University.

Though I fail to remember a classmate by his name, he seems an old acquaintance with his ingrained eccentricities and first signs of geriatric ailments. And the widow, too, as beside him she makes her way slowly cemeteryward, takes shape by virtue of sheer willpower. She'll teach him to stop shuffling.

A long but enjoyable walk, for the widow subdivided it by explaining everything in short, concise sentences and letting out an occasional burst of her bellbird laughter. By the time they had made their way from St. Catherine's and the Big Mill, where the Radaune canal carries very little water—"Stinks," she said, "but what doesn't around here!"—and came in sight of the high-rise Hotel Hevelius, she knew: "I bet gentleman from West has view of city from so high."

The widower opened up as they approached the library, and was still talking as they passed the former St. Peter's High School—both Prussian neo-Gothic structures spared by the war. He admitted that he had been precocious and a bookworm, referred to the barn still being operated as a school as "my old Alma M.," a term he explained most elaborately. And they had passed the Church of St. James before he finished explaining what books in the reading room of the municipal library had infected and at the same time inoculated him. "You can't imagine how I devoured books, every single volume of the Knackfuss monographs on artists . . ."

And then outside the gate of the Lenin Shipyard—just before it was renamed—the square with the three towering crosses spread out before them, where three anchors hung crucified.

"That was Solidarność," the widow said, and added a sentence designed to mitigate the brusqueness of her obituary. "But we Poles can still build monuments. Everywhere martyrs and statues of martyrs." Then she fell silent, without laughter before or after.

In this sentence the widower thought he detected "a bitterness bordering on despair." All she had left were gestures. Then she extracted an aster from the bouquet, added it to the flowers heaped up in front of the memorial wall, and at the widower's request translated, line for line, the poem by Czesław Miłosz inscribed on the monument: a stern poem in praise of futility. Thereupon she associated herself and her family with the poet and his family—all refugees driven from the East to an uncertain West. "We had to leave Wilno, like you all had to leave here."

Still on the square, but already moving, she lit a cigarette.

To abbreviate their walk to the cemetery: Smoking, the widow led the widower out of the city across a bridge, which since the demolition of the fortifications and the construction of the main railroad station arches over all the railroad tracks leading westward from Danzig or Gdańsk or eastward to Gdańsk or Danzig. Since German and Polish spellings are used interchangeably in the widower's notes, I shall follow his irresolute nomenclature and say not Brama Oliwska but: The widow led him out of the city to the Olivaer Tor streetcar stop; then, via the left fork of the highway to Kartuzy, up the gently sloping Hagelsberg to the service station for tourists intent on lead-free gasoline, across from which there is an old cemetery shaded by beeches and lindens, which formerly belonged to the parishes of Corpus Christi, further up to those of St. Joseph and St. Bridget, and on the western edge to various "nonsectarian" religious congregations. Overcrowded for years, it now seemed abandoned. No open gate provided access. They walked along a fence overgrown with shrubbery. Across from the adjacent military cemetery was a Red Army war memorial, on whose lawn some teenagers were playing soccer. The widow knew a hole in the fence.

Once inside—under trees and among overgrown single and double graves—the widower proffered a formal introduction: "Please allow me to introduce myself, as I should have done long ago: My name is Alexander Reschke."

The widow's laughter took time, and must have struck him as out of place, especially here among tombs. Nevertheless, still laughing, she followed suit: "Alexandra Piątkowska."

This entry in Reschke's diary made it clear that fate had a hand in it. What difference does it make that his former classmate, whose only function here is that of a reporter, finds this consonance too much in harmony, suitable at best for an operetta on the well-known model, all right for fairy-tale characters but not for this pair thrown together by chance. But it's got to be Alexander and Alexandra; after all it's their story.

The intimacy of the names, however, must also have alarmed both the widower and the widow, as I have been calling them up to now, though they couldn't have known that they were meeting in a widowed state. Determined to be independent, Alexandra Piątkowska walked into the cemetery, disappeared among tombstones, reappeared, disappeared, reappeared. Alexander Reschke also kept his distance. Avoiding the rustling autumn leaves, he shuffled along moss-covered paths, his beret now gone, now seen again. As though loitering, he hesitated before one tombstone, then another: plenty of diabase and highly polished granite, little sandstone, marble, or shell limestone.

All the stones bore Polish names and indicated dates of death beginning in the late fifties, all, that is, except the numerous children's graves lined up in a field to one side and dated 1946, the plague year. Wooden crosses and headstones. The silence under the cemetery trees was not lessened by the soccer-playing children, or even by the sounds of the service station. I read: "Here I have again grasped the meaning of the words 'quiet as a tomb.' "

Nevertheless, Alexander Reschke was looking for something. On the edge of the cemetery he found two crooked tombstones and then two more, overgrown with weeds, and he had a hard time deciphering what was

14

on them. Death dates from the early twenties to the mid-forties, and inscriptions above the names—"Here Rests in God," "Death Is the Gateway to Life," or "Here Lie Our Dear Mommy and Granny"—evoked the distant past of this burial ground. Reschke notes: "These stones, too, are made of the usual material, diabase and black Swedish granite."

For a while, I leave him with the remaining tombstones. Long enough for Pani Piątkowska to deposit the bunch of asters in a vase on her parents' grave. This double grave, I copy, is bordered by box trees, and less neglected than the neighboring graves. Her father died in '58, her mother in '54. They were both under seventy. I take note of All Souls' activity in all areas of the cemetery. Here and there hurricane lamps on tombstones indicate that visitors have come and gone.

But widow and widower paid no attention to them.

"I was with Mama and Papa. My husband is in Sopot Forest Cemetery." Alexandra Piątkowska said this as she joined Alexander Reschke, whom the other tombstones had distracted from the present time; the voice behind and to one side of him may have startled him; in any case it brought him back.

The pair again. Because she had made it known that she was a widow, he should have talked about the death of his wife and also about the early, too early, deaths of his parents. Instead, he provided her with his professional status, identified himself as a professor of art history lecturing in the Ruhr, and for completeness' sake brought in the title of his doctoral dissertation submitted and accepted many years before—Memorial Slabs and Epitaphs in the Churches of Danzig—and only then, abruptly, dated the death of his wife: "Edith died five years ago."

15

The widow said nothing. Then she came closer, and another step closer, to the crooked tombstones that the widower had found worthy of notice. Suddenly, and too loudly for a cemetery, she exploded: "Disgraceful Poland! Everything with German on it they cleaned out. Here and other places, in Sopot Forest Cemetery too. For dead no peace. Wiped out everything. After the war and later. Worse even than Russians. They call it politics. Plain criminals, I say."

As far as I can make out from Reschke's notes, he tried to soothe the widow by putting the blame on the invasion of Poland, the consequences of the war, and the exaggerated nationalism on all sides, roughly in that order. Yes, he said, the desecration of a cemetery borders on barbarism. He, too, he had to admit, was saddened by these forgotten tombstones. One should expect human beings to deal more humanly with the dead. After all, the grave, and its artistic execution, is the last authentic expression of a person. One has to consider, however, that most of the memorial tombs of German patrician families in the main city churches had been protected from vandalism. Yes, yes, he understood the persistence of her anger. It was only natural that people should want to know that the graves of their closest relatives were in good condition. On his first postwar visit to Gdańsk—"That was in the spring of '58, when I was working on my dissertation"—he had wanted to visit the graves of his paternal grandparents in the United Cemeteries. Yes indeed, it was awful; the place seemed to have been laid waste out of sheer malice. "A terrible sight! Believe me, Frau Piątkowska, I understand your indignation. Nothing was left for me but grief, which, it is true, can also be viewed in the context

16

of facts that are a matter of historical record. After all, such barbarity was first perpetrated by us. Not to mention all our other unspeakable crimes . . ."

The two of them were made for such conversation. He was a master of the lofty tone; she had the gift of righteous indignation. Under towering beeches and lindens, which had survived all manner of political vicissitude, widow and widower agreed that politics was a curse and had to stop somewhere, and that it was most certainly out of place in cemeteries. "Yes," she cried, "dead enemy no longer enemy."

They called each other Herr Reschke and Frau Piątkowska. Relaxed after their exchange of views, they suddenly noticed that all around them other celebrants of All Souls' Day were paying their respects to their dead with flowers and hurricane lamps. And only then did the widow make the remark that the widower noted verbatim in his diary: "Naturally Mama and Papa prefer to lie in Wilno cemetery than here, where everything strange was and is."

Was it these words that sparked it off? Or did ravished tombstones continue to weigh on their cemetery conversation? My former classmate and now doctor of philosophy Alexander Reschke, that past master of elevated discourse, has indeed conveyed to me a whole anthology of somber images—"The autumnal trees provided a wordless commentary in the abode of transience . . ." or: "Thus the spreading ivy has survived the violent depredation of the cemetery and in its own way remained victorious if not immortal . . ."—but only after a critical observation (Did she absolutely have to smoke in a cemetery?) does he confess: "Why do I hesitate to tell Alexandra of my parents' boundless if seldom expressed hope of being allowed to rest in their native soil, though neither of them had any hope of returning in their lifetime? Like Alexandra's parents, they had to accept their foreign surroundings."

The two of them lingered. Their cemetery talk went on and on. Finally they found a cast-iron bench which had managed to survive along with the ivy. They sat in the shelter of yew trees. According to Reschke's entries, the teenagers had tired of their soccer game on the lawn in front of the Soviet military cemetery; only the large service station continued to intrude into their world. And smoking, still smoking, as though memory were stimulated by puffing at cigarettes, Alexandra, as she is called in his papers from this point on, talked about her childhood and youth in Wilno, as Vilnius or Wilna is called in Polish. "Piłsudski took it from Lithuania and gave to Poland. Was white and gold from Baroque. And all over beautiful city was woods, everywhere woods." Then after amusing tales of school, with girlfriends in them, two of them Jewish, and country vacations devoted to rounding up potato bugs, she broke off, and said, "But the war was terrible in Wilno. I still see in street dead people lying."

Again, service station sounds. No birds in the cemetery trees. The smoker, the nonsmoker. The two of them on the cast-iron bench. And then suddenly, because suddenness was her way, and because she wanted to add one more similarity to those of their first names and their widowhood, she surprised him with a declaration about her profession: "I went to same faculty as gentleman. But only six semesters of art history and professorship no chance. But plenty practical experience to make up for it."

18

Reschke learned that Piątkowska had worked as a restorer for a good thirty years and that her specialty was gilding. "All kinds. Matte gilding and bright gilding with gold leaf and ducat gold. Not just Baroque angels, also burnish gilding on marble stucco. Also good at carved rococo altars. All kinds of altars. Three dozen altars I gilded. In Dominican church and all over. We get material from Dresden, gold leaf from People-Owned Gold-Beating Works . . ."

So the iconographer and the gildress of ornate emblems talked shop under cemetery trees that were steadily losing their leaves. He spoke of St. Mary's thirty-eight epitaphs listed by Curicke; she described her gilding work on an epitaph dating from 1588, which had been given up for lost some years ago. He held forth on Dutch mannerism; she decided that the half horse on a red field and the three lilies on blue in the arms of Jakobus Schadius were well worth gilding. He praised the anatomy of the skeletons rising from tombs in the relief; she reminded him of the golden initials on black in the lower broad oval. He lured her downstairs into crypts; she led him from altar to altar in the Church of St. Nikolai.

Never amid tombstones was there so much talk about gold grounds, polished gold, hand gilding, and the tools and accessories of the trade. According to Reschke, who went back as far as the tombs of the pharaohs, gold should have been named the color of the dead: gold on black. This transfiguration, the shimmering between red gold and green gold. "The golden luster of death!" cried Reschke, showing off for all he was worth.

It was not until Piątkowska started talking about the work which some years ago had familiarized her with every detail of the organ screen in the Church of St.

John (evacuated and therefore saved during the war), that her laughter won the upper hand. "More of that we need. You buy with deutschmarks a brand-new organ for Marii Panny Church. We restore old screen with gold leaf that doesn't cost much."

They fell silent. Or rather, I assume silence between them. But this demonstration of how Germans and Poles could collaborate on organs and organ screens rekindled enthusiasm. "That is how it must be!" said the professor. And in his diary noted: "Why can't it be the same in other fields?"

Two or three more cigarettes may have been sacrificed to the cemetery mood. Perhaps her idea first took form and then went up in cigarette smoke. However, it was in the air, demanding to be seized.

Reschke writes that Alexandra then led him, no, invited him to the grave of her parents: "I am pleased if you come to grave of Mama and Papa."

As they stood facing the two hurricane lamps on either side of the vase with the rust-red asters on the broad granite tomb, which bore, incidentally, a freshly gilded inscription—it was the widow who gave the plot direction. As though maternal advice had reached her from the tomb, she pointed at the crocheted heirloom that the professor was still holding, released a short burst of laughter, and said, "Now I make us mushrooms, with parsley chopped fine."

Through the hole in the cemetery fence they crossed into the early afternoon of the present day. Now the widow was carrying the string bag. The widower, obliged to give in, once again ventured no allusion to Chernobyl and its consequences.

———

They took the streetcar, rode past Central Station to High Gate, now called Brama Wyżynna. Alexandra Piątkowska lived on ul. Ogarna, which runs to the right and parallels Langgasse, and which once was Hundegasse, or Dog Street. This street, destroyed by fire like the rest of the city toward the end of the war, with only the tatters of house fronts left, was rebuilt with admirable fidelity during the fifties and, like all the main and side streets of the resurrected city, is in need of thorough restoration: molding crumbling on all sides, blistering plaster peeling. Sulfurous fumes blown from the harbor had disfigured all the pedimental figures hewn in stone, aged them before their time. Scaffolding had been placed against a few façades that seemed especially decrepit. I read: "There will never be an end to this much-admired, expensively maintained illusion."

Since housing in the historic areas of the Old City and Right City was at all times in demand and not allotted without political considerations, Piątkowska's membership in the Polish United Workers' Party through the early eighties, and to an even greater degree the fact that she had been decorated for her work as restorer, must have helped. She had been living there since the mid-seventies. Before that she, her son, and her husband, until her husband's early retirement—he had been with the merchant marine—occupied two rooms in a housing development between Sopot and Adlershorst (eyrie), now Orlowo, a long trip to her place of work in the inner city. Understandably, she put in a complaint with the Party. As a member of long standing—since 1953—she believed, especially in view of her participation in the forthcoming International Youth Games in Bucharest, that she was entitled to lodgings closer to her work. At that time the workshops of the Restorers and Gilders were in Green Gate, a Renaissance structure at the east end of Long Street and Long Market and fronting the River Mottlau.

A few years after the move to Hundegasse her husband died of leukemia. And when, in the late eighties, the president proclaimed martial law and Witold, her late-born only son, went to the West to study in Bremen, the widow was alone but not unhappy in the once cramped, now spacious apartment.

Unlike any other building on Hundegasse, the semi-detached house at ul. Ogarna 78/79 had a front terrace, with steps leading down to the street. During the period of martial law, the government press agency Polska Agencja Interpress had moved into the ground floor, with an entrance of its own, and was now trying to obtain recognition as a private organization. On the street side the spacious terrace had reliefs in sandstone—rococo ornaments and cupids at play. Reschke deplored their condition: "One would like to see these cheerful records of bourgeois culture protected against erosion and moss."

The third-floor apartment was situated at the end of the street, which like all other east-west streets in Right City ends at the Mottlau, from which it is separated by a gate. The slender tower of the Town Hall and the blunt tower of St. Mary's could be seen from the living-room window, though the upper third of both was cut off by the gables of the house across the street. The son's room, now Piątkowska's workroom, looked out over Schnellstrasse to the south. On that side, all that remained of a suburb originally known as Poggenpfuhl (Frog Pond) was the Church of St. Peter. The widow

22

showed the widower the bedroom, which also had a southern exposure, and the adjoining bathroom. In the kitchen, next to the living room, Alexandra Piątkowska said, "You see, sir, I live in luxury, compared with average."

Why, damn it, did I go along? What makes me run after him? And what business have I in cemeteries and on Hundegasse? Why am I involved in his speculations in the first place? Perhaps because the widow . . .

In his notes, immediately after describing the three-room apartment, Reschke thought back on the way her eyes had affected him: "Under the cemetery trees the pale blue of her eyes changed to bright blue, their brightness enhanced by the black of her too heavily made-up eyelashes. Like a tangle of spears, they fenced the upper and lower lids. And then a network of laugh wrinkles . . ." Only then did he quote his remarks to her on living conditions in the West. "I, too, since the death of my wife—it was cancer—and the departure of my three daughters—have been living in a rather spacious three-room studio-type apartment, in an unattractive new building, it is true, with a mediocre view. An industrial landscape, relieved, to be sure, by quite a few green spaces . . ."

Here the long-drawn-out, tragic-sounding chimes from the Rathaus tower invaded the kitchen, interrupting Reschke's comparison of Western and Eastern living conditions. They will often be interrupted just as emphatically. After the last peel the widow commented, "A bit loud. But you get used to it."

From his diary I know that for chopping parsley she tied on a kitchen apron. She cleaned the four thick-bellied, broad-brimmed, humpbacked mushrooms, whose stems were neither wooden nor wormeaten. Little waste. Apart from the mossy lining of the hats, negligible traces of slug damage. He then insisted on helping her peel potatoes. Easy for him, he said, as he had done it since the death of his wife.

The smell of the mushrooms invaded the kitchen and prompted them both to search for appropriate descriptive terms. I cannot tell from Reschke's book whether he or she first ventured the words "aphrodisiac smell." The boletus mushrooms reminded him of his childhood, when he and his maternal grandmother went looking for chanterelles in the mixed forest around Saskoschin. "Such memories stay with one longer than any of the mushroom dishes served in Italian restaurants, most recently in Bologna, when my wife and I . . ."

She regretted that she had never been to Italy, but long stays in West Germany and Belgium had made up for it. "Polish restorers bring hard currency. Good for export, like fattened Polish geese. I worked in Trier, Cologne, and Antwerp . . ."

"She sometimes uses the kitchen as a workshop," he writes, and points to a shelf crowded with bottles, cans, and utensils. The mushrooms had drowned the originally strong smell of varnish as well as "Alexandra's perfume."

After putting the potatoes in a pot to boil, the widow melted butter in a frying pan and cut the mushrooms into quarter-inch slices which she brought to a sizzle over a medium flame. The widower learned to pronounce *masło*, the Polish word for butter. Now she was smoking again, over the stove; that bothered him. He thought it worth noting that not only he in peeling potatoes but she in cleaning mushrooms had resorted to their glasses. At home, she wore hers on a plaited silk string around her neck. I see him opening an elegant, old-fashioned case, grasping the frame, opening it, breathing on the lenses, rubbing them, putting the glasses on, taking them off, folding them, putting them back into the case, and closing it. Her frame—"beautiful present I made myself in Antwerp"—is trimmed with rhinestones, which is supposed to look fetching. His round, horn-rimmed lenses give him a scholarly look. Now they both take off their glasses. Later, when he anticipates the turn of the millennium with his leaps in time, he writes: "Walking with a cane, almost blind . . ."

At first the widow wanted to set the oilcloth-covered kitchen table. "We eat here, yes? Kitchen always cozy." Then decided on the living room after all. Furniture dating from the sixties, some of it rustic. A couch and two easy chairs. The bookcase overloaded and slightly crooked. On the walls framed reproductions of Old Flemish masters, but also a spooky Ensor: Christ's entry into Brussels. On the bulletin board an assortment of photos: the Porta Nigra, Antwerp City Hall, the guildhalls. Among crime novels and Polish postwar literature, a few cumbersome nautical tomes. The tablecloth is of Kashubian linen with an embroidered tulip pattern. The photographs on the glassed-in dish cupboard show the widow's husband in the uniform of the merchant marine; the widow and her husband on the Sopot pier; mother and son at the door of the Oliwa Castle Church, the mother, as Reschke writes, laughing and "starry-eyed," the son morose and aloof; the officer in the administration of the merchant marine looking bored.

"You see," says Piątkowska while serving the steaming dishes, "my husband big. Almost two heads taller."

For almost too long the widower was lost in contemplation of the photographs on Sopot Pier. "Now come and eat; otherwise gets cold."

They sat facing each other. A bottle of Bulgarian red wine was drained. As a finishing touch the widow had stirred cream into the mushrooms, added a dash of pepper, and topped the floury and crumbling boiled potatoes with chopped parsley. Refilling their glasses, Reschke spilled a little. The spot of red wine provoked laughter. Salt was sprinkled on it. Again the electronic chimes from the Town Hall; tragic heroic. "In famous words by Maria Konopnicka," said the widow. "We will never let go the land from where our people come . . ."

No mushrooms were left over. And not until the coffee, served in demitasses and gritty the way Poles like it, were smoker and nonsmoker caught up again in their cemetery conversation.

It started with school stories. Wilno weighed heavily. "Lyceum I was not allowed to attend." They took away my two girlfriends. And Papa lost sugar factory . . ."

It was then that Reschke added another twist of fate, a rather banal coincidence I would call it: he confessed that he and his parents and his brothers had lived diagonally across the street, on Hundegasse, in that plain gabled house without a front terrace, or rather in the original of that house. His father had been a postal official in the period between the wars and had had his desk in the Central Post Office only a block away. "Incidentally, the vault of my paternal grandparents, located in the central aisle of the United Cemeteries, had already been reserved for my parents . . ."

"The same with Mama and Papa," the widow cried.

"They know always where their last resting place in Wilno cemetery will be . . ."

That was when it clicked, when the coin fell. Painlessly a thought was born. Widow and widower together composed an idea whose simple melody was to prove extremely catching, so great was its universal human appeal, in Polish as well as in German.

It must have been a long conversation over several brewings of coffee and several invasions of the Town Hall chimes, which shortly before the stroke of nine kindled this idea, declared it to be their own, and finally expanded it into a thing that would reconcile the nations. She was capable of enthusiasm, he more inclined to skepticism. Begging her to be patient, he took "The Century of Expulsions" as his theme and spoke of all those who had been driven out and forcibly resettled, all those who had fled, all the Armenians and Crimean Tatars, Jews and Palestinians, Bangladeshis and Pakistanis, Estonians and Latvians, Poles and finally Germans who had fled west with bag and baggage. "Many died on the way. Typhus, hunger, the cold. And the numberless dead. Millions. No one knows where their bodies are. Buried by the roadside. Individual graves and mass graves. Sometimes only ashes. Death factories. Genocide, the still unfathomable crime. Therefore today, on All Souls' Day, we should . . ."

Then Reschke spoke of man's need to be laid to rest in the place where his home was before flight, expulsion, or forced resettlement; where he had assumed his home to be, where he sought and found it, where it had always been, since his birth. He said: "What we call home means more to us than such concepts as fatherland or nation, and that is why so many of us—not all, to be sure, but more and more as we grow older—long to be buried in our home soil. A natural longing which for the most part remains cruelly unfulfilled, as only too often circumstances stand in the way of its fulfillment. We should, however, call it a natural right, and it should at long last be included in the catalog of human rights. No, I am not referring to the right to a homeland demanded by our refugees' associations. Our true home has been lost to us forever, a consequence of our own crimes—but the right of the dead to return is something that could and should be urged."

I presume that Professor Reschke uttered these and other thoughts about death and about man's last resting place while striding back and forth in Piątkowska's living room as though addressing a large auditorium. He went on for quite a while before coming to the point, and then cast doubt on the daring statements that had just been made.

That was not her way. Alexandra Piątkowska wanted everything to be clear and simple. "What you mean could, should? Fancy conditionals. I learned all that. It has to be: must, will. Will do this immediately. Will say out loud where politics must stop and human rights must begin, when man is dead with no money only last wish in pocket, as Mama and Papa said as long as they lived, because they were foreigners still, even if Mama sometimes cried out on excursions to Kashubian hills: 'As beautiful here as at home!'"

When the widow was excited—and all that coffee and especially the professor's long, involved sentences must have stirred her up considerably—she dropped articles and stumbled over her word order more than usual. The report that Reschke saddled me with demands that

I quote her verbatim. Now that I'm in it, it's too late to retreat. Moreover, the covering letter contains allusions that compromise me. He claims, for instance, that I won his admiration and that of the other students by swallowing a live toad. All right, I'll swallow another, as demanded.

Reschke must have asked Piątkowska, most likely in the market and at the latest in the cemetery, how she came to know German so well—complimenting her of course. It isn't until later that his diary supplies her precise answer . . . " 'Mother no. Father spoke German.' In Poznań, along with art history she majored in Germanic studies. Her husband, who spoke English fluently as well as German, must have been after her like a drill sergeant. 'Every mistake he corrected, that's the way he was.' Witold, their son, benefited by this. 'Only,' said Alexandra, 'he talks too complicated, much too complicated.' She couldn't be accused of that. True enough. No one who listened to her could fail to recognise that my gildress, exported in exchange for hard currency, had benefited by a number of stays abroad. She says 'Three months Cologne, four months Trier. Every time something stick.' She even sang some Cologne carnival songs recently when we drove to the Island to do taping."

That was later, when her idea had acquired its own momentum. But after the first spirited beginning, when she came to the rights of the dead, Piątkowska soon ran short of words. Sentences and nouns liberated from articles made their way through Polish interjections and exclamations: "Last resting place must sanctity have . . . Finally reconciliation will be . . . I learned German

word: *Friedhofsordnung . . . Niemiecki porządek!* Fine.
Dobrze. We make German-Polish cemetery ordnung . . .
only, we must learn to avoid Polish ordnung and stick
to German ordnung."

I assume a second bottle of Bulgarian red wine from
the widow's kitchen cupboard. In any case, Reschke's
diary assures us of repeated laughter on Piątkowska's
part. He was beginning to count her laugh-wrinkles.
"That wreath of rays!" She must have had plenty to
laugh about. True, no sooner had the idea taken wing,
than they spoke of nothing but funeral establishments,
efficient burials, the transportation of dead bodies, and
the difficulties to be expected in connection with the
shipment of coffins and urns, but Alexandra thought
all that, the name of their shared idea included, worth
a burst of before or after laughter, her bellbird laughter. His proposal was: The Polish-German Cemetery
Association. She, "because Germans are rich and must
be first always," thought her counterproposal, The
German-Polish Cemetery Association, much better.

Finally, because Wilno had to be taken into consideration, they agreed to give the middle position to the
richest and the first: The Polish-German-Lithuanian
Cemetery Association, later called PGLCA, was founded
November 2, 1989, or announced if not actually
founded. Lacking were such indispensables as additional founding members, a draft contract with statutes
and bylaws, a board of directors, capitalization, and a
bank account.

Apparently there was no more red wine or any vodka
in the house, but there seems to have been some honey
liqueur at the bottom of a bottle—as though put aside
for the occasion—just enough for two little glasses. With
that they drank to the new organization. He claims that

he tried to kiss her hand in the Polish manner. She didn't laugh. Finally, the widower took his leave after the widow dismissed him—"Now we on it sleep"—and for the first time addressed him by name. "Won't we, Aleksander?" "Yes, Alexandra," he said in the doorway. "We will, we will sleep on it."

2

It is possible that just once, to show off or because that's what the bored rabble wanted to see and I am good-natured, I actually did swallow a toad. In a country boarding school or some such place. Frogs I can remember, I swallowed them on request in playing fields or beside the Striessbach, vomited them up, and let them hop away. Sometimes three or four at a time. But he claims to have seen me swallow a full-grown toad, a red-bellied toad, without gagging, swallow it a hundred percent with no returns.

That was a hit, Reschke writes. The loony with his loony idea claims to remember me better than I care to be remembered; he claims that I distributed condoms—known as merry widows—in class. Just as I'm ready to go somewhere entirely different, taking with me what words I have left, he drags me back into the old school fug. "Do you remember, just after Stalingrad, old Dr. Korngiebel suddenly turning up without his Party badge . . ." It's possible that early in '43 I met one of his cousins several times—name of Hildchen, he's sure of that—outside the main entrance to St. Dominic's Market. Always after school: Hildchen and me. But here I'm trying to tell you about Alexander and Alexandra. She has just dismissed him after two glasses of honey liqueur at the door of her apartment . . .

And now he's standing on the terrace, alone with

himself. Since in my schooldays I ran myself ragged in the routes that Reschke claims to have covered, for which reason the city faithfully rebuilt from the ruins remains a city where I can find my way in my sleep, and since his detour via Beutlergasse to St. Mary's could have been my detour, I follow him to the Orbis-Hotel Hevelius, adapt to his shuffling gait, make myself his night shadow and echo.

Alexander Reschke avoided going by the covered market. The loneliness and the stagnant smell might have spoiled his exultant mood. He proceeded carefully. I hear him humming: something between *Eine kleine Nachtmusik* and the *Holberg Suite*. He rounded the huge late-Gothic building in a clockwise arc, stopped, hesitated when the Frauengasse opened its front terraces before him, was tempted to drop into a bar, probably the Actors' Club, whose wide-open door announced that it was doing business, for another little drink, resisted the temptation, kept faith with his exultant mood and headed for his hotel.

But once at the Hevelius, he did not feel like going to his room on the fourteenth floor. He walked around the lobby but kept away from the hotel bar. Once again he passed the unconcerned porter and went out into the night with its smell of sulfur. Finally making up his mind, though not without the usual misgivings, he shuffled purposefully in the direction of a bar, a small, scrupulously restored half-timbered little house which was quaintly set in the bushes along the bank of the Radaune, behind the dauntingly tall hotel.

The widowed professor had often stopped here on earlier visits to the city—which despite its poverty was still exceedingly rich in towers—in the days when his studies still amused him and when several religious edifices, such as St. Peter's, the church most recently reclaimed from the rubble, promised the discovery of new memorial slabs.

"No, Alexandra," he said, after a whiff of the Radaune, "it always stank, at least it did in my schooldays." Business was slow, and there was room at the bar. Alexander Reschke later made a note of his "strong though undefined sense that this special day was not yet over. There was more on the program, another scene in the play, which might be pleasant or disturbing. In any case, I felt a curiosity mingled with foreboding. My prescience, my special gift of seeing in retrospect things to come, had been aroused."

Nevertheless, his barroom acquaintance struck him at first as "merely odd." Reschke was addressed across three empty barstools by a gentleman on his left, dressed like a Southeast Asian diplomat, whose strangely gargling English suggested a Pakistani or Indian with a university education. The dainty but obviously energetic man in the blue-gray Nehru jacket introduced himself as the holder of a British passport, born in Pakistan, who after his flight from that country had grown up in Bombay, but one branch of his far-flung family was at present located in Dacca and another branch in Calcutta; he therefore regarded himself as more or less a Bengali, even though he had studied economics and nineteenth-century English literature in Cambridge and had acquired his first business experience in London, chiefly in the field of transportation. He moved one stool closer and said—I quote freely from Reschke's translation: "Please look upon me as a person with nine hundred and fifty million human beings, soon a round billion, behind him."

Reschke, too, moved a stool closer, until there was

only one seat between them. Physical proof of the cosmopolitan's figures was not in sight. But since the widower had spent the whole day and part of the night in conversation with the widow, preoccupied by the dead and their last wishes, he may have been appalled by this image but was pleased, at the same time, to meet someone who had so many living people behind him. I imagine Reschke in the confines of the tiny bar, overwhelmed by the futuristic sight of space-devouring multitudes.

Reschke now introduced himself, not forgetting to mention his professional activity or the endless diversity of Baroque emblems. As his models, he mentioned such great names as Cassirer and Panofsky, and said that when he had studied in London, the Warburg Institute proved invaluable for his research. He then tried to make a show of wit: commenting on the most recent political changes, he called the possible reunification of all the Germans "a German one-pot meal." At the same time, he admitted that the concentration of eighty million of his hard-working compatriots in the very center of Europe worried him a little. "That may not sound like much compared to your impressive figures. Nevertheless, the mind boggles."

Mr. Chatterjee, who like Reschke was drinking Export beer, was soon able to dispel his new friend's anxieties. "As long as the old European order prevails, there will indeed be problems. But it won't last. As the ancient Greeks knew, all is flux. We shall come. We will have to come, because it's getting a little cramped over there. Everybody pushes everybody else; the end will be one great push that will be impossible to stop. Several hundred thousand are already on their way. Not all of them will make it. But still others are packing their bags. Regard me, if you please, as a forerunner or billeting officer of the future world society, in which the egocentric worries of your compatriots will be lost. Even the Poles, who just want to be Poles, always Poles and never anything else, will learn that next to the Black Madonna of Częstochowa there is room for another black divinity, because of course we will bring our beloved and feared Mother Kali with us—she has already taken up residence in London."

Raising his beer glass, Reschke agreed. "I take a similar view." Indeed, his highest hopes were not confirmed by this proof of what he called "Asia's silent invasion." "Nothing," he cried, "is more to be desired than the symbiosis of Kali and Mary, than a double altar consecrated to both."

Although in his scholarly pursuits the professor had specialized in memorial slabs, he had a general idea of Hindu theology, and even knew the goddess Kali under the names of Durga and Parvati. It was not just to be polite that he said he had seen this or something of the sort coming. He hoped that the international amalgamation process would ultimately lead to an exchange of cultures. A future world culture would not be too different from the world society envisioned by Mr. Chatterjee.

At first, Reschke's incorrigible English and the Bengali version of the once dominant colonial language were too incompatible. It was only when the girl behind the bar, described by Reschke as pretty, asked the two gentlemen in her Polish-accented school English whether they wanted more German beer, and when Chatterjee answered in Polish and then asked, in a startling German, if he could buy the professor another beer, that a full-voiced, gargling, percussive, moist-lipped, palatal

Europe, interpolated with warring sibilants, made itself heard.

The three of them laughed. Even when she laughed, the pretty barmaid was pretty. Chatterjee's small-boned hand fusing with his beer glass. Reschke's slightly oblique dolichocephalic skull. He had forgotten his beret at the widow's. The girl behind the bar, her name Yvonne, claimed to be a medical student, able to work here only twice a week. Chatterjee praised Export beer. Reschke identified the Ruhr as its source, then asked the barmaid to put two more bottles on his tab. The medical student let them treat her to a scotch. Uninvited, and half a dozen barstools away, I might have ordered a vodka.

They talked rather randomly about the weather, the dollar exchange rate, the permanent crisis of the ship-building industry. Their main topic had been exhausted; there was nothing more to be squeezed out of Asia. Even when he spoke, Chatterjee's unevenly veiled eyes remained expressionless. "Sadly absent," writes Reschke. Yet no silence set in. It seems they even recited poems: the Bengali quoted Kipling; the professor remembered some lines by Poe.

After questioning each other about their ages, the gentlemen asked Yvonne to guess. The forty-two years of the Bengali-British businessman, born when the Indian subcontinent was partitioned, turned out to be more surprising than the sixty-two of my former classmate, who like me came into the world when the tower of St. Mary's, found to be in need of repair, was encased in scaffolding up to its blunt top. Mr. Chatterjee's sparse hair contrasted with the vigorous if graying mane of the soon-to-retire professor; but when he gestured, gently pleading or suddenly forceful, making use of all ten fingers as he related episodes of a circular Oriental legend, the businessman grew younger. By comparison, the professor had few gestures, all equally dismal, such as the speechless raising or lowering of the hands in the way of aging men; that, at least, is how I rhyme the two of them.

They stopped at the third bottle of Export. When Chatterjee maintained that he went in for sports in order to keep fit, Yvonne found this laughable. Apparently her acquaintance with the Bengali went beyond serving him beer. Her laughter, which kept reinfecting itself, did not improve her looks. When she called him a bicycle champion with, as Reschke noted, an insulting snap of her fingers, Chatterjee took it lying down, but paid at once, barely waiting for Reschke.

It was shortly after midnight when the two gentlemen parted outside the small half-timbered house. "We'll meet again," cried the small-boned Bengali with the British passport as, recharged with energy, he disappeared into the night along the bank of the Radaune. Reschke had only a short way to go, past the hotel's parking lot.

The Bulgarian red wine, the small glass of honey liqueur, and three bottles of Dortmund Export were not enough to make the widower quite ready for bed; at any rate, he was sufficiently awake to give a pedantic account of himself in his diary. He recalled every conversation of that day, omitting not a single variation in mood. A slight headache was important, as well as the likelihood of heartburn, for which he had tablets, drops, and lozenges in his suitcase: Reschke's traveling pharmacy.

I'm not going to make him take his glasses out of

their case again, open them, breathe on the lenses and wipe them. He wrote fluently. Whenever he felt that he was growing longwinded, for example, in singing the praises of the mushroom dish while taking account of its possible aftereffects, he summed up his misgivings like an experienced taker of minutes. "Once again acted against my better judgment." He even reduced Mr. Chatterjee's prophesied Völkerwanderung—the inexorable waves of immigration, which could have justified a more dramatic flow of images—to the essential: "That Bengali who pretends to be British painted a graphic picture of the Asian overflow. When he referred to the Indian subcontinent at least, there was no contradicting him. Is disaster threatening, or is our old Europe heading for a radical, much needed rejuvenation cure?"

Interestingly enough, in his diary Reschke always started with what he had experienced most recently. Enthusiasm turned a mere barroom acquaintance into a "crowning encounter," and his tendency to exaggerate led him to call Chatterjee, who had introduced himself as a businessman interested in transportation, a "transportation expert" and "amiable to boot."

Only then did he write about tripping near the buckets of flowers, about the rust-red asters, the predestined widow. Frau Piątkowska soon became Alexandra. He described her as vital, inclined to sarcasm, interested in politics, though also embittered, not without obstinacy, but worldly wise and warm-hearted. "I have the impression that Alexandra uses her charm to atone for a contrariness that may sometimes strike one as childish. An amusing duel, in which I enjoy participating. She makes a point of being 'modern,' which shows in her rather loud makeup. Several times she said I was old-fashioned, 'of the old school,' but evidently takes pleasure in my admittedly exaggerated good manners."

After a long digression on the poverty inherent in the Polish street scene, the devaluation of the zloty, the rate of inflation and the disproportion between wages and prices, and after deploring the thriving black market, the children begging outside his hotel, the condition of the sidewalks, the unreliable street lighting, and the increase in crime "since the collapse of the Communist state," and after deploring the increased power of the Catholic clergy, forgetting neither the stench of sulfur nor the cloud of exhaust fumes over the city, he turned his attention again to Alexandra Piątkowska. He called her irresistible. He used expressions such as "a good looker," "small but oh." The apartment on Hundegasse was "all in all a cozy little place." "With her I feel alive again." It is only after an elaborate description of the cemetery on Hagelsberg that he comes to the point, which is the Polish-German-Lithuanian Cemetery Association proposed by the widow. He calls it "our no sooner conceived than born" idea, evaluates the Lithuanian component as "sensible and desirable," though "hard to put into effect."

Still, he develops the concept further: "The Wilno project will have to be financed. We must find means to counter all the reservations that may be raised in Vilnius. After all, we stand together or not at all. The Poles as well as the Germans must recognize the right of the dead to repatriation. It is a human right that knows no frontiers."

Resounding words. All that smug self-righteousness in the service of the dead stank in my nostrils. I took his fountain pen and wrote in the margin, "Look here, Reschke, this idea stinks." All the same, I stayed with it.

Something the widow had said caught my fancy. "No room for politics in cemetery." You could only agree with that. Her certainty intrigued me. Now I was curious whether they would succeed or fail.

Something else spurred me on; the fact that they were both widowed spoke in their favor. If their story had been larded with the usual adultery, if one of those ridiculously hyped-up affairs had taken up space in Reschke's papers, if there had been talk of ingeniously deceiving a wife or routinely cuckolding a husband, believe me, Reschke, I would not have been able to oblige you. But with both of them widowed for years, set free by the death of a spouse and again solely responsible for their affairs, unencumbered by children, who have grown up and left home, they are accessible to me. I can follow them.

Toward the end of his entries under "All Souls'," the widow's string bag again became important to him. He returned to that heirloom in repeated flights of fancy: How glad he was to carry Alexandra's loaded bag. How that outmoded household article touched him. How many sentiments, ardent some of them, could find room in it. Here is one: "I feel as if I had walked into her net."

Counting the knotted or crocheted meshes of all the string bags the widow had inherited from her mother, the widower probably fell asleep in the end; or was it the nine hundred and fifty million people behind Mr. Chatterjee that he had begun to count from left to right? As for Alexandra Piątkowska, we may assume that she lay awake working out the cost of the Cemetery Association by mental arithmetic. After computing the initial capital—"half million deutschmarks, about"—she probably drifted off into dream calculations with even more zeroes.

Outside a wide window stand six pillars whose concrete cores are covered with ceramic. On the kitchen side, additional pillars covered with antiqued red brick. Otherwise, smooth wood paneling. In the background, an embossed relief.

Shortly before nine A.M. Reschke found a free table in the hotel restaurant and ordered tea, which he preferred to the gritty Polish coffee, and ham and cottage cheese. A frilly-white waitress approached hesitantly, as if overcoming some inner resistance. No sooner had he ordered than a man sat down at his table, a fellow countryman, as it soon turned out. The newcomer had not, like most of the predominantly middle-aged men and women at neighboring tables, come with a package tour, but was traveling for a private health insurance company, with headquarters in Hamburg. They struck up a conversation.

This gentleman, who remains nameless in Reschke's diary, was trying, with the help of the magic formula "joint venture," to establish business connections. He was looking for attractively situated vacation homes, offering a share of the capital as well as prospective buyers. His company, he informed Reschke, was proposing a time-share program for curative or recreational purposes in Eastern Europe, especially in the former German provinces. There was no lack of demand. As owners of a number of medium-sized homes, the state-controlled trade unions at least showed an interest. "What would you expect? They're in hot water up to their necks."

But Reschke's table companion complained of Polish

unwillingness to cooperate. He realized that the question of ownership might be a sore point at the moment, but felt sure that even allowing for a certain amount of distrust, which was understandable, there had to be the possibility of long-term leases with an option to buy. "Otherwise," he said, "it won't be long before the whole place is dead. They should finally get that through their heads. On the one hand they say they want capitalism and on the other hand they behave like innocent maidens. These Poles still think they can get something for nothing."

Reschke, who for a day now had been entertaining similar plans, wanted to know if by and large the prospects were good for such joint-venture deals. "That is essentially a political question. The time has come for us to recognize their Oder-Neisse boundary. With no ifs, ands, or buts. Forget about the handful of professional refugees left. Then everything will be possible here. After all, now that everything is going to the dogs in the GDR, the Poles are panicking. They need us. Who else can be expected to lend them a helping hand? The French? See what I mean? Take it from me: in three or four years we'll rule the roost here in Poland. They can't ignore the D-mark. And if the Poles don't want us, we'll go to the Czechs and Hungarians. They're more open . . ."

As he stood up, the venture capitalist, a man in his late forties who had ordered too much and had hardly touched his soft-boiled eggs, said: "But this area would be best, even if the Baltic isn't what it used to be. I've looked at a few trade union homes. On the Frische Nehrung on the Hela peninsula. Those pine woods. Or the so-called Kashubian Switzerland. All excellent health resort terrain and more familiar than foreign places.

Full of memories for those of our people who had to leave here once upon a time. And there are plenty of those. My own family, for instance. They came from Marienwerder. I can still distinctly remember the flight, though I was very little at the time . . ."

Reschke left the hotel. The weather continued to be unusually warm for early November. It cost him an effort to give something to the begging children. He bought six exorbitantly priced picture postcards from a boy who was leading his little sister by the hand. Undecided whether to spend his last day in Gdańsk paying another visit to St. Mary's or aimlessly strolling, he hesitated too long at the hotel entrance; for no sooner had he decided in favor of the memorial slabs at St. Mary's than he was addressed by name in the special English of his midnight barroom acquaintance, the Bengali with the British passport.

This is what I read in Alexander Reschke's notes: "At some distance from the row of waiting taxis Mr. Chatterjee stood beside a bicycle rickshaw. With what self-assurance he held the handlebars. In a jogging suit, he stood beside the rickshaw which, though not one of those notorious vehicles powered by coolies on foot, nevertheless seemed out of place, at least at first. He beckoned me to approach and admire his rickshaw—yes, it belonged to him. Spotlessly clean. A folding red-and-white striped top for the protection of his passengers in inclement weather. The frame dark blue, without a rust spot or any sign of peeling paint. Chatterjee explained: Sometimes he parked in front of this hotel, sometimes in front of another. Pure chance that we hadn't met sooner. No, the rickshaw was not imported from Dacca or Calcutta; this Dutch-produced vehicle was designed to meet European requirements. The Sparta trademark

45

was a guarantee of quality. Sophisticated gears. He owned six others, all brand-new. But only two were in operation in the city at the moment. Yes, he had a license for the inner city and part of the pedestrian zone and recently even for Allee Grunwaldzka in both directions. There had been difficulties at first, but he found ways of ingratiating himself with the local authorities. Oh yes, it's the same all over the world. Unfortunately, it's hard to find pedalers, or rickshawwallas as they call them in Calcutta, although, as you see, the taxi drivers are almost all unemployed. The Poles' exaggerated pride keeps them from engaging their labor force in his transportation business. Which is expanding. In fact, he has ordered six more vehicles from Holland. 'Because,' cried Mr. Chatterjee, 'the future belongs to the bicycle rickshaw. Not only in impoverished Poland. All over Europe.' "

Reschke saw at once that the Bengali's business was big business and therefore worth entering in his diary. Moreover, as he looked through his notes, he saw a parallel between his breakfast companion's projected vacation homes, the environment-friendly bicycle rickshaw business, and the cemetery association. He writes: "All three projects have one thing in common: they serve human beings, older human beings in particular. They are, as it were, senior-citizen-friendly."

Mr. Chatterjee, spurred on by Reschke's questions, held forth on the impending collapse of the automobile traffic in all the urban centers of Europe and on the advantages of the highly maneuverable, virtually noiseless, and, it goes without saying, exhaust-free bicycle rickshaw for short-to-medium distances in cities, then spoke more generally on the revitalization of Europe by new blood from Asia, and finally, if only ironically, he invoked the capitalist concept of untapped markets. And reality adapted itself to his vision: powered by the one Pole who had thus far gone into rickshaw cycling, a vehicle of the same model pulled up in front of the hotel, bringing a smiling old man back from his morning tour of the city; whereupon two smartly dressed ladies—both about Reschke's age—engaged Mr. Chatterjee's services and giggled like little girls while fitting themselves into the narrow seat.

Reschke notes for my benefit: "The West Germans are the least inhibited about using rickshaws. Most of them grew up here and come back in order to refresh, as they say, old memories. I gathered from the women's chatter that they wished, after a short tour of the city, to take Grosse Allee from Danzig to Langfuhr and back, as they did years ago in their schooldays; evidently old friends, they had often covered this ground on bicycles. Indeed, they amused themselves rattling off street and place names; and Mr. Chatterjee nodded."

The Bengali put on a bicycle racer's cap. Reschke wished him a pleasant ride. The two school friends cried out: "It's great fun. We can't recommend it too highly. You're from here too, aren't you?" And stepping powerfully on the pedals, as if transporting two portly ladies in his well-sprung vehicle were part of his fitness program, he cried out again: "See you, Mr. Reschke."

All right, if you insist. As a schoolboy I swallowed toads on request. It's possible, too, that I necked on park benches with Reschke's cousin Hildchen during the blackouts, or even during air-raid alerts until the all clear sounded. Yes, Reschke and I may well have sat next to each other in school, and it's probably true that he let me copy from him in math and Latin. Still, having to follow him step by step is too much. Everybody knows he shuffles. Not all his detours must be mine. I let him go, just as he is, without beret and camera case, while my thoughts for a moment follow the rickshaw which, wherever it may be, is rolling toward the future . . .

The few tourists and a sprinkling of pious Poles were lost in the three-aisled church, whose newly raised dome will be supported by twenty-six octagonal pillars until the next destruction. The last time the dome came down, a few memorial slabs cracked under the debris. Nevertheless the passage along the side chapels, through the central nave or transept and past the sanctuary, has famous pavingstones full of meaning. According to Reschke, the dog growing out of vines in the Neuwerg escutcheon still gnaws a bone of stone despite the crack, as it has done since 1538, when the embossed slab of Sebald Rudolf von Neuwerg was laid.

Once again, as though to take leave of the smooth-trodden objects of his assiduous research, the professor walked over the floor slabs whose raised inscriptions, now barely legible, gave the names and death dates of once-powerful patricians as well as Bible quotations in Baroque German. Family arms and heraldry, all worn flat and smooth by generations of awed churchgoers and later by tourists. For example, right next to the Beautiful Madonna is the memorial slab in the floor of the north lateral nave, whose ornamented shield shows, in the left half of a vertically bisected field, two stars above a tree, and in the right a crown over an hourglass, and below, a skull with a swan looking over the shield—an allusion to the "Silesian Swan," as the poet and court historian Martin Opitz von Boberfeld, whom the Plague placed under this slab in August

1638, was called by the members of the Fruit-Bearing Society.

Reschke, and not for the first time, was irritated by the inscription added in 1873 from stupid local patriotism: "To the poet, from his countrymen." But he took pleasure in the inscription engraved in 1732 on the memorial slab of husband Mattias and wife Lovise Lemman: "Their bones are still green and their name will be praised in their children, to whom it is bequeathed . . ."

Then something extraordinary in the diary: "I have encountered my tomb, in the central nave, to be exact. On a gray granite slab, quite smooth, I saw my name freshly chiseled in cuneiform though spelled in the old way, expanded by the first names of my brothers. Thus I read my name as Alexander Eugen Maximilian Rebeschke. I read it over and over again, in the end aloud though under my breath. Without a date, of course. Nor was I favored with an epitaph, let alone an escutcheon. Unable to bear the thought of lying under granite, I fled as if I had gone mad, my steps echoing on the flagstones, so that worshipers looked up in dismay and stared at me. Familiar as I was with the postulate of mortality since my earliest student days, I could not endure this anticipation. So I ran, ran away from myself and out the southern side door, ran as I hadn't run for a long time, and was glad to know where I was going . . ."

For Alexander had an appointment to meet Alexandra Piątkowska at the stroke of twelve at the Neptune Fountain on Long Market. The widow had taken half the day off. They would find a suitable spot in which to hammer their idea into shape, since the widower had to start for home the following day.

He arrived breathlessly on time, didn't say what had put him in a sweat, but cried out while still running, as though to keep up the momentum of his flight: "We'd better take the car . . ."

Reschke in the driver's seat. No photograph shows him at the wheel. Though I have many photographs of the couple, they are never in front of a car. No Mercedes star in the picture with them. His diary says nothing about the car of his choice. Never anything but: "We took the car . . ." or: "After leaving the car at the attended parking lot . . ."

So I can only guess, or type something or other at random. Was he driving one of those Skoda limousines that make an exotic impression west of the Elbe? Since Reschke indulged in extravagances, such as a velvet collar on his tailor-made autumn coat, a nostalgic Peugeot 404 with leather upholstery but an expensive catalyzer might have been right for him. For when Reschke tanked up, he tanked up on unleaded. I definitely do not see him driving up to the Hevelius in a Porsche.

So I'm left with his "We'd better take the car . . ." Since he was pursuing his study of the city's principal churches on foot, he had left the car in the hotel's parking lot. When widow and widower met under Neptune's curved trident, Piątkowska brought a complete plan for the afternoon, which could only be carried out with the help of a car. Before they left the parking lot, Alexandra wiped the sweat from his forehead—"Why, Alexander, you are all outworn!"—and only then did she put on his head and adjust the beret he had forgotten the night before.

Reschke explains briefly that at first he considered the country between Brentau and Matern suitable for a woodland cemetery, especially because "the tall beeches are well spaced and provide the project with a natural setting. Only a few need be cut down. But much underbrush will have to be removed. Because the homecoming dead are to be sheltered beneath a canopy of leaves, not hidden away."

The only objection to this ideal cemetery site was the proximity of the Gdańsk airport, whose runways occupied level ground where once the farms of the village of Bissau had gathered its rolling fields around them. And Rembiechowo Airport was sure to expand as far as Matarnia. Plus the noise of planes taking off and landing. Who wants to take his eternal rest in a flight path?

Unfortunately the long valley to the west of Oliwa was also unsuitable. Where Reschke remembered forest clearings and Sunday family outings, tentlike wooden houses huddled together amid community vegetable gardens. Neatly as the cheerful community gardens were fenced off, dense as the mixed forest was that covered the valley, the trees barely touched by blight, Reschke nevertheless suggested that they turn back. There was no room here. This beautiful land all wantonly built up . . .

They drove back in the early afternoon. I see driver and passenger silent, pensive if not disappointed: their idea bruised, their decision, scarcely made, stymied, and their enthusiasm, which had flared up only yesterday, decidedly dampened.

As they rode down Grosse Allee, which is now called Grunwaldzka and links the suburb of Wrzeszcz to the city, and passed the former Sports Stadium on their way to the attended parking lot, Reschke slowed down and pointed at the large park to the right: "That's where the United Cemeteries used to be, where my paternal grandparents . . ."

Piątkowska told him, no, ordered him to stop: "Not worry, will be again cemeteries, same as before . . ."

"But Alexandra . . ."

"But what? We just get out."

"But it is now a public park . . ."

"Exactly. Now is only now . . ."

"But we can't reverse the course of history."

"We'll see if we can't."

While Reschke parks the car and the two of them discuss the reversibility of historical facts, I have to survey in retrospect the United Cemeteries, leveled by government decree, giving their acreage: An area circumscribed on the one hand by the Polyclinic and the Engineering School and on the other by St. Michael's Lane, leading to the crematorium and the parallel Grosse Allee, this area, later named Park Akademicki, encompassed the roughly four-acre cemetery of the St. Bridget and St. Joseph Catholic congregations, which, like all the other cemeteries, was leveled starting in 1966. On the adjoining eight-acre Evangelical St. Mary's Cemetery, where it fronted St. Michael's Lane, the Szpital Studencki was built. The roughly nine acres of what used to be the Evangelical Cemetery, at the east end of several new buildings of the former Technische Hochschule, now belong to Politechnika Gdańska. The Catholic cemetery of the congregations of St. Nikolai and Royal Chapel measured about six acres, and there was a roughly four-acre crematorium cemetery situated on the other side of St. Michael's Lane, where the crematorium, an imposing Dutch-brick building with a chapel and two chimneys, still stands. This crematorium cemetery was also leveled in the late sixties and then renamed Park XXV-lecia PRL, which means Park of the Twenty-Fifth Anniversary of the Founding of the People's Republic of Poland, and thrown open to the public.

More might be said about other leveled cemeteries on the opposite side of Grosse Allee; for behind the Small Drillground (later named Maiwiese) and St. Stephen's Park lay the United Cemeteries of St. John, St. Bartholomew, Sts. Peter and Paul, and the adjoining cemetery for the Mennonites—and then came railroad tracks, the Neuschottland Housing Development, the shipyard, and the harbor. But since Reschke was thinking only of the particular area where the double grave of his paternal grandparents had been reserved, he parked his car near the brick and half-timbered building which once housed the cemetery administration and guarded the entrance and so remained etched in his memory.

The widow remembered too. "Was in Gomułka time when last German cemeteries they bulldozed. Why didn't I get out of Party then, instead of already too late when came martial law?"

The avenue, bordered by evenly spaced linden trees, still led from the brick building to St. Michael's Lane, and there, on bulldozed burial ground, or, as the widow put it, "On dead people bones," stood the newly built, flat-roofed Special Hospital for Students.

Halfway down the avenue of lindens was a traffic circle, from which other avenues of lindens branched left and right. Thus four large burial grounds, with single trees and clumps of trees, could still be imagined. These formal cemetery avenues created a cross from which radiated all the main and secondary avenues. Tall, shade-promising trees, chestnuts, elms, weeping willows. Dilapidated park benches occupied by men busy with beer bottles and by mothers with small children. Here and there people reading newspapers, a student couple, a lone student who, Reschke maintained, was reading poems in French under his breath.

When widow and widower had paced the length of the avenue of lindens from the Engineering School entrance to the Polyclinic on the city side and roughly calculated the size of the Academic Park, during which expedition Piątkowska counted Reschke's measuring strides aloud in meters, he gazed at the hospital built in the early twenties and said, "That's where they took my tonsils out. And then they wouldn't let me eat anything but ice cream." And she said, "Funny, me too, both tonsils out, when I was teenager already."

After surveying the whole area, Alexander and Alexandra estimated the total size of the alienated cemeteries. She exaggerated. His twenty-five to thirty acres came close to the official figures. The sight of all this fallow land filled them both with enthusiasm. Having the gift of looking into the future, Reschke saw burial ground merging with burial ground. When she spotted additional ground for tombs and urns beyond St. Michael's Lane—today bearing the name of Traugutt, the leader of the insurrectionaries—and the crematorium, her enthusiasm increased by a good three and a half acres. This area, too, they paced off. Right behind the disused crematorium, whose chapel, Alexandra seemed to remember, was used for Orthodox services by the Ukrainian minority that had settled in Gdańsk since the war, there was a broken-down fence, and then the park gave way to community vegetable gardens. "Farther on," writes Reschke, "there are big athletic fields, all part of the Soccer Stadium."

54

In his diary he sees fit to remind me that soon after the Anschluss year 1939 the Heinrich-Ehlers athletic fields were rebuilt and later named after a gauleiter from Franconia, who had been favored with the reichsgau of Danzig-West Prussia.

Yes, Reschke, you're right: We students of St. Peter's were often present at the annual Reich Youth Games in the Albert Forster Stadium. Sweat, whistles, commands, boredom. Hideous memories . . .

I can only add to those recollections. I remember soccer games—Danzig, hardly a first-class team, against visiting clubs, Breslau, Fürth, even Schalke. The names of then-famous players such as Goldbrunner, Schön, Lehner, and Fritz Szczepan come to me. And I remember that on June 21, 1941, a Sunday, the day the Russian campaign started, I witnessed from my place in the standing area in that sunken bowl a game I don't remember against whom.

"This is where," said Alexandra Piątkowska when they returned to the traffic circle. She took in all four burial grounds, pointed a short arm in each direction. Alexander Reschke was impressed by her sweeping gestures of taking possession: "Not only I but Alexandra as well saw what until then had been a mere idea. She spoke of rows of graves and of German names on rows of tombstones. She even murmured, in a tone of incantation, inscriptions such as 'Rest in Peace' or 'Here Lies . . .' Her eyes reflected her words: 'Here, right here will be return of dead Germans!' Much as I hope that her too-loud exclamation—people were looking at us— will come true, nevertheless her vision frightens me."

The widow must have calmed his fears. Nothing could put her off. Convinced that the dead had a right to come home and that her idea was convertible into reality, she said, as they finally left the park: "Must no more be terrible, Alexander. We Poles with bulldozer was terrible. Because politics is everywhere always sticking its nose in, and I saw too late what Communism was supposed to be but wasn't. Terrible everywhere. What now comes brings happiness, believe me, because is human. But account must balance. You understand, *rachunek?*"

On the former burial ground, among the evenly spaced linden trees, and on the way to the parked car, Alexandra Piątkowska talked about the yield of her almost sleepless night, about the money that would be needed as initial capital. Now she high-heeled ahead, now she stood still. She counted on all her fingers. The gildress's short, powerful fingers, practical and eloquent: Since the zloty was worthless, the foundation of her idea, now an enterprise, must be the currency of the West German state. That's the way it was, since everything, even death, costs money. "With deutschmarks it works. Already I see how beautiful it will be!"

As they were riding toward the city, night fell. Mentally calculating, they forged ahead. As an experiment, I imagine the two of them in a Saab. She says, "A million deutschmarks we need to start." A solid car that guarantees safety. Both belted up, exuberance and all. Now they are silent. Just before Oliwa Gate, Reschke thought he passed a bicycle rickshaw with two passengers. All that registered was the rickshaw and Chatterjee's racing cap ". . . I'm sure it was he who was powerfully plying the pedals. I only hope that we progress as auspiciously with our cemetery plans . . ."

Saab or Volvo, or Peugeot for that matter. Never mind what kind of car. He parked it in the hotel parking lot. But a hug must be added before action again speeds up their story. The widow, Reschke reports, hugged him as, standing at the traffic circle, she beheld the future cemetery. The embrace came as something of a shock to him. Standing on tiptoe, the small, firmly built woman rose to almost his height. He felt awakened, revived even in a region from which he had ceased to hope for much. She threw her arms with all their many constantly clinking bracelets around his neck, kissed him on both cheeks, and cried, "Oh, Alexander! Now all we need is a space in Wilno!" His arms would not obey him. "I stood there moved, but stiff as a board."

The widow's physical exuberance may have irritated the widower, but he withstood the assault of her body clad in skirt and tweed jacket, felt its warmth, and did nothing to oppose the joy she had communicated to his body. Later—in Bochum on November 9—he went so far as to answer Alexandra's contention about plenty of deutschmarks with, as he admitted, a frivolous sentence: "Dear Alexandra, let me worry about that. It would be too absurd if I were unable to come up with the required sum. In times like these, when everything is uncertain, one must learn to take risks. We shouldn't be reckless, of course, but not too timid either. In any case our joint venture calls for total commitment."

When Reschke parked the car to one side of the Hevelius, the city was shrouded in November darkness. Not rickshaws but taxis waiting as usual outside the hotel. He knew well that bittersweet mixture of exhaust fumes and sulfur. Undecided what to do with the early evening, the widower asked the widow to join him for a drink at the bar behind the reception desk. Because the Orbis buses with flat-rate tourist groups had not yet returned from their day excursions to Marienburg and Pelplin, Elbing and Frauenburg, the two of them were alone at the bar long enough for a first, then a second whiskey. After so much recent intimacy, they may have felt somewhat awkward. The clinking ice in their glasses, I would think, spoke for them.

As the bar filled up in rapid-fire succession and bursts of merriment erupted, Reschke paid up, unwilling to subject Piątkowska to that crowd. The gentlemen casually dressed, the ladies in traveling outfits with lots of jewelry. Listening to their voices, Reschke thought he could identify most of the flat-rate tourists as of local origin. "More loudly than need be, they showed off their familiarity with the city. Most of them no younger than we, in other words at an age that will make them beneficiaries of our venture—sooner or later."

In this speculation he was not alone. The widow shared his thought and whispered too loudly, "Every one will be customer soon."

"Alexandra, please . . ."

"Certainly have plenty deutschmarks . . ."

"But this isn't the place . . ."

"All right, I didn't say nothing."

Then her laugh. Alexandra was not to be suppressed. She would have been quite capable—after only two drinks—of launching an outright publicity campaign, if he hadn't asked her to dinner in the hotel restaurant.

She declined. "Expensive as sin and food no good," and invited him out instead. "All right. We go."

It wasn't far, only a few steps past St. James's Church. She had reserved a table for two in a small restaurant. They ate by candlelight, and as Piątkowska had promised, "Real Polish cooking like Mama's in Wilno."

During the meal—appetizer, main course, dessert—the two of them behaved like a couple who have a great deal to say to each other. Not that he spoke of his dead wife or she of her husband who had died so young. Nothing that rankled, only well-digested memories. Brief reference was made to her son, who was studying philosophy in Bremen, and to his three working and more or less married daughters. "The man you see before you is twice a grandfather."

The conversation was a little disjointed. It touched briefly on politics—"Now soon the Wall comes down"—exchanged national clichés for a while, the qualities that are supposed to be typical of Poles and Germans, and slipped back time and again into shoptalk, particularly since Alexandra had for months at a time been busy gilding the inscriptions and ornaments of wooden and stone epitaphs, most recently in St. Nikolai. The names and escutcheons of extinct patrician families, from magistrate and alderman Angermünde to merchant Schwarzwaldt, whom Holbein painted in London and whose escutcheon, despite the red of the tongue and the blue of the helmet, was basically black and gold, to Johann Uphagen's coat of arms, in which the knobby beak of the silver swan held a golden horseshoe—she was familiar with them all, including Ferber and his three pigs' heads, down to the most finicky curlicue and helmet ornament. The gildress moved with less assurance in the field of smooth-trodden memorial slabs, so it was not out of mere politeness that she asked Reschke to send her his dissertation someday. "You see, Herr Professor, when people get as old as us, feeling is not enough. We have to know. Not everything, but lots details."

If I am to believe his notebook, Reschke felt hurt at being addressed as Herr Professor. It was only at dinner—they were drinking Hungarian wine—that the widow in the heat of an argument resorted to the affectionate diminutive of the academic title; they were discussing whether the graphic artist Daniel Chodowiecki, who hailed from Danzig, should be admired as a Pole or reviled as a Prussian government official. Several times she said "Professorchen," and then over their glasses not only said but whispered "my dear Professorchen." Reschke felt, as he later noted, "somewhat surer of Alexandra's affection."

Actually, they came close to quarreling over Chodowiecki. Piątkowska was capable of strong national feeling. She called the draftsman and etcher, who toward the end of his life reformed the Royal Prussian Academy, "a traitor to the Polish cause" because, when he found himself in dire need after the partition of Poland, he offered his services to Berlin—Berlin of all places.

Reschke disagreed. He termed her view too "narrow" and evaluated the artist as important and of European stature, "because he pointed the way beyond the Baroque." Though a Protestant, Chodowiecki remained loyal to his Polish origin. True, he trusted the Huguenots who had emigrated to Prussia more than he trusted the Catholic clergy. "Nevertheless, dear Alexandra," he cried, raising his glass, "you should take pride in him as a Polish European!" Whereupon the widow clinked glasses with him and gave in for the first time. "You reconcile me with great Polish artist. Thank you, Professorchen! You dear Professorchen."

They had come to the dessert. It couldn't have been one of his favorites because it isn't mentioned in his papers, though he gives the borscht, the piroshki, and the carp in dark-beer sauce their due.

Then complications. She insisted on paying. He had

to give in. But when she took him the short distance back to his hotel and was about to return to Hundegasse alone through the poorly lit streets, he asserted himself, took her arm and shuffled along beside her, while she clack-clacked in her high heels, as far as the steps of her front terrace, in whose sandstone relief the games of the putti and little cupids were barely discernible.

From street corner to street corner they seem to have spoken less and less. He notes only her sudden fear that when the Wall between West and East came down, everything might be more difficult. "In Dresden no more People-Owned gold leaf. Shortages will be . . ."

And then the widow dismissed him with a quick kiss and a routine "Write if you feel like it . . ." Left standing at the door, the widower started shuffling back to his hotel.

No, Reschke did not take refuge in the half-timbered house by the Radaune. Shortly after eleven, he asked for his key, took the elevator to the fourteenth floor, opened the door to his room, changed into the slippers that accompanied him on every trip, washed his hands with his own soap, sat down, bent over his notebook, opened his glasses case, and put on his reading glasses. Then shut the case and reached, as if in a hurry to gain written assurance of his own existence, for his fountain pen.

It might have been the memorial slab in St. Mary's with his name on it that made him invoke in writing the patron of the square highrise hotel, the astronomer Johann Hewelke, known as Hevelius, and his wife Catharina, née Rebeschke, also known as Rebeschkin, in order, as his father had tried in vain to do, to follow a line of kinship with the brewery-owning Rebeschkes back to the seventeenth century, and thus lend some meaning to the terrifying apparition of his own tombstone, when there was a knock at the door. Twice softly, once loud.

"It's me again," said the widow Alexandra Piątkowska when shortly before midnight she called on the widower Alexander Reschke.

She arrived breathless, carrying not only her shoulder bag but also a loaded heirloom, Mama's string bag. This time it was a brown and blue one with a zigzag pattern. In haste, as if someone had lit a fire behind her, she had picked up this, that, and the other, and without stopping to catch her breath run after Alexander, who by then must have been passing St. Dominic's Market, run with short, clattering high-heel steps.

"I completely forgot. You take this on your trip."

The contents of the string bag: a jar of pickled beets, a few dried boletus mushrooms on a knotted string, and a walnut-size chunk of amber "with a gnat in it!" She took off her mouse-gray raincoat and her jacket and stood before him in a glossy light-blue silk blouse with dark sweat stains under the armpits, still breathless.

Should I be there holding a lamp in spite of the hotel room lighting? He saw her sweat spots. She saw him in bedroom slippers. She let the string bag with contents slip to the floor. He took off his glasses and still found time for the case. She took a short step, he a stumbling step, then she another, and he likewise. And they fell, lay in each other's arms.

That's how it must have been. Or how I see their fall, though Reschke confided few details to his diary. Immediately after the horror of treading on his own tombstone and the speculation about his family tree—

"Unfortunately Hevelius's first marriage remained childless . . ."—came the string bag, the dried mushrooms, the pickled beets, the amber with the gnat, and the dark-blue spots of sweat. As the widower noticed next morning, the widow had brought her toothbrush—"an astonishing but sensible precaution," he called it. And in the solemn tone reserved for glad tidings, he cited Alexandra's words, laughingly spoken after midnight or early in the morning: "We are lucky, Alexander, because, my change of life gone by already." "How frankly Alexandra calls a spade a spade."

Then references to the narrow single bed and the repulsive spots on the carpet. And after the barest suggestion of a disagreement—he wanted to turn off the light, she didn't—his confession: "Yes, we loved, we had the power to love, and no one stopped us. And I— O God—I was capable of love!"

That's all. I have no intention of crowding into that narrow hotel bed any more than my classmate revealed. In the light of day or in the half-darkness: he thin but not withered; she firm and round but not fat. They'll do as a couple.

Alexandra and Alexander slept little. They seem to have mastered the task of making love. At their age patience is needed and the kind of humor that ignores the possibility of defeat. As they were able to assure each other at breakfast in the hotel restaurant, neither snored during their brief spells of exhausted sleep. At a later point in their story, however, he noted her only moderately bothersome snoring, and she no doubt was equally tolerant. I owe her suggestion, that they finally get some sleep, that is, lie back to back, to his note: "Suppose we make double eagle."

Did they talk intermittently about their idea? Was

there at least some passing mention of cemeteries in Gdańsk and Wilno, of adequate supplies of deutsch-marks? Or with all that love was there no room in the narrow bed for cemeteries here or there? Or was their idea, still short of fuel, oxygenated by love? When Reschke asked her at breakfast whether she had ob-tained his room number at the reception desk, her an-swer, followed by laughter, was: "But you tell me how high your floor and number when we argue about great Polish artist in Prussian Academy."

They handled their parting quickly. After paying for the single room he said: "Have no fear, Alexandra. You'll hear from me. You'll never get away from me now."

And as his suitcase stood beside them ready to be picked up, she is reported to have said: "I know, Alex-ander. And on highway don't drive too fast. Now I am no longer widow."

Piątkowska left before Reschke carried his suitcase to the parking lot. That's what they had arranged. He tipped the porter, but didn't allow him to carry the suitcase. A sunny to partly cloudy morning. A north-west wind blowing the sulfur stench of the docks in the harbor to other places.

When Reschke stepped out of the hotel shortly after eight o'clock, there were no taxis but across the street three rickshaws stood invitingly in the sun. Chrome and enamel gleamed. The three drivers were talking. One of them was Chatterjee in his cap. The third driver looked foreign. Chatterjee noticed Reschke carrying the suitcase and was beside him in three steps. He intro-duced the Pakistani as a new employee. "There are more outside the Novotel."

My former classmate offered congratulations, all the more so as a second Pole had swallowed his pride.

Chatterjee said: "When will you be back, Mr. Reschke? I invite you to a tour of the city. You know what I always say: If anything has a future, it's the bicycle rickshaw."

Reschke's account of this parting makes several references to the Bengali's sadly remote look. Chatterjee gave Reschke one of his brochures—*Chatterjee's Sightseeing Tours:* "For your friends in old Germany. Gridlock, stress, noise! The solution? Ask Chatterjee. He has the answer for the cities."

Alexander Reschke put the brochures in his glove compartment. On the passenger's seat he laid his other present: a crocheted string bag full of little mementos, such as dried boletus mushrooms.

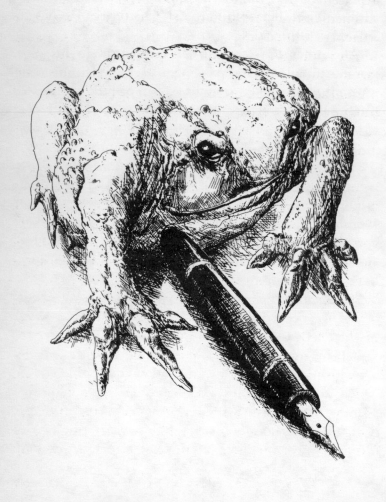

3

Now this could be the beginning of an epistolary novel, one of those crackling exchanges in which the voice is replaced by omissions, by eloquent gaps. Candor restrained only by punctuation. Famished interrogative sentences and passion narrowed strictly to two persons, which achieves expression on paper with no commentary from outside . . .

But their idea has already taken wing; it is on its way, bringing in other participants who, as the bylaws provide, want to join in the discussion and not just whisper indirectly. Soon there will be demands for an agenda.

Since my former classmate put his fountain pen in with the rest of his junk, I am able to specify the make of pen (whereas the brand of car was up to me): a black Montblanc, as thick as a Havana cigar, with a gold nib, and which he, for my use, filled by suction with blue-violet ink. Ah, Reschke, I write, what stupid business have you got me into?

Still dated in Poland—Hotel Merkury, Poznań, where, being overtired, he interrupted his journey and wrote his first letter. I'm not going to make things easy for myself by reproducing his pages-long handwritten letter with its even margins and clear, neat penmanship, which would merit an "excellent." This is not the beginning of an epistolary novel. For one thing, the unabridged publication of such a document might give offense, since, on three of the five pages, written on both sides, Reschke, in fits and starts, lives through a night in a single bed, in which connection he comes up with circumlocutions of all kinds, some in bad taste, others inventive, all concerned with the sex organs of two lovers. Rhapsodic flights flow from his pen but give little idea of the actual feats performed in the narrow bed, though they do make it clear that sex reduced him to a state of geriatric adolescence. As if a pipe had burst, obscenities, too long contained, pour forth in a flawless hand to fill page after page. Here I must admit that only once does the professor's free-flowing imagery appeal to me—when after a baroque accumulation of adjectives he refers to his penis as "a retarded young fool." He is positively itching to go the limit, and with school-boyish abandon. In one or two passages he uses words or expressions that Alexandra whispered to him in the heat of action, e.g. on completion of the act of love: "Please, in my junk room stay little longer."

Understandably, Piątkowska, in her reply, which took ten days to reach Bochum over intricate Polish pathways, protested. Yes, the night in the narrow bed was unforgettable, and she hoped for "happy returns and soon." But she never again wanted to read such crude outbursts, especially those dictated to her by passion. "Is question of manners, and not because I am afraid of censorship still."

Then she takes up the last third of the letter, the content of which was more businesslike and called for few exclamation marks. Reschke, cautiously, and still with hedging ifs and buts, nevertheless had made headway toward the future of their common idea: "After all the injustices that people have inflicted on each other, it should be possible—now that the horizons are brightening and much that seemed unthinkable only a year ago has become reality—not only to open up a better future for the living but also to secure the rights of the dead. The expression 'silent as a tomb' has often been used negatively; now it should take on new meaning—no, Alexandra, I can see your frown—it *must*. The Century of Expulsions will come to an end under the sign of homecoming. Only in this way can that end be fittingly celebrated. We must hesitate no longer. As I promised you, dearest, on my return I shall contact individuals and groups, not least those of religious orientation, and at the same time start setting up a card file . . ."

Piątkowska had something similar in mind: "You must know that in Gdańsk and Gdynia, no, in whole *województwo,* more than third of people come from Wilno and they like to lie there when their time is up. Not all, but many. In Church of St. Bartłomieja right near your Hotel Hevelius they have meetings of friends from Wilno and Grodno. I will write to Bishop, who sits in Oliwa, and ask him, carefully because with Church you must be careful always, because in Poland Church is *wszystko,* everything . . ."

Reschke restrained himself in the letters that followed. Nevertheless, the affair between Alexander and Alexandra, called by him "our incomparable love," assumed vast proportions. He no longer put the sex organs of the two lovers in a variety of costumes, but let their "transcendental juxtaposition and introition" resound, now with the fullness of an organ blast, now with the delicacy of a plucked instrument. "Our late communion, our joyous Gloria, our restrained Credo, never cease to reverberate within me. And even your laughter, which I often thought mocking, finds ever-new echo chambers, though it makes me painfully aware of your absence."

While Reschke's penmanship has been found praise-worthy, it must now be admitted that I find it hard to decipher Piątkowska's letters down to the last hen-scratch. It is not her word order or economical use of articles, which she rejects on principle as a "typical German tor-ture," that gives me trouble, but the way her pen either storms forward or lurches backward. Her words, and the letters, too, seem to be suffering from epilepsy. They step on one another's heels, they push and shove, leav-ing no space between lines or words. Or they dance in ecstasy, a performance not lacking in visual charm.

Yet what emerges from this scribble-scrabble seems perfectly sensible and to the point, for example, her attempts to channel the outpourings of her Alexander: "Maybe we had a little luck because we chanced to meet in market, which made us argue right away about flow-ers and money. But I knew even then that funny gentleman next to me is something special."

I admit that I take more interest in Alexandra than a reporter should. My feeling that a different man might have been better for her is beside the point.

In her letters from first to last she writes their first names in the Polish way. It's always Aleksandra writing to Aleksander. She never writes Alex, or Aleks. No nicknames have come down to us. "Shuffler" would have been conceivable. Only "dear Professorchen" turns up now and then, when his lecturing invites it.

The letters exchanged by our couple at Advent, at Christmas time, and at the end of the year give a rough idea of the direction of their efforts. Piątkowska reports that the Catholic Church, in the person of the Bishop of Oliwa, has not only shown interest but has characterized "our idea" as "pleasing to God" despite anticipated difficulties. "Important," she writes, "because in Poland Church here always is and government sometimes is and sometimes not." True, she met with a good deal of headshaking amazement among her Polish-Lithuanian compatriots, but also with some support. "Many want to finish in Wilno cemetery. And some burst in tears because thought is so beautiful."

Reschke writes about his first contacts with refugee organizations. "These people are not as reactionary as certain articles in their church bulletins would lead one to think." Some local groups with headquarters in the cities of Lower Saxony and Schleswig-Holstein reacted positively; other reactions were not without suspicion. One letter expressed vital interest in "a return to the homeland, if only for the dead." The idea of the cemetery association was surprisingly well received. Conversations with dignitaries of the Lutheran variety—"No interview with the Catholic clergy has as yet taken place"—met with initial success. "A consistory councilor from Elbing, who wished to take an active part, told me that the mere mention of such a cemetery in his birthplace cheered him immeasurably. You see, dear Alexandra, our idea, though devoted to death, contains a life-affirming element, which gives hope to many; just as the medieval Dance of Death motif gives not only a macabre but also a cheerful relevance to death as an egalitarian principle. Consider if you will the Lübeck Dance of Death, unfortunately destroyed by the war, and that of Master Bernt Notke, preserved in Reval: this endless round dance of the walks of life, from patrician to tradesman, king to beggar. They all dance into the pit, as they do today, and today, dearest, is a time of great change whose outcome is unknown. I see waves of barbaric power approaching us directly and by devious ways; some may be salutary. Yet I cannot share the present exuberance of mood without reservation—it is almost certain to swing to bitterness. Although the end of the Wall is a source of satisfaction, I fear the worst. Yes, I vacillate, I feel hot and cold, I'm glad there has been no bloodshed here as in Romania, but I do not exclude the possibility of a special kind of brutality, because in Germany, there is always . . ."

Thus the correspondence between Alexander and Alexandra was increasingly burdened by the events of the day. In one of his December letters—four in number—Reschke reports at length on "further initial successes, likely to advance our cemetery idea," but then: "I see signs of a unity which, though longed for, is beginning to look alarming . . ."

Piątkowska opposes this view with confidence, as if all Polish fears for the future have evaporated with the decline in the value of the zloty. "I don't understand you, Aleksander. As Pole, I can only congratulate with whole heart your people. Anyone who wants Polish nation undivided must also want German nation one. Or do you want to build two cemeteries in Gdańsk with Rest in Peace East and Rest in Peace West?" But then it occurs to her that the border between the two antagonistic nations must be made secure: "Otherwise unity will be dangerous, as often was for whole world."

One might suppose that this assault of historic reality would detract from their barely kindled love, the unmannerly intrusion of politics, the "hoofbeat of the mounted Weltgeist" outgalloping the dreams of men, the ubiquitous banners and slogans. Didn't the increasingly amplified shouts of "We are one people" drown out the lovers' whispers, their gentle vows of "We are one flesh"?

The Monday demonstrations in Leipzig traveled around the world. When New Year's Eve was celebrated on and under the Brandenburg Gate, the slums of India and Brazil joined in the celebration, and the worldwide family of nations looked on in amazement. In Bochum and Gdańsk, Alexander and Alexandra saw what the TV brought into their living rooms. At such a moment, who could turn off the TV and gaze instead at a photograph showing mushrooms, or hold up a walnut-size piece of amber to the light?

Their love remained unharmed. In her Christmas and New Year's letter, Piątkowska, usually all common sense, recalls the skinny body on top of, under, and beside her. Her love is still palpably with her when she writes of her pleasure in fingering and counting her "dear Aleksander's ribs." "You have body of boy!" She counts the sparse hair on his chest as profit. In one letter Piątkowska uses an expression that the exported gildress must have picked up in Trier or Cologne: "You fucked me good and I hope it is more and often . . ."

Reschke on the other hand refrains from bodily allusions, adumbrating their love with the help of sublime concepts, as though to put it on a pedestal. Even the momentous political events of the day he harnesses to that frail vehicle. At the start of the New Year he writes: "And what happened there on New Year's Eve, on and under that classical structure, long sealed, now at last open, what happened on the stroke of twelve, when a bloody decade bristling with weapons to its very end passed away, what suddenly broke free, and what then irrevocably began with the new decade, which I saw coming with fear and hope, set off a bellowing—

for the people in Berlin and elsewhere seem to have gone wild—which was reduced by a large-circulation newspaper, that harangued this people day after day, to a single word in bold type: Madness! Yes, Alexandra, the new decade was rung in with this word. When people meet on the street, they greet one another with, 'Isn't it madness?' Yes, it's madness. Whatever happens, madness must have a hand in it. If something inexplicable happens, madness explains it. Madness is the lid that fits every pot. And it may well have been madness, my dearest, I'm referring to the sublime madness that lends wings to love, that brought us together outside that flower stall, that led us to the cemetery, tempted us with that fragrant mushroom dish, brought us together again, and fitted us together in that narrow bed. But to this madness, to *our* madness and its melody, I say yes and again yes . . ."

From this point, roughly since the middle of January, much becomes obscure. If I see them at all, it is as silhouettes. True, not a single letter is missing from my mountain of documents. But amusing as this correspondence may be to an outsider, alternating between billing and cooing and mortuary matters, it seldom goes into anything of substance. To keep their story flowing, I have to grasp at dependent clauses and milk single words dry.

I shall try to explain this deficiency. Reschke and Piątkowska carried on a large part of their correspondence by telephone. Next to nothing is known of these conversations, though the letters and his diary give an idea of the difficulties encountered in telephoning between East and West. These quarters of the compass are not at all neutral; they divide good and evil, are imprinted like watermarks on their writing paper. While she bemoans the poverty of the East, the rising prices, the soup kitchens—in Poland at present the needy can get soup by presenting a *kuroniówka,* named after Jacek Kuroń, the minister of social affairs—he complains about Western oversupply and the unyielding hardness of West German currency, which he refers to, borrowing Alexandra's language, as "the German mark." And if she calls it disgraceful that she stayed in the Communist Party as long as she did, yet holds Communism responsible for all subsequent disasters—she even blames Communist iconoclasm for the persistence of Catholic dogma—he believes capitalism is responsible for all failings, including his own. After buying a computer for tax reasons—"Such things are deductible here"—he sees himself succumbing, compulsively as it were, to the principle of capitalist accumulation. "And to think that the university has a superabundance of data-storing devices . . ."

How dismissive he sounds, and yet this computer which, as he himself admits, he "hardly knows how to operate," will help him bring their idea to life. A so-called PC, probably an Apple. Here again I lack details, because he omits the technical information which I, stubbornly at work without a computer, cannot pull out of my hat.

Be that as it may, his "useful acquisition," as he soon calls his nameless contraption, begins to spit out elaborate extrapolations based on statistics as well as input coming to him from an increasing number of local homeland associations. For the first time he speaks, without a trace of irony, of "burial-ready persons," basing his calculations on the assumption that 30,000 people will be willing to advance as much as DM 1000, and in addition make further contributions as well as eventually sign over payments from health and life insurance policies, so that, given the availability of an authorized cemetery, a capitalization of some 28 million would be assured. True, a third of that sum would have to be set aside for the cemetery in Wilno and deposited in an escrow account, since it seems certain that Lithuania will want the return of burial-ready Poles to be paid for in hard currency. "Yes, dear Alexandra, that's how it is. Only with the help of the deutschmark can we provide our idea with concrete form . . ."

The majority of the former inhabitants of Danzig and environs, which until 1939 formed a Free State and was then incorporated into the Reich, had found reasonable accommodation if not a home in Schleswig-Holstein, Hamburg, Bremen, and Lower Saxony. Another 15,000 burial-ready persons could be expected as soon as Reschke fed figures for the East and South German settlement areas into his computer. My former classmate did not exclude the possibility of further increase after reunification, "although in that case the most that could be hoped for is a deposit of 500 deutschmarks. After all, East Germany is groaning under inherited burdens similar to those of Poland, even though it is true that recovery here should be quicker than in Poland. You, after all, have a big brother who knows the answer to everything."

Playing with the computer must have amused Reschke. Words like *network, monitor,* and *mouse* slipped into his letters. ROM was explained to Alexandra as Read Only Memory, RAM as Random Access Memory. Since their idea struck like a bombshell, a flood of programs poured through the mail, and he loaded them all on to his hard disk. He soon filled dozens of floppy disks. Not that his PC replaced his distant loved one in his affections. Nevertheless, he speaks fondly of his new acquisition: ". . . and as my buzzing companion, who stutters knowledgeably and yet so discreetly, recently whispered, we can start our cemetery association with a capitalization that promises to be far larger than my first extrapolations led me to believe . . ."

I wouldn't have thought him capable of such easy familiarity with software. At first Reschke felt obliged to justify his acquisition as required for his academic work. Passages from secondary sources, flowery jumbles of Baroque iconography struck him as worth storing, but in the end it was only the Polish-German-Lithuanian Cemetery Association and its plans that the professor entrusted to the memory of the "capitalist monster."

Having gone through numerous issues over several years of the monthly *Our Danzig* in the university library, he fed his PC—I see him in bedroom slippers sitting at his Apple—with information gathered from the back pages of that organ of local patriotism. There he found death notices and messages of congratulation on round-numbered birthdays, silver, golden, and diamond wedding anniversaries, and "well-deserved retirements." Photos of class reunions with captions told him how many surviving, now very senior schoolboys might still want to travel. There were also class photos from various elementary schools, junior high schools, and high schools, listing the boys and girls squatting in front, then sitting, then standing, then in the last row elevated. Their side-parts and pigtails, their cabbage bows and Schiller collars, their knee stockings and striped socks, their grins and timid smiles, and so much pinched gravity, flanked by the school principal and the class teacher—conveniently pre-assorted sources of information for Reschke, because these and other sources told him something about the longevity of former refugees. My classmate hesitates between categories and says "resettled" when he means "driven out," or he blurs the issue by classifying our aging compatriots as "resettled refugees."

As proof of this above-average life expectancy, he sent Piątkowska photocopies of birthday and anniversary notices as well as death notices, showing that a Herr Augustin Habernoll had celebrated not only his ninety-fifth birthday but the seventy-fifth anniversary of his career as an organist, or that Frau Frieda Knippel had reached her eighty-sixth birthday in the best of health, or that Herr Otto Maschke, age ninety-one, had "quietly passed away after a long illness."

Alexandra read: "Is not the longevity of resettled refugees trying to tell us that people are waiting impatiently, no, longing, for the Cemetery Association to be founded? Nay more. I believe that the dread prospect, increasing with each year, of having to lie in foreign soil, mingled with the hope of one day finding their last resting place in a native churchyard, has prolonged the twilight of my countrymen's lives. The waiting bench is steadily growing longer. It is as though the old and the very old were crying out to us: 'Hurry! Don't make us wait any longer!' How fortunate that these jubilarians along with their former addresses are communicated to my otherwise obscure homeland paper, whose editors still believe that the course of history can be reversed, e.g.: 'Formerly of Danzig, Am Brausenden Wasser 3B, present residence 2300 Kiel 1, Lornsenstrasse 57.' I have stored over a thousand addresses. Most local refugee organizations answer my circular, expressing interest. They provide me with raw data. And I am grateful that nearly all of them distribute my questionnaire. Seventy-two percent of the replies indicate burial-readiness in the context of our Cemetery Association. Fifty-one percent of these wish to make the full deposit as soon as possible, while only thirty-five percent prefer to pay in installments; the remaining fourteen percent are undecided. Several times I have checked these figures, and every time I am amazed to see what wonders computer technology, which I long believed to be soulless, can accomplish. Soon we will set up one of these magic boxes on Hundegasse. I feel sure that my Alexandra will learn to use it more easily than I did."

Her reaction upon the arrival of the new piece of furniture: "Yes, German gentleman has to tell Polish people always how to make everything all right . . ."

That was toward the end of February, when the East German state was threatening to drain in a westerly direction and Reschke was feeding the daily emigration figures into his PC, whereupon it spat out the information that this depopulation gave reason to fear an Anschluss of the vacated territories in the near future. I read: "More and more the events of the day make me fear that our idea will suffer under the burden of German incompatibility . . ."

By return mail a reply that is meant to comfort him arrives. Piątkowska compares the permanently worried face of her prime minister with the West German chancellor's standard expression: "Why you complain, Aleksander? If poor Poland has knight of mournful countenance, you have only blubbery Sancho Panza always grinning . . ."

Now I want to unload my rage. What are their letters to me! Why should I join in his computer games? What is it about the couple's story that continues to intrigue me? Isn't their love getting banal, and isn't their business with the dead contrived? How many more toads do I have to swallow?

Neat and spidery, their February letters justify my bad mood. Piątkowska writes that her son, who is studying in Bremen, has dismissed his mother's and her lover's plans for the Cemetery Association as a "typical product of petty bourgeois wishful thinking." "Witold says our idea is false consciousness because he has to tease me always, he is Trotskyite because I was too long in Party, and he won't have girlfriend like I want him to have." Reschke then complains about the "injudicious egoism" of two of his daughters, one of whom accuses him of an "anachronistic homeland cult" and the other of "revanchist necrophilia." "The youngest keeps out of it; obviously our idea means nothing to her."

He further deplores the bureaucratic pettiness at the university, the electoral defeat of the Sandinistas in Nicaragua, the weather, the neonationalist attitudes of his colleagues; she, on the other hand, reports uncomplainingly on her work, now in St. Mary's. "There stands astronomical big clock, made, as you know, by Hans Düringer, but legend says he smashed it all, because council of patricians put out both his eyes and blinded him to stop him making wonderful clocks in other places. And now I get to fix it . . ."

The gildress's task was to restore the traces of the

original gilding, specifically in the numerals of the ecclesiastical feast days. Piątkowska wrote this letter in December, whose feast days are: St. Barbara, St. Nicholas, the Immaculate Conception, and St. Lucy. The Golden Number, the lunar cycle running from 1 to 19, the twelve golden numerals for the hours on the outer circle of the clock, and the few traces of gold in the signs of the zodiac on the inner circle still had to be restored. "Especially Leo has most gold left over from first gilding. I am looking forward to Leo because my birthday comes when Leo dominant . . ."

Our professional pair. I'm getting curious about them again. Luckily, they were not entirely obsessed with their idea. While Piątkowska was gilding time that had stopped, Professor Reschke was inventing exercises for his students. "The charming gift from your hand," he writes, "has inspired me to channel my anger with the university and its intrigues into useful activity—that is, to give a seminar on the objects created for buying and selling. Everything that appears in works of art can be categorized in this way: baskets, panniers, bags, sacks, nets, carryalls, knapsacks, which are again in fashion among the counterculture people, as are, sorry to say, those wretched plastic bags. As you might expect, the Dutch Little Masters have a great deal to offer. Money pouches, visibly displayed and often magnificently executed, can be seen in woodcuts since the late-Gothic period. And contemporary art, down to Beuys, positively celebrates these objects; no felt slipper is safe from it. Incidentally, any number of these useful articles figure in the etchings and drawings of our mutual friend Chodowiecki—I'm sure you recall our little quarrel—I am thinking in particular of the drawings he did on his journey from Berlin to Danzig and during his stay there, for example, the charming sketch of a maid with a wicker basket. My students are crazy about these drawings. And they were ecstatic when, with your permission, I hope, I brought your dear gift to my seminar. What interests me in all this is the visual quality and the possibility of building bridges between art and everyday life. No wonder that two of my female students and a little later a young man started crocheting a string bag with a zig-zag pattern. They use your bag, which I am now glad to call mine, as a model . . ."

Daily association with the astronomical clock may have made the otherwise down-to-earth gildress reflective, for in her first March letter she writes: "We must move. Or time runs out. Not only because Germans soon unite and will not want to think about cemetery, but because also general shortage. I mean time shortage, same as meat shortage and sugar shortage used to be. Now in stores there is too much, only too expensive, because money is short. Time runs out if we do not move . . ."

This was in line with Reschke's own fears, though he was less concerned about the passage of time than about the weather. "On January 25, the first storm, coming from England across Belgium and northern France, caused considerable damage. There were fatalities. And this storm was followed by five more, which created a hopeless chaos in our already ailing forests. Fear is widespread. In Düsseldorf and elsewhere, the Monday carnival procession had to be called off; that never happened before. To make matters worse, the weather is mild between storms, too mild for February. We haven't had a normal winter for years. Since the middle of the month, crocuses and other flowers have been blooming in front gardens and parks. Take my word for it, Alexandra, I'm not alone in worrying about the present climatic changes; in spite of the caution that science imposes on us all, a number of university colleagues working in this field regard the so-called greenhouse effect as the cause of the violent storms we have been having. I'm sending you under separate cover some articles on the subject, because I don't know whether or to what extent your newspapers report on changes in climate. Here, in any case, we fear the worst, but I suspect that you have other worries . . ."

Reschke and the university. Perhaps I should try to give a more rounded picture of my former classmate than can be pieced together from his letters. Some information comes from the material he left with me. Other information I have gathered through inquiries. I vaguely remember our shared schooldays. Two Hitler Youths on the same school bench but not in the same troop, parading in columns at morning festivities or in front of the rostrum on the Maiwiese, as the Small Drillground beside the stadium came to be called . . .

He studied in Heidelberg and took his degree in Hamburg, where his father, soon after fleeing, found work in the post office. Alexander Reschke got tenure late, at the age of forty. That was at the Ruhr University in Bochum. The political changes in the late sixties may have helped; quite a few assistants, instructors, and chairless professors managed to wangle careers at that time. In any case, his ideas—on university reform, on student participation in decision making, and particularly on the interpretation of art history—were timely and not devoid of radicalism. He called for the study of the workaday world as reflected in the industrial as well as the fine arts. His doctoral dissertation on memorial slabs reads like a draft of his later theses. Burial customs and the social distinctions revealed by them are treated at length: the gradient between the paupers' cemetery and the burial vault of princes.

But Reschke was only moderately radical. As a faculty member and as an individual in the sit-ins common at the time, he opposed the formulating of excessively revolutionary aims. After a certain amount of to and fro, which for a while brought him close to a Communist splinter group, he adopted a left-liberal position which in the course of two decades underwent some change but remained recognizable. He was not the only one to justify his inconsistency by the well-known adage that life goes on.

In the eighties his views were enriched by contact with new generations of students, with the result that to what remained of his left-liberal views he added ecological convictions. The broad range of his opinions often brought him into conflict with himself. He complained about narrowness and stuffiness, for like other professors he had acquired, from exchange professorships overseas and periods of study in London and in Uppsala, the degree of cosmopolitanism that enables one to regard one's home as provincial.

Popular with his students, but also ridiculed as a veteran of '68 by some who thirsted for a more authoritarian system, Reschke felt himself, in the early days of the correspondence between widower and widow, to be "profoundly split and without perspective." The university and, as he wrote Piątkowska, "even more so the teaching routine" disgusted him. Small wonder that the idea born in an abandoned cemetery appealed to him at once. Though at first limiting it to one region, he soon endowed it with global significance. Later, Reschke spoke of an "epiphany"; he tended to construct lofty concepts as pedestals not only for objects but also for feelings, daydreams, mere coincidences, even mirages.

A woman student, who had attended his seminar on baskets, string bags, and plastic bags, said to me: "He cut a fairly melancholy figure with his everlasting beret, but he wasn't unattractive, you know, only kind of old-fashioned, the way he'd shift his thousands of details around like the pieces of a Chinese puzzle. On the whole, we liked him. What more can I say? Sometimes he stood around like a spare prick at a wedding, and he kept shooting his mouth off rather negatively, about the future, the weather, the traffic, reunification, and so on. He was right in a way, don't you think?"

What Professor Alexander Reschke didn't know: the students had a nickname for him. They called him Jeremiah.

To sum up, he seems to have been divided, incapable of linear action, a shillyshallying Reschke wasting his energy, reacting to every topic like a jumping jack. On the question of unification he was able to line up as many pros as cons; on the one hand, it was "desirable from a purely emotional point of view"; on the other hand, he feared German immoderation and—as he writes in a letter to a newspaper—"This colossus in the center of Europe oppresses me like a nightmare."

The fact that after the Second World War millions of Germans were driven from their homeland—Silesia, Pomerania, East Prussia, the Sudetenland, and (like his parents and mine) the city of Danzig—also divided his mind, though without tearing it apart; for if Reschke suffered from feeling that he had "two souls in one breast," it also would have left him soulless had one of them been surgically removed. In a letter to Piątkowska he confessed to being a "German Hamlet"; this made him feel justified in saying one thing and something entirely different in the same breath. He spoke alternately of "being driven out" and of "resettlement," whereas Piątkowska spoke of Poles and Germans, regardless of whether they had been driven out of Wilno or Danzig, as "poor refugees, the lot of them."

After stumbling over these contradictions in his diary and in his unpublished memoir, "The Century of Expulsions," I couldn't help but wonder: How could this split Reschke become obsessed with an idea that exhorted him night and day to carry it out unswervingly and without misgiving? What transformed him, the procrastinator, the Jeremiah, into a man of action?

My research informs me now that once, in the course of his academic career some time ago, he had an idea that he put through obstinately, ruthlessly in fact, despite the opposition of colleagues in other fields. This idea advocated a "praxis-oriented" course of study for art historians. Basing himself on statistics, Reschke demonstrated that many students left the university unprepared for professional life. Why? Because, he argued, they were without practical experience. Since museum jobs were rare, art-book publishers reluctant to spend money on readers and editors, and since as a rule the municipal authorities picked their cultural advisors on a political basis, the art historian of the future had to find new ways to plan his career.

Reschke's curriculum provided for courses in adult education, mass tourism, leisure activities, and cultural guidance for senior citizens. Experts, such as the manager of a travel bureau, the female manager of an amusement park frequented by millions, and the program director of a so-called summer academy, were invited to give talks. The cultural needs of hotel chains, golf clubs, and old people's homes were explored.

He was successful. His praxis-oriented courses were called exemplary. When Reschke's idea had acquired a well-funded place in the university budget, the minister of education for North Rhineland–Westphalia, a woman, spoke of "an act of social responsibility . . ." In the press a good deal of praise and a corresponding amount of criticism: some spoke of the leveling of university studies. The university should not become an employment agency. And so on.

But Reschke won out. His praxis-oriented course for art historians was copied at other universities. I am beginning to see my former classmate more clearly in retrospect. Wasn't it he who during the war organized the compulsory campaigns against potato bugs and achieved success by devising an effective method of rounding up those noxious insects? It seemed that Reschke, the split Alexander Reschke, could act with a sense of purpose, aggressively tackle reality, and creatively turn ideas into facts.

Thus I am not surprised to read in a letter dated early March that on the basis of his forecasts of "declared and undeclared burial-readiness" he had scheduled meetings with former refugees in Bonn, Düsseldorf, and Hannover. Interest was shown. A German-Polish relaxation of tension, if not outright reconciliation, was seen in the idea. His plan was characterized as constructive and worthy of encouragement. A long-term program of this kind, it was thought, might even act as a kind of flanking movement in support of reunification. A clause to that effect should not be absent from the boundary treaty with Poland, a treaty that could no longer be postponed. Now the unavoidable concessions had to be put to profitable use.

Official documents confirm that Reschke was able to suggest to all burial-ready persons the possibility that the initial deposit of DM 1000 might be tax-deductible. He enclosed proof of this in his letter. "You see, dear Alexandra, our cause is making headway. Even in my correspondence with the central office for Danzig affairs in Lübeck I can speak openly. There and elsewhere, no reservations. Furthermore, conversations with the management of two reputable funeral companies have shown me that large-scale operations are receptive to new methods; one has already entered into negotiations with a firm in the GDR which, in line with the local linguistic usage, calls itself the People-Owned Earth Furniture Consortium and produces cheap coffins. Soon, that is, after the conclusion of the currency union, this enterprise too will be faced with marketing problems. If our Cemetery Association were already in existence, I would be tempted to invest in the production of 'earth furniture.' It would never have entered my head that putting our idea into practice—computing transportation costs, drawing up plans for future cemeteries, studying coffin catalogues, and preparing for discussions with so-called professional refugees—would amuse me so much, no, would give me such moral satisfaction. Incidentally, both funeral companies are interested in working with a Polish establishment in a joint venture. Also—if and when the time comes—in transportation from Gdańsk to Wilno . . ."

From Wilno Piątkowska had received bad news. In principle, of course, they were interested in transactions that would pay them in hard currency. On second thought, however, they decided that the whole enterprise was not practicable. Alexandra writes: "No go in Wilno, because Lithuanians want own state first. I see their point; they want to be out of Soviet Union first. You report fine first success, and here I must wait until politics says yes. But let's start anyway German-Polish Cemetery Association. Here many people want to talk to you. Sad part is we depend on Soviets still. Even people from *województwo* and Church. Even assistant director of National Bank don't want to wait no more. You must come, my Aleksander. With all my heart I want you here soon . . ."

But before his next trip to Gdańsk they met in Hamburg's Fuhlsbüttel Airport. After a congestion-impeded taxi ride to Central Station they took the next train to Lübeck. There Reschke had reserved in the Hotel Kaiserhof two adjoining rooms with a view of the nearby Mühlentor and the city's towers. I got all this from the hotel bill, which is on my desk along with xerox copies of the air tickets, the railroad tickets, several taxi receipts, and other documents. Reschke got receipts for everything, even their stand-up snack at the Hamburg station.

They had arranged their meeting by phone. Apart from the date, March 15, I don't know much. Certain assumptions can be made from letters written later. It is certain that the day after their arrival and their night at the hotel (in adjoining rooms), they visited the city, the Behn-Haus, the cathedral and its astronomical clock, then took lunch in the Maritime Club and kept an appointment that afternoon in the "Angel's Den," a room in the House of the Hanseatic City of Danzig and the headquarters of the Homeland Association, "with a number of leading citizens of both sexes."

Between lunch and appointment there may have been time for a visit to St. Mary's, where Reschke may have told Piątkowska the story of Malskat, the art forger, and explained the scrubbed and derisively empty perspective plane high up in the choir. I hear him talking and talking: his old-fashioned diction, with its tinge of hurt feelings, his digressions . . . Authenticated is Piątkowska's only comment on the Malskat case. "Why wipe it all off if beautiful? We painted on façades lots of things never there before. Isn't art always forgery a little? But German art, of course, has to be one hundred percent always."

Apart from the receipt, my only record of the lunch at the Maritime Club, a restaurant where the customers sit on long benches under authentically rigged models of ships, is a menu, in the margin of which Reschke wrote in a small, neat hand: "Alexandra wanted to eat something exotically North German: Labskaus, a seaman's dish. She tasted my matjes herring and liked it better; she also liked the rote Grütze we had for dessert . . ."

I assume that our couple scarcely touched on politics at table, though at that time carloads of visitors from Schwerin and Wismar were coming across the nearby border, now open, more to see than to buy—what would they buy with? Actually, I wished the two of them at the long table hadn't restricted their conversation to private matters, especially since the newspapers were already carrying stories about xenophobia, in particular hatred for Polish border crossers. No, the couple were still savoring their night in the Hotel Kaiserhof, the visits from room to room, the return of their stored-up passion. In all likelihood it was only after the rote Grütze that Alexander and Alexandra began to discuss political developments—he the impending Volkskammer vote in the GDR, she the high cost of living in Poland—and finally their forthcoming appointment in the House of the Hanseatic City of Danzig.

Though subsequent letters yield few details concerning their second night together—who cares how pleased they were with the hotel, which Piątkowska recalls was "all nice and clean and smelled good"?—they both comment in detail on their afternoon appointment. After going on at length about an exhibition of old prints, panoramic views, and faded documents in vitrines, he writes: "We have taken a not inconsiderable step forward," and she: "I wouldn't think your officials could be so polite and talk not least bit revanchist . . ."

That doesn't tell us a lot, but this much is certain: Reschke was able to display not only his computer's diligence in spreadsheets and extrapolations but also commitments from funeral companies and burial funds, plus letters of approval from high-ranking government officials, fiscal affidavits, and a blueprint of the future cemetery. Piątkowska produced letters from the *województwo*, from the Gdańsk branch of the Polish National Bank, from two deputies of the Sejm, and from the diocese. Add to this Reschke's practiced delivery: eloquently he populated the former United Cemeteries, row upon row, all in accordance with the German Cemetery Regulations.

I found out later that the refugees' association, officially the League of Danzigers, Inc., had promised discreet support, consisting apparently of making their membership list available. Staff collaboration was an item under discussion, with the understanding that no further entitlements were to be expected. No one was to profit personally from the philanthropic community work of the German-Polish Cemetery Association. A certain Frau Johanna Dettlaff said: "We are interested only in this modest patch of home soil." All were agreed that the proceedings would further peace and understanding among nations.

The diary contains complete minutes, recording even the coffee, the Bahlsen biscuits, a few little glasses of aquavit served during the session, and the fact that Frau Dettlaff, a sturdy woman in her middle sixties, was adorned with a necklace of outsized amber beads. Finally, Piątkowska's gift to the League, a copy of a mug, partly gilded and of beaten silver, of the Danzig Brewers' Guild, with a dedication dated 1653; and the League's gift to Piątkowska, a copy of the *Selected Etchings* of Daniel Chodowiecki, published by Velhagen and Klasing in 1907, a book no doubt mischievously suggested by Reschke.

They left in the late afternoon. A bill documents the fact that they spent the night of March 17 at the Hotel Prem in Hamburg, this time in a double room. Their visit to the large, parklike Ohlsdorf cemetery is also a certainty, for Piątkowska exclaimed later with enthusiasm: "So glad I am to see that! German cemetery in Gdańsk must be made lovely as Ohlsdorf. Naturally not so big, but kept well to make it pleasure to go for stroll, to look for last resting place . . ."

After that the pair spent several days settling down in Bochum. There is no record of further visits to cemeteries. A brief note on the results of the Volkskammer election, which Reschke calls "a Pyrrhic victory for the coalition parties." Nothing about the Ruhr District, but the widow must have liked the widower's apartment, because immediately after she returned home, she wrote:

"Real surprise it was to see my Aleksander's apartment so neat, not just books, everything, towels, sheets. Hard to believe he is bachelor . . ."

From this first visit to Bochum there are photos of the two of them alone and with others. Reschke took Piątkowska to the university and introduced her to some of his colleagues and invited her to speak at his praxis-oriented seminar. "Alexandra's improvised talk about gilding as a trade and her comments on the necessity of rebuilding the old cities destroyed by the war were well received by my students, which is no surprise. She used her charm to make them forget the forgery underlying all reconstruction . . ."

They were constantly on the move, and not always for pleasure. In the presence of an important official from Bonn a preliminary contract was signed and notarized, which made it possible to open an escrow account in the Deutsche Bank. The atmosphere was unbureaucratic but serious. Since the Bonn Ministry for All-German Questions had already recognized the still-to-be-created Cemetery Association as a worthy cause, funds were set aside as seed money, for which a special account was opened. In Reschke's financial report the figure given is DM 20,000. Mention is made of widely distributed membership application forms, offering the option of paying the full fee up front or in installments. Should the Cemetery Association not be fully funded by the end of the year, reimbursement was guaranteed.

A photo shows the two of them standing outside the door of a house, beside which a notary has his office hours inscribed on a brass plate as if for all time. Piątkowska in a tailored suit, burgundy, bought in Essen and often mentioned in the diary. He in his usual beret. Both without string bags. An attaché case dangling on his right.

On March 21 Alexandra left. The first deposits in the escrow account had just been made. The computer had predicted correctly: only a third of the subscribers opted to pay in installments. On March 31 the balance stood at DM 317,400. Not a bad start. The idea was paying off. There would soon be an even million.

One may wonder why widower and widow did not meet again sooner, at Christmas, for instance. Had it been a question of her taking too long to get a visa, he could easily have made the trip by car or by plane. Or they could have met elsewhere, on so-called neutral ground, in Prague, say. No impromptu meeting is mentioned in his diary. Much as they longed for each other in their letters and found sparkling words for their desire, they didn't want to rush things. In his best handwriting, we read: "At our age, experience counsels caution."

From her hen-scratchings I make out: "Our love is not little and won't run away."

He in December: "We have waited years for each other; what do a few months matter?"

"Do you know," writes the gildress, "when I sit in scaffolding with astronomical big clock in front of me, the time just slips away."

He wants to be like the gnat in the walnut-size chunk of amber. ". . . enclosed in you . . ."

"And I in my Aleksander . . ."

"Ah yes, Alexandra, each in each . . ."

"But longing is great . . ."

"No, dearest, we mustn't. Not yet."

Besides, both had family obligations. She had her son

94

Witold with her over Christmas—"He was very sweet and I spoiled him like child"; he spent the holidays with his youngest daughter and for three days surrendered himself to the mercies of his grandchildren. "The two boys," however, "were not as exhausting as their parents with their passion for long-drawn-out conflict."

I don't know whether they had sworn in Gdańsk, perhaps over breakfast at the Hevelius, not to see each other until their idea had learned to fly on its own, but obviously they decided that when in doubt they would give precedence to the Polish-German-Lithuanian Cemetery Association. In one of his April letters I read: "Duty is duty and schnapps is schnapps." So they let the Easter holidays go by and did not arrange to meet until mid-May. By that time, they assumed, everything would be in place for incorporation.

He traveled by car. Three other persons flew from Hamburg: Frau Johanna Dettlaff, 65, wife of a retired manager of a district savings bank in Lübeck; Herr Gerhard Vielbrand, 57, a mid-rank industrialist from Braunschweig; and Dr. Heinz Karau, a consistory councilor of the North-Elbian Lutheran Church. These three persons had agreed that once the incorporation went through, they would occupy the three German seats on the board of directors. A legal adviser, whose name was not recorded, arrived at the same time.

Piątkowska reserved rooms for them, and a conference room on the seventeenth floor of the centrally located Hevelius. I have in my possession copies of itemized bills for expenses paid out of the account opened with the seed money from the All-German Ministry. Out of this account twice fourteen lunches were paid for. The dinner that concluded the conference after two days of meetings—"The atmosphere was relaxed, speeches were made," according to Reschke—must have been paid for by the *województwo* or the Polish National Bank. I find no documentary evidence.

Much remains unclear: Why did Reschke and Piątkowska wish to be considered only executive partners without voting rights? What was the legal basis of those meetings? I do not possess a copy of the contract of incorporation. But this much is certain. With the exception of the site occupied by the Students' Clinic, the entire area of the former United Cemeteries, in other words, the Park Akademicki, a tract of land amounting to twenty-five acres, was leased for sixty years, with option to buy, to the Association, hereinafter referred to in brief as the German-Polish Cemetery Association. In compliance with the size of the units required by the German Cemetery Regulations, it was specified that the area, fully occupied, would comprise 20,000 plots, including smaller plots for urns. However calculated, the lease amounted to DM 484,000 per annum, payable November 2. The total rent for the duration of the contract came to DM 6 million and was to be paid within two years. All additional expenses were the responsibility of the Association.

I assume that the two of them put their November date into the contract, though making no reference to the private significance of All Souls'. It goes without saying that burial expenses and grave maintenance in the now-German cemetery, to be known officially as the Cemetery of Reconciliation, were to be borne by the beneficiaries. The ground rules, worked out by Reschke, were accepted. After revision by the legal advisors— paragraphs concerning the length of interment periods and the right to be buried anonymously—Alexandra

Piatkowska and Aleksander Reschke signed the contract as executive partners. The Lithuanian part of the concept, the "Polish cemetery in Wilno," with its financial structure based on the deutschmark, was reserved for a separate clause—a compromise which Piątkowska had to accept.

He writes: "We met in a shabbily furnished conference room, but the view from the seventeenth floor of the resurrected city with all its towers made the scope of the enterprise clear to those present. Toward the end of the meeting, the atmosphere became festive. I don't know who ordered, or paid for, the champagne."

The board of directors consisted of the shareholders Dettlaff, Vielbrand, and Karau, and, on the Polish side, of the shareholders Marian Marczak, Stefan Bieroński, Jerzy Wróbel, and Erna Brakup. Erna Brakup, it was thought, would make up for the preponderance of Poles—four to three—because she was of German descent. As Reschke writes, "This was a friendly gesture on the part of the Poles, all the more so as Erna Brakup is no ordinary woman. Well into her eighties, she blabbers nonstop . . ."

The following day, the incorporation was announced to the press. My former classmate, who called his idea-become-contract "the work of a century," was nettled when anyone failed to agree with him. He shooed away like flies the criticisms of the press—the journalists had not been allowed to ask questions until the contract was signed. "We'll just have to get used to these troublemakers." In the end, however, he found the press conference satisfactory. "The questions were pointless more than malicious. When the editor-in-chief of a student newspaper observed that the Western border of Poland had not yet been recognized, I was able to refer to the clause in the contract—voted with no opposition and only one abstention—which stipulates that in the event of nonrecognition the contract becomes null and void."

Reschke speaks of Marian Marczak as helpful in dealing with the press. In his capacity as vice president of the National Bank, Marczak insisted "firmly but gently" that in the interests of Poland accommodation to the laws of the marketplace could not stop halfway, unless the intention was to restore the principle of Communist penury in all its glory . . . "I like this Pan Marczak, though I don't fully agree with his economic liberalism . . ."

Piątkowska's remarks about the distant goal of a cemetery to be leased in Wilno were applauded. Since reconciliation between Lithuania and Poland was in order, that cemetery too could be called a cemetery of reconciliation. I believe that she made this statement first in her language and then in her German. "We have all enough suffered!"

And yet Reschke saw fit to deplore her violent (his word was "rude") anti-Russian outburst, which true enough did not occur during the press conference but immediately after. "It grieves me to hear Alexandra speak that way. Understandable as the Russophobia of many Poles may be, our idea does not permit blanket judgments. For my sake at least she should dispense with them . . ."

Otherwise nothing clouded our couple's month of May. Alexander Reschke made little use of his single room at the Hevelius. The three-room apartment on Hundegasse was always open to him. Alexandra was delighted with his present from the West, a laptop computer. She was soon able to use it.

Directors Dettlaff, Vielbrand, and Karau departed

after the Board had voted a constitution and bylaws and elected the vice president of the National Bank chairman. Despite certain organizational problems that remained to be worked out, there was time for our couple to make excursions to Kashubia and to the Island as far as Tiegenhof. They took the car. But when my former classmate wanted to hire a bicycle rickshaw for the short ride to the newly leased burial ground, a quarrel erupted, which might have marred their happiness.

According to the diary, Reschke gave in. And Mr. Chatterjee, whose firm by then was operating more than thirty rickshaws in the Gdańsk area, offered the prospect of a future ride.

Actually, the short quarrel between Alexander and Alexandra was brought on not by the rickshaw question alone. If Chatterjee's sprightly employees had consisted entirely of Pakistanis and Bengalis, or even of Russians, Piątkowska would have risked the little exotic adventure. But because Poles, and by now exclusively Poles, were keeping the three dozen rickshaws on the road, the widow's "no" was motivated by national pride and for that reason riled the widower. "I should live," cried Alexandra, "to see Polish men doing coolie work."

4

My former classmate has written down a good many names for me: Marian Marczak, a tailor-made vice president, Stefan Bieroński, priest in jeans, Jerzy Wróbel, town clerk, who in his everlasting windbreaker is said to be a fact-finding bloodhound, and Erna Brakup in her cloche hat and galoshes, who is now coming to life for me.

Herren Karau and Vielbrand and Frau Johanna Dettlaff—who, according to Reschke, distinguished herself during the negotiations by her ladylike smile and rapid-fire mental arithmetic—have left town, but will return whenever Marczak summons the board of directors. Surrounded by people eager to vote, to meddle, and to supervise, Alexander and Alexandra were allowed only a little time together; so little time left.

Piątkowska began filling in the traces of gold on the outermost rim of the astronomical clock. Reschke continued discussions with the Polish members of the Board, most often with Marczak, who promised liberal terms from his bank, which was located in the old building on High Gate, where the coffered ceiling supported by granite columns created the illusion of permanence. With its ornamentation entirely in ceramic tile—the outer fields in green, white, and ocher, the center field in shades of brown, ocher, and white—the building had offered a secure home to varying currencies, and to that home Reschke now had access.

His computer had to be fed now and then with the hard work that had accumulated in Bochum. From the Interpress Bureau on Hundegasse, he was able to make long-distance calls and, at a later date, send faxes. Someone, probably Wróbel, advised caution—someone might be listening in, old habits die hard—but Reschke was unperturbed: "We have nothing to hide." Day after day his diary reports ever new activities, and yet the couple find time for two weekend excursions: a car trip across the Vistula to the Island and a drive to a lake.

At the beginning of May, earlier than usual, the rape was in bloom. "Too early," he writes. "A magnificent sight it is, as if yellow were celebrating yellow, but I still suspect that this spring, foreshadowed in February by violent storms, is fooling us all. Alexandra may laugh at me and call this monochrome floral splendor a gift from God that one should not complain about; I still say that sooner or later we'll get the bill for our commissions and omissions. I see the time, perhaps around the turn of the millennium, when, as Chatterjee says, the bicycle rickshaw will have driven the motorcar from the cities. Strict laws are in force. Much of what we can't do without today will be obsolete luxuries. But *our* idea, which now has a definite address, will not be affected by the great change, because it serves the dead, not the living. Nevertheless, in landscaping the cemetery, whose reconciliatory name we owe to consistory councilor Karau, a man of God who speaks in metaphors, preference should be given to plants that can withstand the future warming of the earth's surface. I must admit I don't know much about this. I will study and learn. Which plants withstand dry weather, even periods of drought. While crossing Tuchler Heath, reputed to be sandy and barren, my attention was drawn to those round juniper bushes; they immediately struck me as hardy, just the thing for our cemetery grounds . . ."

But it was not just the too-early-blooming rape that fed his forebodings. My classmate, who even during the weekly two-hour art class would scribble terrifyingly prophetic pictures on his Pelikan pad—in the middle of 1943 he did a sketch of our until then untouched city beneath a hail of bombs, all its towers in flames— was now finding a wider field for his talent. On the flat Island and along the shores of the Kashubian lakes, in the drainage ditches of the low-lying country and in the reeds along the shore, everywhere toads clamored, and Reschke identified them by their mating call, as red-bellied toads, the so-called fire toads. He writes: "They're still here. And in the higher lakes and ponds there are even yellow-bellied toads."

When Piątkowska, proud of her vocabulary, exclaimed, "Regular frog concert all over," the art history professor was prepared for more than a zoological lecture on spadefoot toads, common toads, midwife toads, frogs of all sizes, natterjacks, and horned toads: "Do you hear how the red-bellied call stands out against the others? It sounds as if a glass bell was struck. Over and over again. That plaintive double note after a short strike. That everlasting lament 'Oh, woe to you!' No wonder the call of the toad, even more than the screech of the barn owl, has given rise to superstitions. In many German fairy tales—in Polish fairy tales too, I'm sure— the call of the toad foreshadows disaster. We find it in Bürger's ballads, we find it in Voss and Brentano. In the old days the toad was believed to be wise. It was only later, as the times grew steadily worse, that toads became the harbingers of calamity."

No one could have been on more intimate terms with the subject than Reschke. In the rushes along the lakeshore near Kartuzy, and on the road from Neuteich to Tiegenhof where they stopped the car to photograph the rows of osier willows on the bank of the Tiege, or along the drainage ditches, with toads providing the accompaniment, the professor recited from the romantic poets, and his last quotation, from Achim von Arnim—"And the frogs and the toads sang on and on, celebrating the fires of St. John . . ."—brought him back to the too-early spring. If Arnim had the toads celebrating the fires of St. John, he was undoubtedly referring to the time of the summer solstice; but what was heard here in mid-May was the ominously premature call of the natterjack, or Bufo calamita. "Believe me, Alexandra, just as the rape is flowering too early, so are the red-bellied toad and the yellow-bellied toad calling too early. They are trying to tell us something . . ."

After this disquisition on their meeting with premature nature, Reschke's diary tells us that Piątkowska laughed at first, then scolded—"Why can't you just say rape is pretty! You big toad yourself"—then went on puffing cigarette after cigarette, growing increasingly taciturn, and in the end stopped talking altogether. "I've never known Alexandra so silent." The only request she had left was: "Here is little spooky. Let's go back to town."

The diary does not say whether she uttered this request on the shore of a lake or among osier willows. But on a tape Reschke's voice tells where he went with his recorder and sensitive microphone to capture the distinctly glass-bell-like calls of the toad. In Kashubia, near Chmielno, I hear Alexandra's voice over those ringing bells. "Mosquitoes eating me alive." And: "Now is enough nature sounds, Aleksander. It gets soon dark."

"Right away. Just a few more minutes, to compare the intervals . . ."

"Bites all over . . ."

"I'm sorry . . ."

"I know. All must be perfect."

Thanks to audio technology, his identification on the tape of time and place, her complaints, and the song of the toads all blend into a beautiful trio. From this I have learned that red-bellied toads call at longer intervals than yellow-bellied toads; that my classmate's voice is soft and warm, rumbling in a register between bass and baritone, but always as if he had a slight cold; and that she trumpets her words challengingly in harmony with the singing of the toads.

With the same technology Reschke captured the prolixity of a woman who, as a Polish citizen of German descent, belonged to the board of directors of the German-Polish Cemetery Association. Erna Brakup was also the speaker for the Ethnic German Minority of Gdańsk, which until then had been reduced to speechlessness; minorities had not been allowed.

A tape which records Erna Brakup's babbling right after the toad calls evokes warmed-up memories. That was how my paternal Grampa and Grandma talked. That was how our neighbors talked, and the beer truck drivers, shipyard workers, Brösen fishermen, the women who worked in the Amada margarine factory, housemaids, marketwomen on Saturday, garbage collectors on Tuesday, they all yapped their words querulously, and even the schoolteachers yapped, though in a more refined way, and the postal and police officials, and on Sunday the pastor in the pulpit.

"It wasn't just the government that tortured and badgered us . . ." After more than five decades of repression, the flow of Erna Brakup's speech—few speakers of that dialect are still alive—contains rarities and peculiarities that are threatened with extinction: Who today knows what *perlushken* are? She spoke a dying language. "And that is why," Reschke writes, "there was every reason to appoint her to the board of directors of the German-Polish Cemetery Association. She is close to ninety. When she goes to her grave, that pronunciation will be buried with her; one more reason for putting Erna Brakup on tape."

I have more than half a dozen cassettes. But before I hasten to transcribe the first, we need a better understanding of this old woman, which calls for a brief detour to the world of high politics. No sooner had the negotiations for the founding of the Cemetery Association begun, than an official visit was announced, first in Warsaw, then in Gdańsk. The president of the West German Republic was coming to Poland in the hope of smoothing over, with a few well-formulated speeches, half a dozen blunders made by the chancellor, and of creating a favorable atmosphere for the day when these two peoples, who had so much to forgive each other, would be neighbors.

Erna Brakup was in the crowd when the distinguished guest, with retinue, coming down Long Street, appeared to listen to interpretations of past and current events, and cast knowing glances in all directions; he submitted to the inner and outer circles of security guards and photo journalists as a fact of life, was finally escorted up the stairs of the Right City Rathaus and, after waving down the stairs with reserved bonhomie, disappeared into the building. There treasures would be shown him, including some which, newly gilded by Alexandra Piątkowska years before, had recovered their former radiance. In the crowd of tourists and local curiosity seekers, who all stood still under the president's gaze, Erna Brakup remained outside.

And this is what she said later on Reschke's tape in her priceless dialect that cannot here be reproduced: "I'd have liked to talk with him. Now with the century coming to an end it would have given me pleasure. I hope to live to see the German Cemetery back where it used to be. And so does my younger sister, who hightailed it across to the West right after the war and is now living in Bad Seeberg, Gorchfock Street No. 4. She will be able to come and lie here when it's all over with her. I just wanted to say: many thanks, Herr Bundespräsident, for all your trouble in putting the German Cemetery through and satisfying the heartfelt wish of my sister Frieda. And I, too, I'd have told him, after being Polish for so long, hope, when our Father in Heaven calls me, to be in the German Cemetery and not with all the Polacks that put us through the wringer till there was nothing left. But there was such a crowd that I couldn't catch him."

Not only Erna Brakup but also Alexander and Alexandra were standing at the foot of the Rathaus steps flanked by stone candelabra. The tourists clapped when the statesman waved gently down at them, his silvery hair glittering in the sun. The citizens of the visited town were impressed by his grandeur but didn't feel like clapping; even Reschke held back, though well aware that this official visit was propitious to the Cemetery of Reconciliation. The vice president of the National Bank, like Erna Brakup, was convinced that the visit of such a notable figure would be helpful. And Alexandra Piątkowska assured Jerzy Wróbel that her Aleksander had been instrumental in coordinating the president's brief visit with the cemetery negotiations.

Later, long after the visitor has departed, I hear Piątkowska say on tape, against a background of rushes and over the calls of the toads: "What beautiful eyes, your president. Doesn't need to wear dark glasses like ours. Good he came at right time. German Cemetery otherwise might have gone kaput."

For obvious reasons and because he was fed up with the university anyway, Professor Reschke took a leave of absence. No sooner was he back in Bochum than he entrusted his praxis-oriented seminars to his assistants and canceled all his teaching activities for the following summer. This did not require him to tighten his belt. At the incorporation meeting, the board of directors of the Cemetery Association had voted the executive partners a flat salary; with that to fall back on, he had no qualms about leaving the university and his colleagues.

There were smirks of course, but Reschke didn't let that bother him. His colleagues were now convinced that his carefully catalogued collection of hand-forged coffin nails, acquired over his long years of researching Baroque tombstones in North German cemeteries, was something more than a whim. The nails that gravediggers and sextons had brought him, crooked as well as straight, some corroded with rust, some with defective heads, and some that remained bright and sharp, most a good forefinger long and dating from the early Baroque to late Biedermeier, pointed to Reschke's present enterprise. To Alexandra he wrote: "I never would have thought that this by-product of my doctoral thesis would take on importance . . ."

He set up an office in his bachelor's apartment, which soon provided his university secretary with space and empty shelves. His collection of hand-forged coffin nails, along with his books, had to move into the living room.

Only then did Reschke check his wardrobe and, as the receipts bear witness, purchase a black worsted suit, black shoes, black socks, several gray-on-gray patterned ties, a black Borsalino, and a black umbrella to match an asphalt-gray raincoat, both made in Italy; for the Cemetery of Reconciliation was to be solemnly consecrated in the second half of June, with the first two burials taking place at the same time.

On his return to Gdańsk, his gift for her was a porcelain sink with accessories. While Reschke was taking care of everything, Piątkowska complemented his meticulous planning: while he and his office, for the time being on a half-day schedule only, were in communication with the visa division of the Polish Embassy, she, through the Orbis tourist bureau, reserved many single and double rooms for the mourners expected in the near future.

The bodies were to be shipped by a funeral company which had found a counterpart in Gdańsk and had already signed a contract with it. It had proved impossible to do business with the East German firm of the People-Owned Earth Furniture, whose coffins were at best adequate only for cremation. However, cremation, if desired, could take place close to the former home of the deceased. The restoration of the old crematorium on St. Michael's Lane, whose furnaces had only recently been dismantled, was unthinkable at the moment.

Luckily Reschke entered all sorts of day-by-day trivia in his diary: "Now at last the leaky sink on Hundegasse can be replaced, and Alexandra is pleased that with all my other activities I did not forget her wish."

Then the day came. Since the Bishop of Oliwa had accepted then suddenly saw fit to decline the invitation owing to a previous engagement, the Cemetery of Reconciliation was consecrated by Father Bieroński, the parish priest of St. Peter's, and by consistory councilor Dr. (of philosophy) Karau, who together acted as an ecumenical doubles team. The presence of a Catholic and an Evangelical cleric reflected not only the denominational composition of the board of directors but also their determination not to segregate the burial ground by faith, as had been customary in the days of the United Cemeteries. The event was not widely publicized. Very little press, no television. Reschke did, however, commission a private film to tape—from a respectful distance—the consecration of the cemetery and the first burials. The materials in my possession include a videocassette with a running time of at least half an hour. After playing the tape several times—though admittedly it has no soundtrack—I can say that I was almost there.

The consecration took place on the first day of summer, and was immediately followed by two burials in the far corner of the large area where the avenue leading to the main building of the Engineering School borders the Cemetery of Reconciliation. Despite fine weather—sunny to partly cloudy—only few curiosity seekers attended: some old women keeping shyly to one side, a few unemployed. In any case, the camera focused only on the mourners and Reschke, of course in his worsted suit, his Borsalino slightly tilted, and his rolled umbrella over his arm. Beside him, the gildress in mourning black, under a broad-rimmed hat, not without elegance. Then Frau Brakup, small, wizened, covered with a pot-shaped mushroom, her legs in rubber boots. And behind the couple, Jerzy Wróbel. Bald on top, but with long wavy hair on the sides, the picture of a perpetually bewildered artist. His windbreaker, which, Reschke never fails to point out, he wears on every occasion, has to suit every occasion.

Since on June 21, at the same time though elsewhere high politics was enacted, someone later said: The Reschke-Piątkowska team know how to link their interests to important dates; those two weren't born yesterday. However, Reschke says in his diary that it was not intention but chance, pure chance, or providence if you will, in the choice of date for the first burials—a most gratifying providence: "The fact that on the same day, even at the same hour as the consecration of the Cemetery of Reconciliation, the Bundestag in Bonn and the Volkskammer in East Berlin officially recognized the western boundary of Poland, as established by international law, was extremely favorable to our enterprise. After August we were able to use the chapel of the former crematorium for funeral services. The White-Russian congregation had enriched the once boring emptiness of that starkly utilitarian room with Orthodox pomp."

Then they were standing beside open graves. It was as if our couple had hand-picked the first two corpses: an elderly man of the Lutheran persuasion and an aged woman of the Catholic faith were buried so close together in time that both groups of mourners were able to attend both burials. In addition, the weather was such as to invite them to linger. The sunlight, filtered by shade

111

trees, as the video bears witness, fell upon the mourners.

Returned to earth were: Egon Eggert, formerly of
Danzig, Grosse Krämergasse 8, last residence Böblin-
gen, age 82; and Auguste Koschnick, formerly of Nas-
senhuben, District of Danziger Niederung, last residence
Peine, age 91. One coffin black, one walnut. Bieroński
and the servers in white and violet. Karau in gown and
bands.

According to Reschke's report, not only relatives and
friends of the deceased were present; several branches
of the Homeland Association had sent observers; the
League had sent Frau Johanna Dettlaff. Their purpose
was to make sure that the German burials were conducted with dignity in Polish surroundings, to study the
cemetery conditions, and report on the maintenance of
the graves. Special interest was shown in double graves.
Because Frau Martha Eggert, the widow of Egon Eggert, was present, she was able to secure a place by her
husband's side when the time came. All questions were
asked in an undertone. And in a soft voice, always ad-
justed to fit the expression, Jerzy Wróbel answered like
a dignitary.

Reschke's diary entries still echo the emotion of the
first burials. In the video I seem to see Piątkowska
weeping under a broad-rimmed hat at both the first
and the second memorial services. Touching, how the
boyishly gawky priest of St. Peter's apologized at the
beginning of his brief funeral oration for his "very in-
sufficient German." Consistory councilor Karau's ser-
mon was rather too long, his sentences in constant search
of metaphors, and terms such as "return" and "home
soil" overemphasized. Frau Dettlaff, whom I believe I
recognize in an imposing lady dressed in good quality

mourning, after the consecration wished, in her capacity as the speaker of the League, to deliver a prepared speech, but Reschke managed to talk her out of it. Would she kindly deliver her contribution on another occasion less open to misunderstanding. He too had to restrain himself, for the occasion inspired many a pertinent thought. It all went very tactfully. On the whole, in the judgment of the press, the first burials in the Cemetery of Reconciliation were felt to be dignified and mercifully free of political static. While condolences were being expressed, the cameraman with slow panning shots captured the cruciform avenues of lindens, the large traffic circle, several clumps of trees, elms and chestnuts, the weeping willow and a copper beech, and finally he showed a certain Polish bias by including those who used the park, women with small children, pensioners, readers, a lone drinker, and a group of unemployed card players, none taking much notice of the burials. Then came the brick house like a witch's cottage at the entrance to the park-cemetery, and with it the brass plate mounted on yellow brick, making it known in both German and Polish that in future the park would serve as a Cemetery of Reconciliation, a Cmentarz Pojednania.

Older mourners found it offensive that some of the younger mourners, among them the great-grandchildren of the deceased, had chosen to ride from the hotel to the cemetery and back in Chatterjee's bicycle rickshaws, though Reschke notes that "nothing unseemly happened, for the rickshaws like the taxis covered the distance, which was the same, though the fare was much less, with crepe blowing on the side."

What used to be called the funeral feast was held at the Hevelius. Both groups of mourners sat at long ta-

113

bles reserved for them at the restaurant. Reschke mentions in his notes that on this occasion Frau Johanna Dettlaff managed to make her moderate (all things considered) speech. Unfortunately I possess neither the text nor a recording. But when, in the course of that double feast, member of the board Erna Brakup came to life, the tape was running. Under and over the interference, I hear: "All right, I'll take another slice of pork, our Heavenly Father gave me hands and no one has to press me . . . But I liked the burial, even if it wasn't the same as it used to be, when it was called the United Cemeteries. It really made me hope to be lying there soon. Jessesmaria. Never mind, I can wait awhile . . ."

What can Reschke have been thinking when in his diary, describing the funeral feast, he compared the burial rites of the Mexicans and Chinese and ended by listing the advantages of cremation as practiced by the Hindus? He praises the minimizing of the corpses and has no qualms about speaking of "the need to save space." Was he afraid that the Cemetery of Reconciliation might someday be full, in fact, overcrowded? Did he, one who expressly rejected mass graves—"Never again must that be allowed!"—have a vision of future mass funerals?

After escorting further burials in his new suit—with umbrella in rainy weather—joined by Piątkowska in expressing condolences but at the same time keeping a discreet eye on the orderly progress of the ceremonies, he broke off his stay in Gdańsk and busied himself at his headquarters in his Bochum apartment, providing the Cemetery of Reconciliation with a steady flow of material. In a short letter that seems to have been written in haste, we read: "It was right, my dearest, to set

114

up the office so quickly, even if that makes my apartment too small for you and me. Frau von Denkwitz has proved helpful with the new work here. She has been my secretary for many years, and I can trust her implicitly. The bank balance is gratifying. Soon it will come to a round four million. The number of the burial-ready is mounting. Moreover, numerous small gifts, considerable amounts, including some from overseas, have been deposited in the bequest account that was opened early in June. Frau von Denkwitz is now working full time . . ."

The business was doing nicely, but my former classmate's success was not unclouded: the mail brought a good many insulting letters. The newspapers were full of "malicious wit" and "cynical sallies." So incensed was Reschke about such comments that I wonder whether my neighbor on the school bench could have been the same gangling, pimple-faced boy whom the slightest criticism reduced to tears. Better than average in almost all subjects, he let his friends copy from him, but wanted to be praised for it, above all praised. And when his crude drawing, with its prophetic vision of the city going up in flames under a hail of bombs, brought him blame and only blame from all the students and teachers, he burst into tears—yet, come to think of it, he had foreseen correctly.

In any case Reschke thought it absurd that he of all people should be reviled as "an incorrigible revanchist," as "profiteering at the expense of the dead." One of the lampoons, headlined GERMAN CEMETERY PEACE ASSURED, accused him of aiming at "reconquest through corpses." Reschke, an experienced writer of letters to the editor, replied, characterizing his organizational efforts as "the ultimate in international understanding."

Obviously this Reschke can't have been the lanky, pimple-faced boy so intent on praise. I see my former neighbor rather as a zealous troop leader who, in addition to organizing the potato bug campaigns, distinguished himself by setting up a collecting point where during the first or second winter of the Russian war woolens and other articles for the soldiers on the eastern front were collected and packed: sweaters, wristlets, long underwear, fur coats, ear muffs, and even skis. But that terrible drawing was also the work of troop leader Reschke, the Reschke who alone knew what the future would look like . . .

Anyway, the flood of supportive articles and enthusiastic letters outweighed the insults. Compatriots wrote even from America and Australia. Let a quotation from one letter stand for them all: ". . . and not so long ago, it gave me joyful satisfaction to read in our bulletin, which always arrives weeks late, that the United Cemeteries on Hindenburgallee have reopened. Congratulations! I am still hale and hearty; though going on seventy-five, I'm right in there at shearing time, but I'm thinking of accepting your generous offer. No! I don't want to lie in foreign ground . . ." Soon bodies were arriving from overseas.

Reschke answered this letter personally. But he was able to entrust his secretary with most of his correspondence; for years, her letter-writing style had been his. There was no more than that between them, no sticky intimacy, nothing to upset Alexandra . . . and anyway, I refuse to bring in a subplot.

Erika von Denkwitz, of whom I have no photograph, was five years old when her mother, with her and three other children and the estate manager and his wife, all left Stuhm with two jam-packed horse carts and headed west. Two of her siblings and the wife of the estate manager died on the way. Only one horse and wagon made it. Erika lost her dolls.

Reschke in his notes expresses surprise that "the details of West Prussian rural life should be so deeply embedded in my secretary's childhood memories." Interestingly enough, she did not wish to be entered in his card file of the burial-ready. He claims to understand her reluctance, makes no attempt to win her over, praises her "unswerving loyalty regardless of deep-seated doubts," and after less than two weeks leaves town, putting her in charge of the office. My former classmate was good at delegating; otherwise I wouldn't be saddled now with this report.

Back in Gdańsk, Alexander had to reassure his Alexandra, who because of the recently enacted currency unification was worried about poor Poland now doomed to live next door to the deutschmark. "What will we do when you come with fat moneybags to buy us?"

Reschke was sure the deutschmark would have its hands full putting the East German economy on its feet. "There won't be much left for Poland. But even so, I'm confident the Cemetery Association will not be seriously affected by the changing economy. Preparing for death frees one from worry about economic trends. Believe me, Alexandra, no one economizes on his funeral."

This conversation took place one weekend soon after his arrival from Bochum. The two of them had driven to Kashubia. A fine summer day, though the rape was no longer in bloom. There were still poppies and cornflowers and peasants with horse-drawn plows. The cock out of the picture book was crowing on his dunghill.

117

Alexandra had bought food for a picnic, which she prepared on the shore of a lake near Zuckau and spread out on a pretty red-and-blue embroidered tablecloth: coarse garlic sausage, cottage cheese mixed with onions and chives, a jar of mustard pickles, radishes, too many hard-boiled eggs, mushrooms in oil and vinegar, bread and butter, nor did she forget the salt shaker. She put four bottles of beer in the lapping water by the shore. They found a sandy bay between clumps of rushes, small enough for the two of them. Both sat barefoot on folding chairs, he with rolled-up trouser legs.

No, no toad noise. Once in the distance, a motorcycle. Dragonflies over the water, bumblebees, cabbage butterflies, what else? Little by little it grew dark. Now and then a fish jumped out of the water. Cigarette smoke against mosquitoes. And then suddenly the call of a single toad! More a ring than a call. "When we had almost given up hope, the bell struck three times: short, long, long . . . The still surface of the water made the ringing especially clear. Where did it come from? I couldn't say; from near, from far. No other sound, except perhaps larks, who held the stage from morning till night over the prematurely ripe fields. And sacks of white cloud drifting from the northeast were part of the Kashubian summer. The toad call went on and on . . ."

And into the silence and over the endless croaking Piątkowska said, "We should stop now."

It seems to have taken Reschke a moment to answer:

"You mean what we began can't succeed?"

"Only what I said. Stop now, because it's going well still."

"But we've just begun . . ."

"I still say."

"We haven't yet filled three rows of graves . . ."

118

"Believe me, Aleksander, any better it won't get."

"We'll have to let the business take its course, because no one can stop it now . . ."

"Just because we had idea?"

". . . which will be a mess if we leave it unfinished."

Alexandra Piątkowska put an end to this dialogue which paralleled the croaking of the toads. Her laughter is recorded on Reschke's tape.

It goes without saying that they went on—and damnit, even I now want them to go on—but the suggestion that they stop while it was going well marked a turning point in their story. Later I find entries that confirm this caesura. "It was the solitary toad that advised Alexandra to put an early end to our endeavors. Should I have listened?"

Of that picnic it remains to be reported that the four beer bottles refused to cool in lukewarm lake water. "We should have brought bathing suits, as I had advised," writes Reschke. But I personally am glad they didn't, because it spares me the need to portray the art historian and the gildress, the widower and the widow, the pale and skinny Reschke and the lean-to-overflowing Piątkowska, that belated pair, in bathing suits.

With rolled-up trousers and hiked-up skirt they dabbled in the shallow water by the shore. He might contemplate his feet in the water, how they blur, how, distorted this way and that, they seem strange and remote to him. She smokes with her left hand while holding her skirt with her right.

Now Reschke has picked up flat, barely wet stones from the sand. "In my youth there were crayfish here," he said, when nothing stirred under the stones.

Piątkowska said: "When I was here with Mama and Papa just after war, there were lots of crayfish still."

And added: "They're gone now." And Alexander agreed: "Gone forever."

The next day Reschke had to put on his suit for special occasions. Three burials were on the agenda, two Protestant, one Catholic. In each case the mourners had brought their clergyman, pastor, priest, which the rules of the Association permitted.

Mourned by numerous family members, women far advanced in years were buried. The burial according to the Catholic rite would start the fourth row of graves. To judge by the photos taken by Reschke and dated on the reverse side, the Polish pallbearers might just as well have been German. By that time, in addition to the gravediggers two cemetery gardeners had been hired. In the brick building facing Grosse Allee there was now a guard, who in the daytime provided visitors with information and was also in charge of the hearse and the gardeners' and gravediggers' tools.

Frau Brakup would gladly have filled this post, which at first seemed peaceful. Jerzy Wróbel had a hard time convincing her that a job in the cemetery was incompatible with her position on the board of directors. It was only when he impressed on her her high degree of responsibility as speaker for the German minority and promised good money for her taped monologues that the old woman was satisfied. "Oh well, if it can't be done, it can't be done. But I'd have fixed the little house up comfortable and made it cozy. Nice at night, too, when it's spooky dark outside. And I'd have kept a lookout for rowdies wanting to raise the roof. It don't matter. But I sure always wanted to watch over a cemetery."

It wasn't only Reschke who loved listening to her, when possible with the tape recorder. At the end of the war, Jerzy Wróbel, who came from Grodno, drifted to the ruins of Gdańsk, grew up amid scaffolding, and was keen about stories from the old days, because he lacked the East Polish background of his parents and grandparents and his only source of information about the past of this city that had grown up from the rubble was the piles of documents at the registry of deeds. Teachers and priests led him to believe that Gdańsk had always been Polish, a hundred percent Polish. When cracks appeared in this childhood faith, Wróbel wanted to know more than could be found in documents. The bundles of German-language litigation concerning boundaries and rights of way, the obsolete property deeds and estate papers, the accumulated fug of centuries-old claims to rightful ownership did not satisfy him. But Brakup could provide him with details that had smell and taste. Her adage—"Speak well of what's foreign, but don't go where you're foreign"—bore witness to a life of unbroken roots. From time-displaced memories she dredged up gossip and political sludge. She knew who had lived in the patrician houses along the Allee, that is, in the neighborhood of the United Cemeteries: "Directors all and filthy rich, with cooks and nursemaids and handymen. Take here, Hindenburgallee up as far as Adolf Hitler Strasse, which is what they had to call Hauptstrasse. I still know all about it, because I went to Doctor Citron's villa for my heart. I tell you, Pan Wróbel, he was a fine doctor, never mind if he was a Jew. They gave him a bad time, they wouldn't let him be a doctor, so he got out to Sweden . . ."

Everything that was important to Wróbel, even the routes of streetcar lines and which preacher in what church had been permitted to speak out and for how short or how long a time in praise of God or the

Führer—he only had to ask Brakup. Married to a ship-yard worker who was killed in the Crimea in 1942, she knew who hated whom during the Free State years. "Let me tell you, Pan Wróbel, here in Schichau and in the railroad car factory it was hell. Red fighting Brown, and the Brownshirts with their clubs fighting the Red Front. Until Adolf came along and made them all equal . . ."

Wróbel couldn't hear enough of that. If Piątkowska was there with Reschke when these endless stories were being told, she would draw comparisons with a great-aunt who, whenever she got started on ancient history, ended up with Marszał Piłsudski marching into Wilno, his eyes blazing, his mustache bristling, and his white horse dropping turds. Alexandra laughed. "To believe all that we don't have to." And Reschke wrote in his diary: "We shouldn't stir up these old stories too much, because, as Brakup says: 'You step into a bog, and you splatter yourself with mud.' The cemetery is mission enough. Our idea is forward-looking, even if all it does is promise the dead a narrow patch of home soil."

With this evocation of a fully occupied cemetery only coffin burial could be meant; but by the end of July an urnfield had to be added to the Cemetery of Reconcil-iation, because an increasing number of burial-ready persons preferred cremation. Many applications from the provinces of East Germany, which by now had all but ceased to exist as a state, requested cremation, mak-ing no mention of a Christian funeral service. Without calling themselves atheists, the applicants from Stral-sund, Neubrandenburg, or Bad Doberan wished "only a simple burial without a priest or speeches at the graveside." This probably because of the lower cost, since only urns had to be shipped, particularly as the new currency, convertible on a one-to-one basis only to a

122

limited degree, may have not yet lost its shine but was becoming scarce.

Since it was not possible to reactivate the old crematorium on St. Michael's Lane—a video rental establishment had moved into the basement rooms—the first urnfield was laid out in the western part of the Cemetery of Reconciliation, parallel to Grosse Allee.

The urn burials were attended by fewer mourners, often only members of the immediate family. The reduced attendance is also explained by the practice, which soon became common, of shipping the ashes of persons long dead. Undoubtedly such belated shipment was done in accordance with a wish expressed in the lifetime of the deceased, that is, to make one's last resting place in the land where one was born. Such wishes from beyond the grave would soon create problems for the board of directors of the German-Polish Cemetery Association; but let's not anticipate.

So far everything was running smoothly. Yet Reschke, an aesthete by training, was bothered by the urns that were arriving. He therefore sent a letter with revised Cemetery Regulations to all persons stored in his computer. By prohibiting the use of synthetic urns, he was able to promote the production of urns made of hard-baked potter's clay.

Then it became necessary to discuss the nature of the tombstones to be erected after the graves had settled. Through Piątkowska, Reschke made contact with some stonemasons who were doing restoration work for the city. Because restoration of the terraces had been completed, most particularly on Brotbänkengasse, they complained that work was becoming scarce. On receiving the promise of an interest-free loan of DM 200,000, which the board of directors approved after a brief dis-

123

cussion, partly by telephone, a group of stonemasons set up business on the site of the former crematorium and soon began to build stock for the Cemetery of Reconciliation.

Reschke insisted that not a single stone violate the Cemetery Regulations, which in separate paragraphs specified that "every tombstone must be stable and firmly attached by dowels to the pedestal or foundation . . . It is forbidden to affix photographs, artificial wreaths, or glass or enamel plates . . ." The use of synthetic stone was likewise prohibited.

But Reschke did not content himself with regulations. Some of the models recommended to the stonemasons' workshop—I have copies of them—suggest a revival of the Baroque tombstone. He favored traditional emblems and ornaments. To judge by quotations from his doctoral dissertation, he would have favored pictorial low reliefs retelling Biblical motifs: the Fall of Man, the parable of the Prodigal Son, the miraculous raising of Lazarus, the Burial of Jesus, the Resurrection of the Dead . . . With plenty of acanthus leaves and clusters of fruit.

More difficulties were created by some of the epitaphs requested. Many had to be rejected, which often led to unpleasant correspondence with family members. In the notes of my ultrapunctilious classmate I find a few epitaphs that were never hewn in stone, for instance: "What the Foe from Thee Has Taken, Thou Hast Now in Death Retaken." Or: "Here Rests Our Beloved Father and Grandfather Adolf Zollkau in German Homeland Soil." Or: "Driven Out and Now Returned, Here Rests Elfriede Napf in God and Native Soil." Or short and sweet: "Here Lies in German Soil."

The board of directors had to be consulted, and the

124

industrialist Gerhard Vielbrand and vice president Marian Marczak disagreed when the epitaph "After Injustice, Justice Was Born, His Homeland Now Has Been Restored" came up for debate. Following a short tug of war, in which German self-righteousness and Polish sensitivity seemed evenly matched, Erna Brakup's argument—"I won't talk about justice, because there ain't any, but homeland is homeland and that's that"—seems to have brought about a compromise, according to which the first line of the epitaph was dropped and the second authorized to be hewn in stone.

Vielbrand apologized in writing for using the word "censorship" in a telephone conversation; Marczak in return asked Vielbrand not to attach too much weight to his own outbursts of temper. Piątkowska seems to have shrugged this quarrel off with a laugh. "Why epitaphs? Isn't name in stone enough?"

In many ways August lived up to its reputation as the month of crisis. In Gdańsk and elsewhere tourists were conspicuously absent. True, the zloty had been stabilized somewhere very low (from the Polish point of view) and was now convertible, but prices rose higher and higher, in utter contempt of wages and salaries. The Iraqi invasion of the oil sheikdom of Kuwait, far away but brought close by television, sparked a crisis, which soon became known as the Gulf crisis. Not to mention the worsening of the crises in Georgia, Lithuania, Yugoslavia. But even without looking across the border, the situation was not good: trouble was brewing for the German-Polish Cemetery Association .

Soon after the founding of the Cemetery Association the question came up of putting a fence between the parkland now known as the Cemetery of Reconciliation and the Engineering School and Polyclinic, but it was tabled as not urgent. Then flowers and wreaths began to disappear from fresh grave mounds, and worse, it was reported that the stolen goods, with the ribbons removed in the case of the wreaths, and in every case very fresh, were being sold at stands in St. Dominic's Market. Although the affected families were compensated for the loss, they complained and complained. When an urn was overturned, brutally and maliciously overturned, though not broken, the board of directors, which barely had the quorum needed to make decisions (members Karau and Vielbrand were absent on the German side), resolved—after too little discussion, at the insistence of Frau Johanna Dettlaff, who spoke of "unspeakable outrage"—to protect the cemetery with a fence and moreover engage night watchmen, at the expense, it goes without saying, of the Cemetery Association.

All this because Piątkowska and Reschke had not asked for voting rights on the Board. Their argument that the fence would be a source of quarrels and hard feeling carried no weight. Even Wróbel voted for the fence.

By mid-August, when the Gulf crisis had no more news value than any other crisis report, posts were set up along Grunwaldzka, designed to support a six-foot fence later to be covered with greenery. The press was quick to take up the matter with headlines such as CEMETERY-CONCENTRATION CAMP, and GERMANS LOVE FENCES, and the suggestion that "instead of wasting money on expensive wire, why not import sections of the now dismantled Berlin Wall into Poland duty-free, and set them up again for the defense of the German Cemetery?" Concluding with the slogan: "We need the Wall!"

All in all, there was more laughter than recrimination. No sooner was the fence put up than parts of it were torn down. This was done carefully, avoiding damage to the materials, for the posts and wire reappeared, put to good use in the fencing of community gardens or the building of henhouses. The dismantling turned into a local fete.

"And yet," writes Reschke, "it's an ugly sight." Each day there were eight to ten burials. The seventh row of grave sites had now been filled, and the urnfield would soon have to be expanded. The cemetery was flourishing when the fence trouble struck; small wonder that various groups of mourners began to make inquiries about the safety of their dead. One indignant family left town with the ashes of their father and grandfather. When finally demonstrations were held around what was left of the fence and chanting profaned the quiet of the tombs, the board of directors after a telephone conference decided to reverse their decision and do without fences. No one, they declared, had wanted a political row.

The remains of the fence vanished overnight. No objection was raised to planting a quick-growing hedge—Reschke suggested juniper. The board of directors publicly expressed its regrets, and the media lost interest. In spite of the night watchmen, the theft of flowers and wreaths did not stop entirely, but at least the cemetery was quiet again. Not so the world crises. New weapons systems were tried out in the Arabian desert; the far-flung regions of the Soviet Union were threatening to fall apart. The crisis month of August suffered from an overcrowded schedule; only from Germany came news that claimed to be gratifying: a date was set for the day of unity.

On August 7, Reschke's latest gift from Bochum, a chrome-plated shower set with adjustable spray, was inaugurated far from any crisis. Alexandra's sixtieth birthday started out wet and happy. Reschke writes: "What a capacity for enjoyment! 'Is luxury,' she cried out and absolutely insisted on our standing together under our new acquisition, like children . . ."

Then the couple stood in front of Alexandra's place of work, the astronomical clock. It looked all finished. Not without pride she pointed, among the signs of the zodiac and other symbolic figures, to the Lion, which, like the Crab and the Archer, the Bull and the Virgin, did not glitter with new gilding but shimmered in a matte earth tone. "That's my sign. Leo means I'm frivolous and game for adventure. The Lion wants to dominate, yes, but is always generous, likes to take long journey and celebrate cheerfully with friends . . ."

It was an intimate birthday dinner. One of her colleagues at work and Jerzy Wróbel joined them on Hundegasse. Smoked eel was served, then fillet of perch. They talked about everything under the sun, including crises near and far. Before dinner the couple had mingled with tourists and locals; as usual at the beginning of August, St. Dominic's Market spread into all the streets. Evidence of the couple's private stroll is provided by a cut-out silhouette showing the two of them in profile, side by side, Alexandra slightly overlapping Alexander. Her small nose, his big nose. Her full mouth, his receding lower lip. Her chin arching double over her short neck, his high, steep forehead contradicted by his inadequate chin. The back of his head, a curve balanced by the outline of her bosom. A Biedermeier pair, in keeping with Reschke's second birthday present, a volume illustrated with numerous silhouettes.

In my documents there are no references to travel. After so much life already lived, the two began to discover each other. Yet I don't believe they were given to confessions or revelations. Neither widow nor widower had reason to complain about dead husband or dead wife; photographs of normally happy days were preseved in the apartment on Hundegasse and the apartment in Bochum—some framed, some collected in albums. There was no need to pry into the past, for their few off-the-beaten-path adventures left only vague or misfiled memories. True, he at the age of fourteen and a half was a troop leader in the Hitler Youth and she at seventeen was an enthusiastic member of the Communist Youth organization, but both excused these aberrations as congenital defects of their generation; there were no abysses to be sounded. Even if he, in moments of self-doubt, thought he would always have to combat the Hitler Youth in himself, and even if she wished she had left the Party sooner, in '68 or two years before, "When militia fired on workers here . . ."

After the end of August they seldom attended the burials. They left that to Wróbel and to Erna Brakup, who never missed a burial or a funeral feast at the Hevelius. The Cemetery of Reconciliation was now running smoothly. Piątkowska was putting the finishing touches to the astronomical clock: the sun between Cancer and Gemini and the moon between Libra and Scorpio demanded gold. Reschke concentrated on organizational tasks.

The computer in Bochum was hooked up with the

computer on Hundegasse, feeding as well as questioning each other, and there were seldom breakdowns or glitches when it came to supplying the Cemetery of Reconciliation with raw material. The Polish as well as the German press had calmed down. Other news had priority, such as the constant increase in manpower and equipment being poured into the Gulf, the latest developments in Lithuania, and the oppressive tension between the perpetually gloomy Polish prime minister and the labor leader in Gdańsk, who like many small men felt called upon to do big things. Nevertheless, the bank balance of the Cemetery Association showed that world crises did not impede the reconciliation between the German and Polish dead.

Despite considerable expenses—maintenance and incidentals—the bank balance shot up to unexpected heights. Prudently invested, 16 million deutschmarks yielded so much monthly interest that shipping and maintenance costs—the rest was covered by the health insurance and burial funds—hardly made a dent in the capital. Not to mention the bequest account, used to defray the burial costs of needy persons; they and the German minority in Gdańsk could always count on a final resting place in the Cemetery of Reconciliation; the GPCA worked for the commonweal.

These favorable bank balances apart, it must be said that a third of the capital and interest was reserved for the as yet inactive Lithuanian component; but the Lithuanians' demand for national independence left no room for the wishes of *their* minorities. No space was allotted to the Special Cemetery for dead Poles who had once lived in Wilno; not yet in any case. The Lithuanian people first had to have a state of their own. Later, perhaps, when they got rid of the Russians, a deal could be made on a strictly hard currency basis, but right now . . .

In my classmate's diary I read: "Alexandra suffers from this attitude of total rejection. To do something at least, she has lately been sending Polish school-books across the border through her organization, the Society of the Friends of Wilno and Grodno. We both think that's not much. But she does not allow her sorrow to cast a shadow on our enduring summer happiness . . ."

It was then that those photographs were taken, which Reschke interpreted in a much too dramatic way. The subject presented itself on a weekend early in September. Since the location is not indicated on the back of the photographs, I can only conjecture. It is certain, however, that the couple took the ferry across the Vistula estuary from Schiewenhort to Nickelswalde: a snapshot shows Piątkowska in a light-blue blouse, standing at the rail of the car-ferry. So they must have been on the highway alongside the narrow-gauge railroad tracks, in the direction of Stutthof and Frische Nehrung. A leafy tunnel skirting the forest by the shore. My assumption is based on an entry in the diary. "On the drive through the lowlands one notices how the industrial zone to the east of the city eats its way like a cancer into the flatland bounded only by the Vistula dike. 'Began already in Gierek time,' cried Alexandra. Sulfur smell all over . . ."

In all four photographs the asphalt surface of a highway shimmers. The outline of a flattened toad is clearly stamped into the surface. It's not one and the same toad. Four toads, I am certain, were run over, and not once but several times. Perhaps they were going

131

somewhere in a group, or possibly in pairs. It is also possible that they were a mile away from one another when run over, that it is only the photographs that bring them together. I assume that more than four toads tried to cross the road, here and there or else all in one place. Some were lucky, others were not. Just flattened, turned into low reliefs, but still recognizable as toads. One of those typical roads lined on either side with lindens and chestnut trees, forming a deep-green tunnel in the summer, was a trap for the toads.

All four digits of the front legs, all four digits plus the webs of the hind legs, and even the rudimentary fifth digits both in front and back can be read from the photographs. Flat heads and bulging eyes pressed into bodies. Yet a row of warts can be clearly made out on the back. Desiccated, the body has shrunk into folds. In two of the pictures, the intestines have oozed out and dried on the sides.

From what I know of toads, which admittedly is not much, these must be common or earth toads. But Reschke wrote on the back of the photographs: "This was a singing toad"—"This toad will sing no more"— "Flattened toad"—"Another flattened toad. Not a good omen."

Maybe he's right. Since red-bellied toads and yellow-bellied toads are smaller than common toads, and he reckons the length of the flat bodies one at five centimeters, two at five and a half, and one at six, they must have been anouras and not common toads, which sometimes grow to a length of fifteen centimeters. Since they were squashed on the Island, they were undoubtedly low country toads. If Reschke had carefully detached one of these reliefs from the asphalt, turned it, and photographed the burst underside, I might now be able to speak with confidence of red-bellied toads. But he was content to look at them from above. So sure was the professor.

I assume that they drove no farther toward Stutthof and the memorial to the concentration camp by that name. Most likely Alexandra wanted to go back. Though she went in for godless talk—on a different occasion she said, "Actually I'm still Communist, even if I'm out of Party"—she clung to her superstitions.

No minutes were taken of their meetings. Neither expense accounts nor photographs tell us anything about the frequent sessions. Only Reschke's diary reveals what was kept secret even from Piątkowska: from early September on, he had many conversations with Chatterjee, "because"—as he explains these secret meetings—"this widely traveled, ambitious Bengali always gives rise to hopes, rather ambiguous hopes. From everything that weighs so heavily on us he squeezes a positive essence. For instance, it pleases him to think that rising oil prices are making gasoline more and more expensive, most notably in poor countries like Poland, for which reason more and more customers flock to his rickshaw business. It's true. Day after day, I see his inflation-oriented calculations borne out. Not only in the Old City are the streets dotted with nimble rickshaws, drawn now by unembarrassed young Poles; they can also be seen running up and down Grunwaldzka, doing a thriving business in Sopot and Oliwa, and no longer exclusively used by tourists. Shipyard engineers, city officials, prelates, and even officers of the militia let themselves be driven to work at attractive prices or home again after office hours. Chatterjee comments: 'We are not only environment-friendly, we are also autonomous. Independent of the oil wells that will soon be the target of furious battles, we guarantee a fair price. But things will get even better because they are getting worse. You know what I always say: 'The future belongs to the rickshaw!' —I didn't contradict him. How could I?"

My former classmate appears to have met the Bengali often in the place of their first encounter, the half-timbered little house where they drank Dortmund Export beer together. Their bar conversations: I hear Reschke, whose pessimism has been confirmed by the flattened toads foreshadowing woe, and who foresees dire punishment for every ecological sin, from the Brazilian rain forest to the soft coal mines in Lusatia; and I hear Chatterjee saving the car-clogged cities, Rome and Paris, with his special lanes reserved for rickshaws. The one thing that troubles him is the long wait for Dutch bicycle rickshaws and the constant chicanery of the customs officials.

And I find a statement of what this Bengali with a British passport has quite consistently been up to. "He has bought into the former Lenin Shipyard, as the new liberal laws permit him to do. He plans to make his own rickshaws in two medium-sized hangars left empty because of the shipbuilding crisis. A license from a Rotterdam firm is already in his pocket. He has more than the Polish demand in mind. His aim is export. Already, Chatterjee tells me, he has twenty-eight first-rate Polish shipyard workers under contract and is having them retrained by two Dutch instructors. With the help of their specialized knowledge he intends to develop the assembly line that has always been his aim. The wheels will soon be turning . . ."

Between two bottles of Dortmund Export, the professor in Reschke has pointed out to the Bengali that the city of Gdańsk, during the centuries when it was still called Dantzik, maintained commercial relations with Holland and Flanders, which supplied it with artists and craftsmen. Thus the architect Anthony van Obbergen, hailing from Mecheln near Antwerp, was commissioned by the city magistrate to build the Old City Rathaus, the Big Arsenal on Wollwebergasse, as well as the rectories next to St. Catherine's in the late Renaissance style. And Chatterjee may have remembered that there were Dutch trading posts on the River Hooghly before Calcutta was grabbed by the British, and that around 1870 a Franciscan missionary of Dutch descent invented the rickshaw in Japan, the term deriving from the Japanese "jin riki shaw," which means "vehicle propelled by hand power." If Chatterjee is to be believed, the Chinese brought the rickshaw to Calcutta twenty years later.

This is mere conjecture, but it is certain that the two men soon arrived at an understanding and that in the course of one of their barroom conversations a first financial agreement between the businessman and the executive partner was committed to writing; the thirty-percent participation of the German-Polish Cemetery Association in S. Ch. Chatterjee's Bicycle Rickshaw Company, however, did not come to light until a meeting of the board of directors much later. In any case, Reschke was bold and far-sighted enough to invest in this promising venture. The balance sheet of the Cemetery Association made the transaction possible.

No actual figures are mentioned in the diary. No withdrawals document Reschke's high-handed risk-taking. His diary refers only to "far-reaching discussions." "This Mr. Chatterjee has a way of dispelling my dark forebodings; or he colors them in such a way that be-

fore you know it they are rosy-red clouds. If only I could
convince Alexandra of the humanity of his idea. If only
I could bring them closer together and make her see
him as a human being just like us. I, in any case, have
a vision of how our work, dedicated as it is to people
who have crumbled into dust, can be coordinated with
his project. While our obligation is to the dead, he is
aiming at the survival of the living. While we are thinking about the end, he has a beginning in mind. If high-
sounding words still have meaning, it is in the field of
our common endeavor. The return of the dead, as enacted each day in our Cemetery of Reconciliation, and
the bicycle rickshaw, a vehicle especially favored by our
younger mourners—all this, I am not ashamed to say,
is living proof of the old adage: 'Die and be born again.' "

Alexandra kept out of it. No stretch of Reschke's
imagination could lead her to Chatterjee. Not only did
she refuse to ride in the melodiously tinkling rickshaw,
she excoriated its promoter, who was simply beyond her;
he was uncanny, he had a foreign smell. She wouldn't
trust him by day or by night. "His eyes," she cried out,
"are always half closed." At an early date, even before
the first burials, Reschke recorded her opinion: "Is phony
Englisher. We'll defeat him same as we Poles at gates
of Vienna defeated Turks . . ."

With regard to Chatterjee's origins, Alexandra's mis-
trust was not unfounded. In one of their barroom conversations the "rickshaw man"—Piątkowska's disparaging
name for Subhas Chandra Chatterjee—admitted that
he was of Bengali origin only on his father's side. Not
without embarrassment he explained that his mother
belonged to the merchant caste of the Marwaris, that
the Marwaris came from Rajastan in the north and had
immigrated into Bengal, where they soon cornered the

real estate market, acquired numerous jute mills in Calcutta, and had not made themselves exactly popular. But that was what the Marwaris were like: good businessmen. And he, Chatterjee, took entirely after his mother, while his father was a lover of poetry, possessed by dreams of power, which accounts for the first names he gave his son. But he, Chatterjee, had no desire to emulate the megalomania of the legendary Subhas Chandra Bose, who had failed so abysmally as the leader of India; his mother's child, he staked his future on the business ethics of the Marwaris. "Please believe me, Mr. Reschke, if we want a future, we must finance it."

Not a word of this was said on Hundegasse, where Reschke had settled in with his bedroom slippers. I'm certain that Alexandra smelled his secret. But since the barroom excursions were an exception and the couple seldom went out in the evening, it is safe to say that they were homebodies. Only for a few minutes did they allow the TV to fill their living room with crises. They cooked for each other—here too in harmony—from Italian recipes. He learned a few Polish words. They took turns playing with the minicomputer. When in the kitchen she sized richly carved picture frames and applied fresh gilding leaf by leaf with the help of the gilding cushion, Reschke looked on. And when he waxed emblematic and explained to her the ambiguities of Baroque tombstones, Piątkowska hung on his every word. Sometimes they listened to tapes together, to what was left of their weekends on the Island or by the reed-lined Kashubian lakes, in a chorus or solo: ominous toad calls.

5

In photos I see them hand in hand or arm in arm. This stance, which went with their weekend outfits, their "partner look," was interrupted by Reschke's trip to Bochum. Apart from diary entries and copies of receipts, there are letters which speak only incidentally of love. Busily he writes about "indispensable transactions" and the "necessity of reorganizing the accounts." Between references to the rise in the price of the stock of certain insurance companies, he informs her that it would be advisable "to build up hidden reserves here and there." "The high interest rate and the present political climate," he writes, "make advantageous investments possible." But this sentence he did not entrust to any letter. He wrote it in his diary, in his meticulous handwriting, for no other purpose than to let me know that he knew how to handle money.

Alexander Reschke could always handle money; during the war, for instance, when he organized the then compulsory potato bug operation and renamed it "the campaign against the American Colorado beetle." After submitting a report in crisp military style to the District Farmers' Leader, he succeeded in having the reward for a full-to-the-brim liter bottle of beetles raised by ten pfennigs to approximately one reichsmark; he then put the money into a "hidden reserve," with the result that our troop—I personally was involved in this "Colorado beetle campaign"—was able to afford a few extras such as crumb cake, lollipops, and malt beer at the end-of-summer celebration in the barn of the Kelpin farm.

It was along the lines of these early exercises that the professor of art history now took to operating with the capital of the German-Polish Cemetery Association. Unbeknownst to the board of directors, he demonstrated sure instinct, split accounts, unloaded before it was too late, made profits, and sub rosa laid the investment foundation of the GPCA so that it became a highly diversified, in other words inscrutable, financial structure. Only his office in Bochum had the full picture, although, Reschke writes, "the place is no longer fit to live in. Denkwitz has had to take on a typist and someone to help her with the bookkeeping, which has become very complicated."

His business trip is dated between late September and early October. He calls appointments in Frankfurt, Düsseldorf, and Wuppertal urgent, but political events of those days are absent from his diary. Only in the letter of October 4, the day after the bells east and west proclaimed one fatherland, do I read: "Now we have unity on paper. It means little to the people of the Ruhr District, with whom admittedly I am far from intimate; at the most it is a pretext for the usual bellowing in sports stadiums. You may be right, Alexandra, we Germans don't know how to celebrate . . ."

Then he has more to say about the money of the burial-ready. That it has been entrusted to us; that it must be managed with loving care and foresight. Money that lies idle does not make money. Accordingly, he endeavors to increase its value in hidden ways. "Let politics call attention to itself by noisy demonstrations of being alive; we, dearest, will quietly continue to keep

140

faith with our dead; removed at last from the vicissitudes of history, let them rest in peace."

So much for Reschke's intentions, which he brought from Bochum along with new, different presents, among them a stylish floor lamp. And yet the couple on Hundegasse were not able to live entirely for themselves and their idea of earth-bound reconciliation. Though in November cemetery activity remained in the forefront, in December great events were on the agenda in Poland. The prime minister, whom Piątkowska liked to compare with the Spanish knight of the mournful countenance, did not win in the first two rounds of elections held for the highest office in the land; defeated, he ceded the field to two rivals who were strong on promises. About the victor Alexandra said: "Was good one time for workers' strike. Now he thinks he is little Marszał Piłsudski. Makes me laugh . . ."

I almost admire the way in which both of them, sustained by their idea, lived more and more aloof from their nations; from a great height they looked past them, beyond them, their heads tilted. From their endless nightly discussions I can filter out half a dozen judgments on the German and Polish peoples. Such as: Now that the rich have unity, they are unable to behave like a mature nation; the poor, on the other hand, who were sure of themselves as a nation even when they did not have a state, are only good for resistance and lack democratic maturity. As a result we have runaway immaturity on both sides. "There will be trouble," said Reschke. "Trouble we have already!" cried Piątkowska.

To tell you what I think of these gloomy judgments is not among the tasks imposed upon me by my former classmate. I'll say only that I would have difficulty giving a passing grade to two students of equal immaturity. But pessimists tend to be right. To the credit of our German-Polish couple, however, it might be said that they demonstrated maturity in dealing with the daily problems of wintering in Alexandra's three-room apartment. She forgave him his know-it-allness and never denounced it as "typical"; he put up with her Russophobia by qualifying it to the point where it became disillusioned love. Perhaps it was the world crisis, whose images poured into the apartment, that made the couple so peaceable. Be that as it may, Piątkowska was not bothered by his bedroom slippers, while Reschke gave up trying to put order into her higgledy-piggledy library. More than that: it wasn't only him that she loved but also his camel's-hair slippers. And he loved, along with her person, the confusion of her ramshackle bookshelves. She had no desire to make him stop shuffling, nor he to make her stop puffing cigarettes. The Pole and the German! I could fill a picture book with them: no quarrels, congenial in every way, too good to be true.

There were few visitors. The priest of St. Peter's is mentioned and his one subject of conversation: the missing arch in the still war-damaged central nave of his church. Erna Brakup and Jerzy Wróbel came to dinner twice. Alexandra seems to have tried her hand at a Martinmas goose stuffed with apples and mugwort. On a tape dated mid-November Erna Brakup is heard: "Haven't had a goose like this with apple in a long time. But I remember one time when Danzig was a Free State . . ." And then Wróbel learned about the price in gulden of Kashubian geese, and about all the people who were sitting around the table when Frieda Formella, Erna Brakup's youngest sister, and Otto Prill, a foreman at

142

the Amada margarine factory, celebrated their wedding in the autumn of 1932.

The year dawdled to its end. The autumn went on and on, and the winter promised to be so mild that the Cemetery of Reconciliation, with the ground frozen no deeper than the blade of a spade, would fill up with no effort at all: row upon row of graves, urnfield after urnfield. I could sum up by saying that nothing happened except burials, were it not for the following note: "While in other respects the cemetery was operating normally, a controversy erupted at the November 5 meeting of the board of directors. Trouble ever since . . ."

The trouble started on All Souls', which they had wanted to celebrate quietly at the Hagelsberg cemetery: "More visitors than expected, undeterred by the long trip. The scarcity of hotel rooms caused bottlenecks, because the Cemetery of Reconciliation drew a large crowd. True, Denkwitz had warned me by telephone and by fax, but this onslaught! No end of complaints. The measly selection of flowers outside St. Dominic's Market must have been really upsetting. Nothing but asters and chrysanthemums. At exorbitant prices. I had to promise that we would do better next time, and listen to insulting remarks about 'Polish slovenliness.' It wasn't until the afternoon, less than an hour before dark, that we found time for the grave of Alexandra's parents. Wróbel came with us. Familiar with all the long-abandoned cemeteries between Oliwa and Ohra, he then led us to an adjoining tract of land, the former garrison cemetery, which is in very poor condition. There we saw some true rarities, which Jerzy with bashful finder's pride uncovered for us as relics of gray antiquity. For instance: in the midst of tangled undergrowth, a cross of shells, obviously done by masons who knew their job, with an inscription commemorating the French prisoners of war who had died in camps in the years 1870 and 1871. The arms of the cross terminating in trefoils. In another place Wróbel knew of a tall limestone stele with a rusty ship's anchor in front of it, all hidden in a clump of weeds. In this case the death of several sailors from the cruiser *SMS Magdeburg,* and of a single sailor from torpedo boat No. 26, dated back to the war year 1914. And our friend had still other treasures for us: a travertine plaque embedded in a freestanding brick wall; on it in high relief over oak leaves, a police helmet from Free State days, and below, damaged by blows, the inscription: TO OUR DEAD. Alexandra was puzzled by a dozen polished black granite stones, each engraved with the names and dates of Polonized Tatars, along with a crescent moon and a star. None earlier than 1957. 'What are they doing in military cemetery!' she exclaimed. Wróbel, who like Alexandra showed an occasional chauvinist streak, could think of no explanation; embarrassed, he stood in his windbreaker among the stones and tried to justify the Tatar graves as 'illegal burials.' Not far away were the horrifying wooden crosses on children's graves, where a year ago we had deciphered the plague year 1946 under German and Polish names. I said, 'Do you remember, Alexandra . . .'—'How I not remember, Aleksander,' she said. 'I carried the string bag with the mushrooms . . .'—'And at Papa and Mama's grave we had wonderful idea . . .' That was how we spent All Souls'. Time caught up with us. I searched in vain for formula that would sum all this up; but even Jerzy and Alexandra stood petrified when at the dilapidated fence that bordered on the community gardens we discovered, wantonly daubed with paint, a grave for

Russian prisoners of war from the First World War. So much lethal history and barbarism! So many dead buried in foreign soil. So much ground for reconciliation. And all the while, leaves were falling from old and new trees. A free-falling leaf. All emblems paraphrasing death derive from nature, after all. Suddenly I saw Alexandra and myself looking for our graves on foreign ground. When in the gathering darkness Wróbel led us out of the desolate field, I suggested that we put the place in order, obviously at the expense of the Cemetery Association. Wróbel promised to bring the matter up at the next meeting of the board of directors. Alexandra laughed, I don't know why."

The meeting started off satisfactorily—the vice president of the National Bank confirmed that the rents and fees had been transferred promptly—but then the German contingent, by the mere mention of wishes, sparked a debate based on principle. Time and again elderly mourners, after attending the burial of an equally elderly friend or relative, expressed the wish to spend the twilight of their lives if not in the immediate vicinity of the Cemetery of Reconciliation then at least in the friendly countryside nearby. And now Vielbrand, seconded by Frau Johanna Dettlaff, moved that comfortable retirement communities be installed among beach pines on the shores of the Baltic or the Kashubian lakes.

While Frau Dettlaff was motivated largely by feeling, Vielbrand brought up arguments which he regarded as realistic. "Our elderly compatriots are prepared to move into trade-union vacation houses, formerly state-owned, even if empty or threatened by bankruptcy. Obviously after thorough renovation." Then he proposed, "ra-

145

tionally looking ahead," that plans be made at once for new buildings. More and more interest was being shown in retirement communities set in native surroundings. And family members were more than eager to comply with this wish of their parents, grandparents, or great-grandparents. The question of money was secondary. Insurance companies were prepared to participate in the financing. One could reasonably count on a demand for two or three thousand senior-citizen living units. A large nursing staff would be needed. Jobs would be created. This might well benefit small industries and therefore the middle class. "And what Poland needs," cried Vielbrand, "is a healthy middle class!" But in case you are suspicious of the wishes of these old people— as he gathered from Father Bieroński's remarks—and fear the possibility of uncontrolled reverse migration, and therefore think that we have to seal ourselves off, close the borders—in that case a "twilight of life in the homeland" program could be developed entirely within the framework of the German-Polish Cemetery Association, as essentially we would be installing death-houses, though of course we can't call them that. The term used in the prospectus will be "retirement communities."

Frau Dettlaff quoted effectively from letters. Consistory councilor Dr. Karau called the twilight of life "a time of turning inward and therefore homeward." Father Bieroński began suddenly and inappropriately to talk about the war-damaged arch in St. Peter's. "To the point!" cried chairman Marczak. Whereupon town clerk Wróbel thought of the trade-union homes along the bay, where bathing was prohibited, also in Jastarnia, formerly Heisternest (magpie's nest) on the Hela peninsula, where the Fregata trade-union house would be suitable; and Wróbel offered to show the assembled board of directors a few projects on Pelonker Weg, such as the castlelike summer home of the Schopenhauer family or the Pelonken manor, which had at one time been used as an old-people's home. He spoke like an enthusiastic real estate agent with an unbeatable offer—annexes with many rooms, a colonnaded doorway, and a circle of ash trees in the inner court, not to mention a pond rich in carp at the foot of the Oliwa forest.

As was to be expected, the National Bank in the person of its vice president showed interest; the offer was recommended and finally approved by the Polish authorities. An amendment was added to the contract of association, from which it could be inferred that for the German partners no financial sacrifice was too great.

Projects were inspected, rejected or accepted, among them the Pelonken manor with its annexes and fish ponds, although this complex, after years of military billeting, was visibly run down.

Alexander and Alexandra were present at the inspections. Reschke, who saw decay everywhere and doubtless wanted to see decay, spoke only of decay: "Absurd, this gutted trolleybus between the manor and the servants' quarters. The only thing that works is the sundial. The Schopenhauer palace is even worse; the father's summer home seems to confirm the son's philosophy. And oh my God, the new buildings. As Alexandra says: 'Are from Gomułka time . . .' Ruins from start to finish. Our friend Wróbel would have done better to keep his deed-registry expertise to himself. Simply revolting, the way Vielbrand takes measurements wherever he goes, taps the plaster, inspects the flooring for dry rot. And Bieroński says nothing, because Karau has promised to finance 'an authentically late-Gothic arch.' "

Before the end of the year, the first leases were signed; painful for Reschke, because this "seed-money financing" made it necessary to deplete a few of his accounts, including his hidden reserves. Additional capital was supplied by private insurance companies, later by the Department of Public Welfare. In Bochum Denkwitz had to take on another office worker.

Soon renovation work began on a dozen trade-union homes, some with a view of the sea. Along Pelonker Weg—today ul. Polanki—several large villas and so-called manors were leased and immediately surrounded with scaffolding. Trouble with present tenants was avoided; generously compensated, they found other quarters.

All this was done with the approval of the Board. Only Erna Brakup's lengthy comment was interpreted as an abstention: "But suppose I don't want to spend the end of my life in my home country; what if I'd rather fritter away the few years I have left on an island that's called in German Machorka?"

The executive couple did not respond with a howl of resistance to the decisions of the Board. As far as I can see, both were satisfied, because the "former garrison cemetery" motion entered by Jerzy Wróbel was seconded and accepted without opposing votes. Money, plenty of deutschmarks, would put the place in order.

Perhaps they found the retirement communities acceptable, or even desirable, as a complement to their own idea. Death-houses, in any case, were not discussed in their evening conversations on ul. Ogarna. The couple were of the opinion that at the end of their workday they were entitled to think of themselves, only of themselves. Couples who marry late have no time to lose. So much to make up for. And similar resolutions. In Reschke's diary I read: "Alexandra rarely has a wish that concerns only herself. Everything has to be experienced with me, experienced together . . ."

A little later, however, Piątkowska did have a wish that was her very own, something she had always dreamed of. "Someday I want to travel all way down Italian boot and see Naples."

"Why Naples?"

"Because that's what people say."

"What about Umbria, in the footsteps of the Etruscans . . . ?"

"And then Naples."

Since there must have been an atlas in Alexandra's ramshackle bookcase among all the nautical reading matter, or under a pile of mysteries, I see the two of them bent over the Italian boot.

"Assisi, of course. Orvieto too. And we can't afford to miss Firenze." She doesn't want to travel the length of the boot alone, only with him. He knows so much. He has already seen everything several times: "You can show me."

I see the two of them contented. It makes me happy to see them that way. After roast pork and sauerkraut with caraway seeds, they wash the dishes together in the kitchen like a model couple. Wrapped in cloth, the frame of a mirror is waiting to be gilded. When the electronic chimes from the nearby Rathaus tower have once again died down, it will be time for a cigarette. Alexandra smokes with a holder now. The new stylish floor lamp has found its place. They are sitting on the couch without holding hands, both wearing glasses. The atlas, from the estate of the merchant marine officer, makes proposals. "And after I see Naples, I can right away die." Then her laugh.

Did the couple absolutely have to show themselves to their families? I'd much rather have confined this report to their beautiful idea and its ghastly incarnation.

Were they equal to this trip? In my opinion, which I know doesn't count, they should not have felt obliged to make, at their age, courtesy calls. The embarrassing situations, the awkward apologies.

Wouldn't photos identifying the couple as a couple—on the Vistula ferry for instance, or the snapshot taken with a time shutter showing them picnicking on the shore of a lake—have been proof enough of their late-blooming relationship? And if these family introductions had to be undertaken, did they absolutely have to be ticked off, station after station, between Christmas and New Year's?

Christmas Eve found them still in Bochum, though without a Christmas tree. He gave her a more subdued perfume, she gave him a louder tie. On the afternoon of Christmas Day they arrived, by car, in Bremen. For the 26th a double room had been reserved at Gerhard's Hotel in Göttingen. Confirmation of a hotel room in Wiesbaden for the 28th is documented. On December 30 they were due in Limburg an der Lahn, where they planned to stay until New Year's and visit the Old City. This didn't happen. It was only from the autobahn overpass, at a distance, that Alexandra saw the cathedral. By themselves again back in Reschke's living-room-cum-office, they toasted the New Year, both exhausted, depressed, and reverberating with hurt, but glad to have the effort behind them. "How good that Alexandra, just in case, had stuck three fir branches with candles in a vase."

Reschke's account of the four visits reads like one continuous tale of woe. No rhapsodizing on this trip. Obviously the couple had a wretched time, though the degree of wretchedness varied from station to station. Not that Alexandra's son Witold was grossly offensive to the man by his mother's side; not that Alexander's daughters Sophia, Dorothea, and Margaretha were insolent, disparaging, or rude to the woman by their father's side. As a couple the couple were received with indifference. Only the three sons-in-law, writes Reschke, showed any interest in the German-Polish Cemetery Association: the first mockingly, the second patronizingly, and the third offering advice that was unmistakably cynical. No complaint about food and drink. No lack of Christmas presents for father and mother.

About the first station, Bremen, Reschke writes: "Alexandra must have been hurt when Witold refused to discuss the Cemetery of Reconciliation with us—even in the most general terms. Still, his comment 'It's your pigeon' shows how well he has mastered colloquial German. When I asked him how he was getting on with his studies in philosophy, he said: 'We're taking Bloch apart. All that utopian shit. It's dead!' That was the tone of our dinner in what I admit was the provocatively posh restaurant of our hotel. He made it plain that he'd have preferred a hamburger joint. Over the soup he started scolding his mother in Polish. As far as he was concerned, I wasn't there. He jumped up. He sat down. Some of the diners turned around. Alexandra, who at first had put up some resistance, grew more and more quiet. When Witold left even before the dessert, she cried, but would not tell me what Witold had said to wound her. Smiling again, all she said was, 'So he finally got a girlfriend.' His Christmas present for the gildress, a badger's-hair brush, undoubtedly expensive, lay beside his mother's plate, in a plastic bag."

About their stay in Göttingen Reschke writes: "Only Sophia's children behaved naturally. Shy at first, then affectionate, even to Alexandra. My youngest daughter wouldn't talk—or let anyone else talk—about anything but her part-time job as a social worker. She complained about everything: the job, her cases, her colleagues, the pay. When I asked if I could show her some photographs of the Cemetery of Reconciliation, which I had taken for my archives, she shook her head. 'Christmas and all this holiday stuff is depressing enough.' Her husband, a bookdealer, complained about the 'hordes of Easties' and with a strained smile joked about their eagerness to buy books on labor law and how to succeed in business. His only comment about the cemetery was: 'Looks really inviting.' This with a grin. A cynic who used to be on the far left but now only cracks jokes, for instance about the Peace Movement and the protests against the Gulf War. Since both husband and wife had recently became fanatical nonsmokers, Alexandra had to go out on the balcony whenever she was in the mood to light up. He gave me a paperback about potency in old age. Brilliantly witty of him! Sophia gave me a pair of slippers, which she called comfies, hideous things. Only the children gave us pleasure."

About the courtesy call in Wiesbaden, I read: "What on earth has become of Dorothea? She gave up her profession: pediatrician. Candy all over the house. She has visibly put on weight, become morose and withdrawn. Only her ailments make her talkative: shortness of breath, itching skin, and so forth. Not a single word to Alexandra. Her husband, who has advanced to department head at the Ministry of the Environment, showed interest in our idea and sympathy for the difficulty (God knows) of carrying it out, but said with characteristic condescension: 'You could have bought that a lot cheaper from the Poles. There's no profit in leasing. Now that their border has been formally recognized, you could have asked for outright ownership, at least of the cemetery land. Anyway, all that once belonged to us.' Alexandra kept her mouth shut. I said: 'You forget that we and our dead are guests in their country.' After that the conversation turned to Hessian garbage disposal sites, increasingly petty party squabbles, and the impending Landtag elections. I was given a picture book that I already own, *The Church of St. Mary*, and Alexandra got potholders from a Third World shop. The two of us said nothing."

Finally, the last station of this calvary, which my classmate lined up as systematically as his memorial slabs. One can only admire Piątkowska's willingness to hold her peace all the way to Limburg an der Lahn, to bear with his three daughters and their husbands. She should have called the whole thing off back in Göttingen. Even Reschke said: "My dearest! What have I got you into? Their coldness. Their callousness. We actually planned to spend New Year's Eve with Margarethe and her Fred. That was their wish too. But when my eldest daughter, unsolicited, told us what she thought of our idea, it was too much for Alexandra. Gret, as I used to call her, flicked through the photos and smacked her lips. 'You sure found an untapped market,' she cried. And: 'What's in it for you?' And: 'Certainly a shrewd idea.' That Fred, who thinks he's an actor and has let my stupid Gret support him for years, put in his two cents' worth: 'Exactly. You have to have an eye for it. Where there's cream to be skimmed. My advice to you is to allow reburials. That'll keep you supplied until at least anno 2000.' I should have slapped him. Alexandra says that would be too much honor for him. We left immediately, without taking our presents—for Alexandra candy, for me a fairly attractive eyeglass case—art nouveau. In conclusion, and with the door already open, Margarethe, a dedicated high-school teacher, stooped to vulgarity: 'You can't stand criticism, can you? Taking it as an insult, the idea! Go bury yourselves in your cemetery, for all I care. Cemetery of Reconciliation. Ridiculous. Robbing the dead, that's what I call it!' "

A little later, Reschke writes: "I don't know where Alexandra gets the strength to keep calm, even to be cheerful, after all that. When at last we were back, toasting to the New Year at home, she asked me to put on some good music. While I was looking for something suitable, she lit the two candles on the fir branches and said: 'I understand your daughters. Witold, too. It's different generation. They were never chased out, never had to flee in cold. They got everything and know nothing.' "

I can only conjecture what music he put on. Something classical. In his diary music occurs only as background. He never mentions composers, not even Chopin. Otherwise he writes only that the weather was mild during the holidays, much too mild. "Again no white Christmas . . ."

When at the end of the first week in January our couple came back to the three-room apartment on Hundegasse, the weather turned cold after all. Snow

154

fell and lay on the ground, more and more snow, powdery snow on snow. Reschke wrote: "It would seem as though nature wanted to apologize for the long time without snow. Caps on all the decorative gables. How I missed the sound of running feet on crunchy snow, making tracks in the snow. Alexandra's high heels will have to take a rest . . ."

This entry in the diary accounts for the purchase of fur-lined, "sinfully expensive bootees" for her, and some sturdy footwear that he treated himself to. Thus shod, they were on the move, on the ramparts at Leegen Gate for instance or with Wróbel at the old Salvator Cemetery overlooking the Radaune, where one could imagine under tons of snow a good four acres of cleared cemetery land; or I see the two of them by themselves, because Wróbel is detained by his work, tramping down the left side of Grosse Allee toward the Cemetery of Reconciliation. This couple that I have been saddled with: she as round as a tub under her fur cap, he in his baggy black coat, bent as if fighting the wind, though there isn't any wind in this frosty weather. Since he too is wearing a fur cap, I can't help wondering: Was it bought in response to the weather, or did Alexandra unearth a mothballed article from the years of her previous marriage? Photos bear out assumptions: our couple let themselves be photographed on their way to, and later in, the Cemetery of Reconciliation, several times in color.

The burials had to be halted. The deeply frozen ground made digging impossible. With the thermometer at seventeen below, not even urns could be properly buried. Reschke writes: "We were glad to find ourselves alone between rows of graves. Mound after mound. Amazing how quickly the first rows have lined up. By spring, the upper right-hand quarter of the cemetery will be full. I believe the lower quarter, the urnfield, will also be fully occupied. Though all the plots were landscaped individually to suit the taste of the families, the snow has made them all alike. The simple crosses, which for the time being make known the names and dates of the dead, are confirmed in their uniformity: everything is covered by a thick layer of white, the freshly planted box borders and all the fir branches that cover the graves in winter. The snow caps on the urns made Alexandra laugh. For the first time I hear her laughing across the snow. How cheerful she is again. 'Your pots are funny looking. Nothing like that in Polish cemetery, where everything Catholic.' Later, we weren't alone anymore. Heavily bundled, Erna Brakup came waddling along in her felt boots, and talked and talked . . ."

I'm grateful to him for taking down her word-flow immediately after their visit to the cemetery, and not trying to convert her babble into standard German. "Hey, did the lady and gentleman see on television as how they're making war on the Arabs in the desert?"

That was her greeting. It was through her that the outbreak of the Gulf War was first recorded in Reschke's diary. "That's the way it's always been. When the gentlemen up top don't know what to do, they make war. First I thought they'd show us fireworks like at the end of Dominik. But then I saw they were hell-bent on smashing all the Arabs. And I said to myself: What for? An Arab's a human, ain't he? Even if he's maybe done wrong. Who in the world hasn't done wrong? I ask you, Herr Professor. Will there never be mercy?"

I don't know whether he or she explained the significance of the Gulf War to the old relic. In the diary his approach to the war is circumspect. "Once again," he writes, "Brakup knew what was going on. Amazing, the interest she takes in current events . . ." But that doesn't tell us what he thinks of the new weapons systems glorified on television. I read only that, as usual, he is of two minds: on the one hand he justifies the slaughter and on the other calls it barbarous. While the ultimatum was still in force, he was definitely furious with the Germans for supplying arms to Iraq, but his fury lost itself in generalities after he referred to chemical warfare agents as "German poison." "It is as though human beings were deliberately trying to wipe each other out, until nothing is left . . ."

He took a picture of Brakup in the snow, and the old woman seems to have photographed the pair amid snow-covered grave mounds, white-capped urns, and sugar-sprinkled cemetery lindens. All the photos in my possession speak of January frost, winter sun, and blue shadows on the snow. We already know how the couple look in snow, but Brakup is new. She has wrapped her scarf several times around her small, already shrunken skull so tightly that the muffled ball reveals only narrow-set eyes, the reddened hook of a nose, a sunken mouth. It was this photographed mouth that said across the silence of the cemetery: "And when they stop the war, it'll be the same as it was here in Danzig. Everything smashed, and so many bodies that nobody could count them . . ."

A photo that Piątkowska must have taken seems strange and unsuitable for Reschke's documentation. I see him and Brakup in the center of the cemetery traffic circle, both in violent motion. Slightly blurred, they are throwing snowballs at each other. Firmly planted in felt boots of the kind worn in wartime, Brakup throws and hits—sending up a shower of snow—while Alexander

157

Reschke winds up for a throw, his fur cap slipped to one side. "Snowball fight," he wrote on the back.

The frost held until mid-February. The cemetery was as good as dead. But this slack time was taken up with activities: senior citizens moved into the first of the former trade-union houses. In other houses renovation work was under way. In the large villas and manors on Pelonker Weg, progress was slower. In passing Reschke notes that he and Piątkowska saw nothing wrong with the additional leases—in any case the executive partners had no voting power on the Board.

Advertised in glossy pamphlets under the slogan "Spend the twilight of your life in the homeland," the housing project was a huge success. Applications poured in. Waiting lists had to be made. Leases were signed for eight more buildings, some of them hotels on the brink of bankruptcy, of course with an option to buy. Vielbrand invested a good deal of time in the new project, confident that his own medium-sized business, which specialized in floor heating, would have a part to play.

For a time Reschke and Piątkowska were swept along in these activities. Impressed by the cheerful vigor of many of the old people—over six hundred of them moved without any problems into the first five homes—the two approved the decision of the Board after the fact. He released more of his "hidden reserves" when a plan had to be drawn up for a geriatric clinic that met Western standards. After the brief rejuvenation that came with the joy of arrival, the infirmities of old age reclaimed their usual rights. If anything, the change of scene so ardently longed-for made the old people's health more delicate. The clinic was therefore indispensable, especially as there was no relying on the Polish hospi-

158

tals, which at best could be used only during the transitional period. In any case, the mortality rate in the retirement homes was on the rise. By the end of February, as even Vielbrand had to admit, the situation was critical.

Reschke, whose early misgivings were confirmed by this increase in the mortality rate, nevertheless denied the accusation made in a West German magazine that "a profitable business feeding on the homesickness of old people had produced sad flophouses fit only to die in and which ought to be condemned." In his reply, the executive partner pointed to the advanced or, as he put it, "Biblical" age of the dying. The thirty-eight deaths since the opening of the retirement homes included seven between the ages of ninety and one hundred, while not one was under seventy. "Furthermore, it is safe to say that in every case a long cherished wish had been fulfilled. This wish, expressed in many letters, can be reduced to a few words: We want to die in our homeland."

In the name of the board of directors, Vielbrand thanked Reschke for his letter of clarification. And in Reschke's diary I find remarks casting a more favorable light on the industrialist: "Spoke with him recently in private. Was surprised to learn how much importance he attaches to the economic recovery of Poland. Touching, how excited he gets. Gerhard Vielbrand's standard remark—'What Poland needs is a healthy middle class'—provokes violent nods of agreement not only in Marczak and Father Bieroński; Wróbel nods too, and so does Alexandra; they all nod, and sometimes I nod too."

Yet strife was on the horizon. At the early March meeting the atmosphere was already tense. Balancing,

in his usual way, expense against benefit, and as usual
ending up with a profit, Vielbrand outlined a proposal
which aroused interest only in the vice president of the
National Bank. Space, he said, should now be desig-
nated for the reburial of bodies and bones. Marczak
immediately agreed and set December 1, 1970—when
the first German-Polish pact was drafted in Warsaw—
as the cutoff date. Only those resettlers who died after
that would be eligible to be returned for reburial. In
conclusion Vielbrand stated: "I believe we can handle
well over thirty-thousand as a start. Economies of scale.
It goes without saying that I shall make reburial possible for my parents, who died in the mid- and late sev-
enties. I trust our Polish friends realize that we are acting
in full awareness of the enormous cost. Anything that
furthers the reconciliation of our peoples is worth paying for."

Sums in hard currency, yet with many zeros, were
named. It was made clear that for reburial the basic fee
would have to be drastically increased. Still, despite the
vice president's interest, the Polish faction held back.
Stefan Bieroński, as a priest, said a flat no. Jerzy Wróbel, though obviously upset, gently commented on the
"inhuman dimension" of the idea. Piątkowska seems to
have laughed out loud and asked Vielbrand if he thought
his proposal would improve the health of the Polish
middle class. Angry, heated words passed up and down
the conference table. In all likelihood, the proposal introduced by Vielbrand as Operation Reburial and para-
phrased by Marczak as "cemetery diversification," would
have been voted down, buried under the rubble of as-
phyxiating talk, if the professor in Reschke had not won
out over his better judgment.

Carried away, he treated the assembled board of directors to a lecture described in his diary as a "succinct excursus." Tediously, he brought out his knowledge of church burial customs. Elaborately, he expatiated on the dates chiseled into memorial slabs marking the expiration of interment contracts, then on the transfer of the bones from reopened graves to the charnel house of the parish church, whose small inner chambers did not allow for permanent use, so that the only solution was the installation of crypts filled with skulls and bones, which were, according to Reschke, "the most striking symbols of death."

I am certain that he embellished this lecture, which ruined everything, with the finds to which Jerzy Wróbel had called his attention in mid-February, after the frost let up, in the interior of the ruined Church of St. John.

They had entered, Wróbel in the lead, first through the hoarding and then through the side door of the right nave, which had been only loosely boarded up. Reschke's thrill of horror: "What a sight! There in the dim, broken light amid scaffolding and beams, amid cracked memorial slabs and pulverized Gothic arches, the witnesses of our mortality: bones upon bones, heaped-up fragments of skulls, pelvises, collarbones. I saw knucklebones and vertebrae, as though the war had only just brought them to light when the city crumbled in the firestorm caused by bombs and shells . . . I can see it in my mind's eye, though I left the city when it was still intact . . . In the central nave a worthy hand has started cleaning up, collecting bones in crates. One crate is marked, as Jerzy translates, GLASS, HANDLE WITH CARE! Where to put them next? They can't be left there among cigarette butts and beer bottles. Since we can't afford a charnel house, a special pit should be dug and

161

covered over. Perhaps by the tower . . . And then in the rubble, to the right of the demolished main altar, I found pieces of memorial slabs partially sunk into the crypts, among them one dedicated to two sea captains—St. John's was the church of mariners, sailmakers, and fishermen—and a limestone plaque on which two hands in bas relief hold a key beneath illegible names. Here, too, bones and skulls . . ."

Vielbrand seized on these details, on everything Reschke said about skeletons and charnel houses, and bent them, stripped of their baroque gruesomeness, to his purpose. Obviously, any reburial program involved the problem of space. The large number of applications demanded consolidation. Common graves seemed to him a possible solution, and he proposed repositories large enough to accommodate fifty reburials. The names and dates of the reburied could be arranged in alphabetical order on a simple plaque. In accordance with the esteemed Professor Reschke's suggestion, some of these inscriptions might be cut in stone. There would even be room for traditional symbols, such as the above-mentioned key. Every problem contains its solution. Where there's a will, there's a way.

But the will was not there just yet. Reschke objected to the misapplication of his knowledge and called the above-mentioned charnel house an obsolete model. Consistory councilor Karau confessed that he was "torn." Frau Johanna Dettlaff said: "Frankly, I am uncomfortable with the macabre aspect of the program under consideration." Bieroński and Wróbel stuck to their no. Unable to make up his mind, Marczak said: "Later perhaps . . ." After Reschke's presentation, Alexandra Piątkowska was able to put an end to the discussion by referring to the double grave of her parents on Hagels-

162

berg and categorically refusing reburial, even were it to become possible in Wilno. "Anyone already in ground should stay there."

So for the time being nothing came of it. Marczak tabled the motion. Under "miscellaneous," the last item on the agenda, certain public reactions were mentioned. It was noted with satisfaction that a debate in the Sejm had ended favorably for the Cemetery Association. A former Communist deputy had attacked the German-Polish reconciliation movement as "cryptorevanchism." His denunciation culminated in the cry: "An army of German corpses is intent on conquering our western provinces." Marczak reported that several deputies rejected this denunciation, or, in his words, "unmasked it as a Stalinist horror story." When the meeting was over, he invited the whole board of directors for a drink at the hotel bar.

The conference room on the top or seventeenth floor of the Hevelius may be pictured as two guest rooms joined together. Its only distinction was the view of all the towers in the Old and Right cities. Thanks to Marczak's charm, the tone of the assembled Board seldom rose to the level of an exchange of verbal blows, although it must be admitted that a debate in three languages, Polish, German, and occasional English, often provided plenty of incendiary material. The polyglot chairman, that always carefully groomed quadragenarian whose forehead, heightened by loss of hair, shone as though polished, managed to take the sting out of arguments that threatened to grow violent; with gestures comparable to those of an orchestra conductor he moderated here, pacified there, sometimes in French. He curtailed Wróbel's longwindedness by tossing in questions, hurried Karau's sermons along to the amen by injecting Bible quotations. He softened Frau Dettlaff's repeated insistence that smoking not be allowed, by suggesting smoker's breaks for Piątkowska's benefit. Without irony he summoned Erna Brakup back from an occasional nap to the business at hand. He managed to reduce Vielbrand's motions to a minimum, and even aroused the interest of a bored Stefan Bieroński with an encouraging gesture when Reschke took the opportunity to get back to the original idea of the Cemetery of Reconciliation. Marczak had them under control, even during the session that left the reburial question undecided. Bieroński listened and Brakup woke up when Reschke added a variant to his standard Century of Expulsions theme by provoking the opposition of both Vielbrand and Karau with the assertion: "Reburial is but another form of expulsion." Vielbrand threatened to walk out. Brakup babbled away, though no tape was running. And Piątkowska smoked, though no break had been announced. But Marczak disarmed them all with his helpless smile.

Later in the hotel bar, the atmosphere was relaxed, almost cheerful. I picture Brakup on a barstool.

Just a week after this meeting, Reschke had another talk with Chatterjee, this time not in the small half-timbered house on the bank of the Radaune but conspiratorially in a rundown graveyard behind the Church of Corpus Christi. Here, either forgotten or deliberately spared, the Klawitter family tomb was their place of rendezvous.

"On a gray pedestal, a black granite block rubbed to a high gloss. The spacious tomb is surrounded by a rusty iron railing. The name of the last Klawitter, president of the Chamber of Commerce, is chiseled at the bottom. Of course I owe this discovery to Wróbel. And Chatterjee listened attentively when I told him about Johann Wilhelm, the founder of the first Danzig shipyard . . ."

My former classmate entrusted this secret meeting to his diary as a matter of great importance. Yet it can't have lasted more than half an hour. "He was waiting, leaning against the railing. This vital, often exhaustingly vital man with his life-affirming energy and spontaneity, to whom our preoccupation with the dead is bound to be utterly alien, fascinates me more and more. He calls burial a total waste of space. We could be friends, if only I could manage not to regard him as a threat. Sensible as I find his solution to the traffic problem, and willing as I am, though a motorist, to do without cars and support his bicycle rickshaw as a way to save our cities, I cannot accept his view of the present war and its global effects. No! His conclusions horrify me. Chatterjee believes that the Gulf War is needed to make the pauperization especially of Asia and Africa intolerably evident. The crushing demonstration of military might, he believes, simply highlights the impotence of Western thinking. No one can halt what has now been set in motion. The die is cast. He even tried, by quoting Nietzsche, to make the new era and the transvaluation of all values palatable to me. 'Already we are on the way. Only a few hundred thousand to begin with, poor in luggage but rich in ideas. Just as you came to us, to teach us double-entry bookkeeping, we are coming to you, bringing you something in return.' That led him to his rickshaw principle, the success of which indeed speaks for itself. After a sudden leap and a vault over the railing, which must have been at least waist-high, he spoke well of my seed-money investments and promised, with a glance at the tombstone of the shipyard founder, to revive the founder's spirit of enterprise. After another vault, he tossed figures about with playful earnestness, vaulted over the railing again, this time without using his hands, and swore by Klawitter to turn the shipyard into a gold mine. Theatricals, of course, but this much is true: Chatterjee's rickshaw production is running full tilt in three shipyard hangars. First he means to satisfy the domestic market, then nibble at other countries. With all this planning activity, my business friend has put on a little weight. Unfortunately, he can no longer find time to pull a rickshaw in his own employ; his personal fitness suffers, and that's why he resorts to jumping exercises. Again he vaulted inside the railing, and again back to me, and confided that he had arranged for additional help by procuring visas for six of his numerous cousins—four from Calcutta, two from Dacca—and, in return for small favors, obtained residence permits for them. Three of the expected kinsmen are supposed to be Marwaris, hence especially capable."

All this was heard by the forgotten and spared tombstone of the founder of the Klawitter Shipyard, whose expensive railing the Bengali was using as gymnastic equipment; over and over again he practiced the side vault from a standing position. All around him scrubwood, rusting scrap iron, the remains of a wooden shed, and, farther on, community gardens. Even before Schichau, Klawitter had been active. His first steamship. Only later, much later, came Lenin, who built no ship and nothing but ideas.

And once again hup! and hup! After the twelfth vault—Reschke was counting too—Chatterjee pointed to the polished granite and tapped the first chiseled name and the dates 1801 to 1863: "I'd like to have that man as a partner!" And Reschke, poor Reschke, who wouldn't have dared attempt any vaults but wanted to be a partner in the place of Klawitter, offered further financing from his hidden reserves. Figures and bank connections were mentioned. With the six-foot tombstone behind them, Chatterjee's rickshaw production and the Cemetery Association, the moving and the immovable, the quick and the dead, once again concluded a deal which, to quote Chatterjee, was based "on reciprocity."

When Reschke asked how business was doing in the winter, he learned that even in the hard January frost a good many Poles had responded to the attraction of the low rickshaw prices, among them the vice president of the National Bank. "Mister Marczak is a loyal passenger and always willing to help," said the Bengali after a last leap over the cast-iron railing.

Erna Brakup too enjoyed riding in rickshaws. If the Board was in session, she had herself cycled to the hotel entrance. Her arrival drew a crowd. She was the one, actually, who gave Chatterjee the idea that the rickshaw could be used for small deliveries. Soon an inner-city service for letters and parcels was introduced.

When activity in the Cemetery of Reconciliation resumed with the early spring weather, Brakup could often be seen riding up Grosse Allee to the old brick building beside the gate. She never missed a burial. To all the mourners she expressed her condolences, which boiled down to one sentence: "Let's wish them eternal peace." She is reported to have said to Chatterjee, who pedaled her at reduced rates: "We're both a minority here. That's why we should back each other up. I mean against the Polacks and the Germans from over there. They want to put us through the wringer." And then she made Reschke, who was less than eager, translate her babbling into English. "Especially the part about backing each other up." The parcel service which she suggested became so popular that Chatterjee had special rickshaws built in his assembly plant, and honored his advisor with a book of free tickets.

There were always spectators at the cemetery entrance when Brakup drove up. From there she went to the brick house where the gravediggers and gardeners kept their tools and where the permanent guards were stationed, and picked up her watering can and her little shovel that also served as a hoe.

I have a photo showing Brakup sitting in a bicycle rickshaw with a raised top, although the photo indicates fine sunny weather. She sits as though in a shell, wearing her pot-shaped felt hat and the same old wartime felt boots. Her fingers are braided in her lap. She is not smiling.

Since the driver is not a Pakistani but flaxen-haired, he could be a Pole, and if not a Pole then a Kashubian. Unfortunately, few photos document Chatterjee's rickshaw enterprise. This photo appears as authentic as those black-and-white snapshots in my possession that prove that in German-occupied Warsaw, when all sorts of things were prohibited and no Pole was allowed to drive a car, whether a taxi or privately owned, there existed a legal bicycle rickshaw business operated by Poles for Poles, engaged in the transportation of persons as well as goods. The wheels and crates attached to them look shabby, the drivers morose, and the passengers worried. In another picture, the "driver" pushes an overloaded crate. The writer Kazimierz Brandys has this historical vehicle rolling through his novel *Rondo*. The rickshaw also occurs in some of Szczypiorski's works.

The color photo of Erna Brakup, however, shows a spanking new wheel that was made in the shipyard hangar. To the right of the bicycle seat a pea-green inscription on a ground of white enamel avoids the national language and attempts, through English, to be universally intelligible: CHATTERJEE'S RICKSHAW SERVICE. The raised top is striped in the national colors: white and red, white and red. The driver's dress has a hint of uniform but is actually a sports outfit: bicycle racer's cap, collarless tunic, trousers not unlike antediluvian knickerbockers. A stripe across the chest of the tunic displays the logo of the firm and the number of the vehicle, which is 97.

Like the Warsaw passengers in those black-and-white wartime photos, Erna faces the camera impassively, as if welded into the rickshaw. Reschke must have taken this snapshot, because on the back of it is written: "Thus majestically does the spokeswoman of the German minority in Gdańsk ride to the Cemetery of Reconciliation."

The photo was taken at the end of March. At that time the currency, which had been briefly stable, began again to show an inflationary trend; prices were rising, production falling, and wages stagnating. The new president of the Republic, of whom Piątkowska said, "Now electrician wants to be King of Poland," had got himself a prime minister who lacked the mournful countenance of his predecessor but saw everything, countrywide, in a much more mournful light. Only churches were being built, ungainly churches everywhere.

Reschke writes: "The joint-venture businesses that put on such a show of optimism are already failing. Just as a year ago the Americans refused to take over the run-down Lenin Shipyard, now the Norwegians hesitate to buy into the deficit-ridden Paris Commune Shipyard in nearby Gdynia. At best we see pseudodeals between foreign firms that have post-office box addresses and native factory managers, each taking a cut. This no doubt is why Chatterjee's enterprise, though of medium size, is commanding more and more respect . . ."

And that is why the photo of Erna Brakup riding in a rickshaw suggests more to me than any photo can prove. The Bengali with a British passport had taken root in Poland. There his six cousins, among them three Marwaris, found fertile soil for their activities and established branches in Warsaw, Łódź, Wrocław, and Poznań. Reschke had done widely to put the Cemetery Association's money—never mind how much—into rickshaw production. Even now it might not be unreasonable to ask whether the former Lenin Shipyard, previously the Schichau Shipyard—and in the beginning there was Klawitter—should not be named, if not after the Bengali's black goddess Kali then after the Bengali national hero Subhas Chandra Bose.

In any event, hope moved into Poland with Chatterjee.

If I am to believe Reschke, as I must, the German-Polish Cemetery Association enjoyed comparable esteem, which, however, as sad experience shows, kept being cast into doubt; the GPCA was respected, whereas Chatterjee was idolized as a benefactor. Yet Reschke sees himself as equal in stature to the Bengali. More and more often he refers to him as "my associate and partner in the business of the future." I would not have thought Alex, as we called him at school and later as a Luftwaffe auxiliary, capable of so much foresight, allowing, however, for the fact that he prospered at a time propitious to his idea, when everything was in flux, when the world was out of joint and all certainty gone. He could at least be certain of his Alexandra.

They were no longer a widower and a widow, but a pair. I see them personifying convincingly their idea: at the Rathaus reception, as guests at the Bishop's palace in Oliwa, in seats of honor at the Baltic Opera House, on the podium at debates about "Courage for Reconciliation," or within the milling crowd at Chatterjee's inauguration of his fourth assembly-line hangar at the shipyard premises with free beer and bratwurst. Whatever the program, our couple was present. Side by side and if necessary back to back, since war was in the cards for the next meeting, scheduled to take place in early April.

Since little reliance could be placed on Jerzy Wróbel, who always had his nose in the past, or on Stefan Bieroński, who was interested only in collections for the arch in his parish church, and since they could expect support solely from Erna Brakup, provided all the talk didn't put her to sleep, the session took a turn it shouldn't have taken. The "reburial program" was presented in a motion formulated by Vielbrand. Brisk, businesslike, armed with a brush haircut and rimless glasses, he made himself heard like a general on the eve of battle.

Because the middle-class industrialist took only what he wanted from the professor's recent lecture and adopted the frequently mentioned Baroque charnel houses as a model for his plan, the reburial of mortal remains sounded practicable and not at all offensive. Communal graves of moderate size were proposed, and memorial tablets instead of tombstones. "This space-saving venture," he said, "demands to be handled with the utmost dignity."

Thus was Vielbrand's mill powered by the professor's passion for research. Bieroński was carried off by sweet boredom. Wróbel was tracking down clues to the past. Brakup was fast asleep under her hat. And Reschke confesses: "He beat me with my own words. I had foolishly supplied him with arguments for his loathsome reburial scheme. That always correct advocate of naked interests reduced me to silence. Even Alexandra's protest, expressed in both languages—'Reburial will take place over my dead body'—for all the effect it had, might have been spoken out the window. But no, her protest was not entirely wasted. Erna Brakup woke up, and she, with her choice of words, did have an effect. The priest in Karau thought he heard speaking in tongues. Bieroński and Wróbel sat up. Frau Dettlaff was shocked and Vielbrand petrified . . ."

With her hat on and standing in her everlasting felt boots, Brakup spoke: "If reburial goes on here, ladies and gentlemen, pretty soon there won't be no room for real dead people. And who's going to dig out all the Germans that croaked at the end of the war and right after the war? The devil only knows where the refugees gave up and lay down. And who's going to pay for all that? Nothing doing. There's no justice in it. You only get reburied if you're rich and German. And the Poles make money out of it. But if you're a German and a poor devil you and your bones can stay where they put them in the bad times when there was no justice. Nothing doing. Count me out. If that's how it is, you can bury me somewhere else. For all I care, in the Arabian desert, where they had a war a while back. But, ladies and gentlemen, let me tell you this: First I'll resign from the Board!"

Apart from the objections of the executive couple, the only dissenting voice was that of Erna Brakup. Wróbel and Bieroński abstained. With the three German votes plus Marczak, the motion would have carried, if Brakup's threat to resign hadn't forced a postponement. The next meeting was to take place in two weeks. Vielbrand was in a hurry. He had acted without consulting the executive couple, and spoke of some 37,000 reburial applications with basic fees raised to 2,000 deutschmarks. The vice president of the Polish National Bank, Gdańsk branch, had no difficulty in adding up the numbers.

Mention must be made of the travel plans not only of Reschke and Piątkowska but also of Chatterjee—in three different directions—the Bengali traveling in accordance with a carefully prepared itinerary and our couple in haste, as if to make the fullest use of the days remaining before the next meeting of the board of directors. Reschke's destination was Lübeck, Piątkowska's was Wilno, though her departure was delayed for several days by visa trouble. Chatterjee visited a string of big cities. They all traveled as light as possible. Reschke took the car, Piątkowska the train, and Chatterjee—what would you expect?—a plane.

Though the intentions of the couple were unrelated to the itinerary of the rickshaw manufacturer, all three travelers had one thing in common: each pursued an idea, either to save it or to give it wings. The purpose of S. Ch. Chatterjee's European tour was to open or expand branches; Piątkowska's to make a last try at establishing a Polish cemetery in Wilno; and Reschke's to put a stop to the reburial program.

The businessman was accompanied by two of his six cousins. He proposed with his visionary concept of traffic to help all those immobilized by motorized metal, smothered by exhaust fumes, and deafened by noise; he guaranteed immediate delivery of brand-new bicycle rickshaws, though in limited numbers to begin with. Piątkowska had fortified herself with a financial guarantee backed by a third of the capital of the Cemetery Association. Only Reschke was empty-handed when he protested in Lübeck against what he called "this inhuman reburial business."

Considering the traffic situation in the western and southern European urban centers, Chatterjee's success was assured: political leaders jumped at his idea and— in Amsterdam and Copenhagen immediately, in Paris and Rome after some hesitation, in London with reservations, and in Athens only after receiving certain favors—granted him concessions for inner-city rickshaw routes.

In Lithuania the opposition of the minorities—a few White Russians and Ukrainians, numerous Russians and Poles, who all felt that the independence given to the majority at the last plebiscite offered them, the minority, too little security—did not make for a climate favorable to Alexandra's wish. Tempted as they were by the financial offer, the Lithuanians were unwilling to guarantee a cemetery for Polish citizens of any extraction whatever. Their answer: "First the Kremlin dictatorship must go."

In Lübeck the ladies and gentlemen of the League, among them Frau Dettlaff, listened to Reschke's worries and complaints, but said there was nothing they could do, since the professed willingness of so many compatriots to move the bones of their family members to the Gdańsk Cemetery of Reconciliation could not be negated by any resolution. The matter was settled, and that was that.

If I now say that I'm glad to see Reschke coming back empty-handed—I thought all along that his idea stank—I still feel sorry for Alexandra; she said nothing about her Lithuanian defeat and even kept her "Russophobia" valve screwed tight. Of the three, only Chatterjee, at the next "tomb of Klawitter" meeting, could announce progress, which Reschke called breathtaking. The professor, who as a rule foresaw calamity in everything, believed in the Bengali blindly. An image rises up before my eyes; a spanking new bicycle rickshaw with a toad as passenger, rolling in the direction of the future . . .

I don't know how Alexander and Alexandra comforted each other. Their love was of a long-suffering kind. Frequent embraces and affectionate words may have helped. In the diary I read: "At first she seemed to be sealed up. Not even tears came out. Later her repeated cry of 'Damn politics. Messes up everything' may have relieved her a little. But yesterday she frightened me. She reached for the bottle—as a rule she never takes more than an occasional sip from a liqueur glass—poured tumbler after tumbler of Wódka Wyborowa into herself, and her curses snowballed into such verbal monstrosities that I refuse to quote. Lithuanians, Russians, and Poles all had their turn. To be fair, I cursed the Germans, though without recourse to the vodka bottle. I could only agree with Alexandra's supranational appraisal: 'Learned nothing from past, make double-trouble mistakes.' Right now, for all Wróbel's urgings, we've lost interest in visiting other potential cemeteries. I'm almost afraid that Jerzy in his excessive zeal is creating more openings for reburials; the Cemetery of Reconciliation by itself would hardly be equal to such a flood of mortal remains."

The shipyard, on the other hand, benefited from Chatterjee's travels. Rickshaw production took over even more hangars. Threatened with collapse, all the big cities of Europe—and later the medium and small ones—had to ban car traffic. The melodious three-note bicycle bell developed in Chatterjee's workshops brought to the citizens of numerous towns a concert which, Reschke writes, "on my recommendation echoes the call of the toads. Gradually this sad and beautiful sound has replaced the aggressive honking of horns, at least in the inner cities."

All of which made for more jobs and revived the languishing shipyard, whose world renown was once based on the idea of Solidarność. Chatterjee decided to name a rickshaw model Solidarność, after the now historical working class movement, and it soon achieved striking success on the international market. The Solidarność Bicycle Rickshaw went into mass production and, passing beyond the borders of Europe, was on its way to meeting the needs of Africa, Asia, and South America. This model too rang with the sadly beautiful toad call.

But before that could happen, Chatterjee had to bring over more Bengali cousins, Marwaris included. There were now a good dozen of them, and with them they brought business sense as well as energy. Poles provided the labor force. According to my classmate's notes, which from now on are often prescient, when the thriving plant, still affectionately known as the Shipyard, was in need of a catchy new name, the president of Poland proposed his own. Reschke writes: "The entire work force of the rickshaw plant rejected that offer." And so it came about—"since Chatterjee knew his place"—that before the turn of the millennium, the Schichau then Lenin Shipyard was named after the legendary Bengali national hero Subhas Chandra Bose, in my opinion a more dubious than exemplary individual. But that's another story . . .

It remains for me to report that the reburial program was already in operation before the next meeting of the board of directors. The ever helpful, courteous, obliging, zealous, all too zealous Jerzy Wróbel had come up with suitable land. The large park beyond Grosse Allee offered ample room. On either side of the Soviet tank which stands there as a memorial (for how much longer?) and where in Reschke's and my schooldays the Café Four Seasons was popular, Wróbel paced off the section available for lease to the Cemetery Association. This area, just behind the Steffenspark, had formerly been St. Mary's Cemetery, nine acres under linden, ash, birch, and maple trees, and even a few isolated weeping willows had survived. The tombstones, as Wróbel found out, had been removed in the late forties and shipped from the nearby freight station to Warsaw for other use.

Behind the railroad tracks and working-class dwellings from Imperial and Schichau times, behind the shipyard with its cranes and dry docks, lay the United Cemeteries of St. John, St. Bartholomew, Sts. Peter and Paul, plus the Mennonite Cemetery, occupying an area of some twenty acres. Then came a field covered by

177

barracks: the former Maiwiese, also known as the Small Drillground—in my day used for big parades past grandstands, shouts of Siegheil, march music, commands, and speeches by gauleiters.

And here, a little to the side of Grosse Allee, right behind the still-standing staff annex of the Café Four Seasons, the first shipments of mortal remains, in small, simple wooden boxes, were buried in groups of one hundred in two common graves. Neither Reschke in his black worsted nor Piątkowska in her broad-rimmed hat attended, but many family members were there. Since the speeches made over the pits were short and moderate, the Polish authorities took no umbrage at the German-speaking throng, especially as the crowd quickly dispersed after the reburials and drifted off to the usual tourist pursuits.

Faced with the fait accompli, our couple could only acquiesce in the reburials, though under protest. I have in my possession, over her hen-scratched and his neat signature, their expression of shared impotence on paper: "Disgrace has befallen us! While until now people of their own free will and in their lifetime decided to make their last resting place in the homeland, from now on the dead will be disposed of unconsulted. Greed and sacrilege have the upper hand. More and more German demands are on the agenda. This must be nipped in the bud."

Alexander, of course, had more to do with the wording of this protest than Alexandra, but it was she who insisted on including this sentence: "If all is not put in minutes, right away I resign." No other statements of dissent are recorded. Bieroński and Wróbel kept silent. A single line, however, announces the resignation of Erna Brakup.

She didn't do it silently. She was said to have banged the conference table repeatedly with her fist. And when she spoke, no one could pretend not to hear her. "Disgusting. I saw them lining up those crates; margarine crates, that's what they used to look like. Always neat as a pin. Poshondek! or as the Germans say, there must be order. Well, I don't want to be German no more, I'd rather be a Polack, being I'm a Catholic anyway. All that for boodle. Not for me. Ain't going to sell myself for money. And I'm resigning from the Board this minute. Phooey!"

6

Reschke and me, me and Reschke. "Both of us antiaircraft auxiliaries," he writes, "in the eighty-eight millimeter Brösen-Glettkau flak battery . . ." In those days Erna Brakup was living in Brösen. She was one of the barely six hundred Germans left in Gdańsk and environs. Possibly there were only five hundred who believed they were Germans; later, there were more and more. When hundreds of thousands tied up their bundles and headed west, the five or six hundred, either by accident or because of unshakable roots, had stayed on in whatever houses remained standing, in the midst of smoking ruins or in suburban slums, where no one disputed their right to a corner in a cellar or attic.

At the end of the war Erna Brakup was a widow of forty; her three children had died of typhus in the plague year 1946. She quickly picked up some makeshift Polish and entrenched herself in her hut in the fishermen's and resort village now called Brzeźno. To the right and left of her hut and on both sides of the streetcar line to Nowy Port, boxlike buildings were being put up. As long as the ramshackle casino was still standing, she gave the waitress a hand; later she found work in the cooperative. From the mid-sixties on she eked out her meager pension by running errands, standing in line outside the butcher shop, and performing similar services. She spoke only with her fellow Germans or when tourists came and asked the way to the pier or the bathing establishment, expressing herself in an increasingly odd variant of her mother tongue.

After the changes in Eastern Europe, when the government, with some hesitation, finally authorized the Germans still living in Poland to form associations, Erna Brakup joined and became a far from inactive member. On Jäschkentalerweg she wangled a meeting room for the three hundred-odd members who, having grown old and useless, were bewildered by this sudden turn of events. Now they were even allowed to sing their favorite German songs: O forest glade . . . By the well at the village gate . . . or, in mid-winter, Now comes the merry month of May . . . So it came about that Erna Brakup was given a seat and a vote on the board of directors of the German-Polish Cemetery Association. Her pension was now supplemented by hard-earned attendance pay, for it was she who secured a resolution guaranteeing long-established residents, in return for a nominal fee payable in zlotys, a place in the Cemetery of Reconciliation. She also supplied them with song books, illustrated magazines, mail order catalogues, and other glossy publications, by prying small sums loose from the bequest account. When the Board was in session, her voice was not to be ignored.

"Often," writes Reschke, "the Board members exchange glances when Erna Brakup takes the floor." Frau Johanna Dettlaff, as though her refugee's luggage—her Danziger's Hanseatic arrogance—had doubled in Lübeck, "seems to react with irritation and disgust to Brakup's 'diminished Germanness.'" About Vielbrand Reschke writes: "This businessman with his passion for brevity tried at first to curb Brakup's logorrhea. Her angry response: 'Who's talking here, you or me?'" And consistory council Karau saw her as a character.

Nor could Erna Brakup be seen or heard with equanimity on the other side of the conference table. Her presence was a reminder to the Poles of an injustice that could not as usual be blamed on the Russians. Marczak and Bieroński sat in embarrassed silence when she blurted out: "It was horrible here after the war."

Only Jerzy Wróbel had no compunction about taking his thirst for knowledge to Erna Brakup, sometimes bringing a bunch of flowers like a lover. To him her babbling was spring water. Intent on details, he learned what Brösen had looked like before it was ruined by new buildings on every side; learned which fishermen, and at what prices, marketed the catch from their trawls; and what pieces of music resounded from the bandstand at the afternoon concerts in the casino garden. For Brakup knew who lived in the remaining fishermen's huts and behind the crumbling façades of the middle-class houses near the streetcar stop, how much freshly caught flounder used to cost, and the names of the lifeguards. She told him about the ice floes in the Baltic—"Such winters ain't no more"—and whistled or sang for Wróbel a medley from the *Zarevich* and *Frau Luna.*

Like Jerzy Wróbel, Alexandra Piątkowska took an interest in the forgotten past of her city, whose history, from the Middle Ages to the Baroque, the gildress knew from the carvings on the high altars and the creases in the garments of the ecstatic saints; but as to what stores there used to be in Langfuhr, now Wrzeszcz, or what films with Harry Piel, Zarah Leander, or Hans Albers were shown and exactly when in the two local movie houses, she learned from Brakup. To her Alexander she said: "It was like hole before. Now I know where was Sternfeld's Department Store and how cheap you could buy there pretty things." But only Jerzy Wróbel profited from the Brakup source, profited for the Cemetery Association.

It must have been mid-March when their friend invited the couple for a mad ride from one former cemetery to another in his "Polski Fiat," as Reschke calls it. They accepted without enthusiasm; since the start of the reburial program, they had both lost interest in their idea.

Wróbel drove them to Ohra, a working-class suburb whose only cemetery, now a park, would hardly have suited the Association because of its location on either side of a railroad line. Next they drove to Schidlitz, where just a few fragments of tombstones recall the Cemetery of St. Barbara, which has also been turned into a park. The main avenue and four crossroads, on a slope bordered by lindens, chestnut trees, a single maple, and a clump of birches, are enclosed in what remains of a fence, its gaps filled with a pile of railroad ties.

In upper Schidlitz they climbed through rugged country: "The lower third of St. Joseph's Cemetery, which was not leveled until the mid-seventies, is crisscrossed by a tangle of pipes which with frequent loops carry steam from a central heating plant to a new housing development."

They approached the Bischofsberg from behind, Wróbel in the lead. They stumbled—Alexandra in city shoes that were much too delicate—over several discused cemeteries choked with weeds. Here the all-explaining Wróbel kept unearthing toppled, cracked, or still intact tombstones. No sooner spelled out, names such as Auguste Wiegandt and Emma Czapp née Rodler gave way to other names. On golden-brown speckled granite, a message chiseled for no one: Paul Stell-macher, whose life had lasted from 1884 to 1941.

Only then did Jerzy Wróbel lead them to where—not far from the Stolzenberg housing development on the farthermost hump of Bischofsberg, called Chełm by the Poles—a neglected park on its way to becoming a forest rises steeply to the tragic remnant of an old Jewish cemetery, from which the city below can be more guessed at than seen.

I climbed with Reschke. Still on the rise, a slab of granite misused as a stepping stone bears the name Sil-berstein. Large tombstones toppled backward, their Hebrew and German inscriptions covered with moss, lie buried in weeds, only Wróbel knows where. I agree with Reschke that these stones were overturned "in our time." Wróbel does not contradict us.

Old stones that speak: Abraham Rollgerber was born in 1766. Alexander Deutschland lived from 1799 to 1870. To hear more, you'd have to scratch the moss out of the grooves. Reschke calls it a disgrace, Piątkowska a double disgrace. I know that beginning in 1937 the Danzig Jewish community was forced to sell this ceme-tery and others to the Free State in order to help fi-nance the emigration of its members to Palestine. Reschke and I were ten or eleven at the time. We could have asked childlike questions, could have found out at an early age . . . A quiet countryside to those who don't listen. Just a few toppled stones are left. There are al-ways stones of which people say, If only they could speak.

I can imagine how the couple felt when they were back in the Polski Fiat—"We hardly spoke"—and they were wordless fellow travelers as Wróbel drove past the Salvator Cemetery and the Mennonite church, which today is used for prayer and baptism by the Pentecostal community, to what used to be St. Mary's Cemetery, next to the Schiesstange prison complex, which is still a prison. Alexandra said: "In December 1970 when strike was, they lock up workers here."

She didn't want to see any more cemeteries. Her shoes were not right for walking through any more cemeteries. All this had made her tired and sad. "I have to sit a little and rest my head."

So they repaired not to the Klawitter tomb but to the nearby Church of Corpus Christi, which in the late fourteenth century had become a hospital church; formerly Roman Catholic, since the end of the war it was open to serve Poland's Old-Catholic minority. "In one of the old hospital buildings Wróbel found the priest, who welcomed us, and, as we walked between the pews, acquainted us with his estrangement from the Pope: as a Christian, he refused to bow to His Holiness's infallibility. A bright, almost cozy church, All the floor slabs, which in the mid-eighties had been moved from the nave to the left wing of the sanctuary, were well cared for. Alexandra sat down in one of the pews."

I set aside my classmate's ramblings about the twin tombs of the Mackensen brothers and the large porphyry slab in the center of which a leaping stag invites interpretation; nor do I pay attention to his notes on the runelike signum of the patrician Georg Brothagen, or to Reschke's quotations from his own doctoral dissertation. These are merely diversions meant to keep me from the heart of the matter.

Seeing the freshly moved floor slabs, Reschke inquired about the bones of the reburied, and the priest offered to let his guests visit a crypt under the left row of pews. With a crowbar that lay ready Wróbel pried two floorboards from the supporting joists. Alexandra

decided that she needed to hear and see after all, and
Reschke followed her through the hole. The priest stayed
behind.

"Jerzy soon found the light switch. Cool, dry air. No
smell to speak of. Downstairs, under a masonry vault,
a room no wider than the nave of the church. On the
left, coffins were stacked to the ceiling and, by the steps
where we stood, only halfway to the ceiling. We had
barely room to stand and didn't dare go into the narrow passage. Each coffin was marked with crudely
painted numerals. The numerals in no particular order. Even so, the number of the unsystematically piled
coffins may have corresponded to the thirty-odd newly
laid floor slabs . . ."

Alexandra wanted to know: "Is in there somebody?"

Wróbel was sure the coffins were occupied, and
Reschke conjectured that the occupants must be Brothagen, the Mackensen brothers, the patricians Moewes
and Schmid, and Burgomaster Gralath.

"Can't we open this one?"

"Do we have to?"

"Well, seeing as we're here . . ."

"I don't know . . ."

"Just a little . . ."

And Wróbel raised the lid of the coffin closest to him,
the foot end of it, so that the lid formed an angle of
about forty-five degrees, whereupon Reschke, not in
response to any special wish of Alexandra but purely
on his own, his very own, "because this had to be documented," took flash pictures through the wide opening, several of them, with pauses required by the flash
bulbs. Like this: Lid up, snap, snap, lid down. Wróbel
breathed heavily as he held the coffin lid high—"A little higher, please."

187

In my possession are two photos in color, in brownish gray to be exact. From slightly different angles both show one and the same mummy, hands folded right over left, roughly on the level of the genitals, on a crumbling shroud, once white, now spotted with mildew. They are male, long-jointed hands whose bones, unlike the head, which is reduced to a naked skull, are held together by skin visible up to the folds of the sleeves; three fingernails of the top hand have survived. No ring, no rosary, only sand-colored dust on everything. The pillow, hardened to sandstone, raises the head, so that the chin is pressed against the frill of the shroud. Wróbel's right hand, holding the coffin lid with the help of his left, which is outside the picture, appears in flesh color. I believe I can identify, on the right edge of the coffin, two hand-forged coffin nails that have come loose; just the thing for Reschke's collection.

Of course, he simply had to record in his diary "the touching beauty of that mummified man, the skull slightly inclined to one side, the still sumptuous drapery of the shroud down to the covered feet." "I am grateful to Alexandra," he writes, "for the opportunity to look upon these two hundred years, at least, of eternal peace, assuming the move from the nave to the crypt to be only a brief disturbance."

Having established that this peace cannot be surpassed and is reserved exclusively for death, Reschke conjectured that he had been standing over the mortal remains of Burgomaster Daniel Gralath, who died in 1767 and had gained recognition for planting the trees on Grosse Allee. "There was a dignity about the patrician's mummy. Gralath was one of those who had endowed the organ in Corpus Christi Church, of which only the restored organ screen survives. The organ itself, as the Old-Catholic priest lamented, was removed after the war and shipped to Bytów."

The diary then says that the visit to the crypt and the sight of the male mummy revived Piątkowska's flagging spirits and gave her the courage to carry on in the face of adversity. Outside the classical portal Alexandra seems to have laughed again. "I am better now. Now again idea is right. Only reburial is wrong, because reburial disturbs peace of dead."

Then Erna Brakup resigned. It is only now, to my mind, that she takes this step, though she had already resigned in words before the board of directors of the Cemetery Association. With her last word she started putting on her felt boots, which she habitually wore from autumn to April but preferred to remove in the overheated conference room of the hotel; first the left boot, then the right, not without groans but otherwise in silence.

Up and down the table, the members looked on until she stood booted. Once booted, she walked backward step by step to the door. Heels first, one entire sole after another placed flat on the floor. To keep her balance, she held both arms up and slightly akimbo. And so she walked, not for one bootstep taking her eyes off the no-longer-full-strength board of directors. She wanted to impress upon them exactly what was happening; they all saw and heard, tap, tap, Erna Brakup irrevocably taking her leave. Thus in felt boots that she occasionally removed, and under her cloche hat that she never took off, she meted out her resignation like a punishment.

And Wróbel, as well as Alexander and Alexandra, may have felt punished when Brakup found the door, opened it backward, and, once in the corridor, slammed it after a last hard look. Reschke writes: "A long silence. It would probably have been even longer if Vielbrand hadn't cried out, 'I call the meeting to order.' "

If I, too, were to continue my account seamlessly by saying that the remainder of the board of directors came to order, I'd come to the end of my story too soon. That won't do. I can't drop Erna Brakup so quickly.

In addition to the progress report which Vielbrand finally gave to the members, a photocopy of a hand-written letter has come into my possession, which on the day of her impressive resignation the old woman penned in a somewhat trembling hand in that variant of the Sütterlin script which Reschke and I also had drilled into us in our schooldays, and which stayed with us until some time after the war, when, thanks to democratic reeducation, we lost it along with other bad habits.

Sharp angles, bold loops, yet not entirely free of Brakup's intonation. "Honored Directors," I read. "I was excited when I had to resign, so naturally I forget something else that I beg to tell You most respectfully. I've always been sincerely in support of the German Cemetery. Because Germans got to lie with Germans and Polacks with Polacks. But what is being done now ain't human. It's a kick in the face of humanity, like has often happened, before the war and after the war. I know, because I seen it. But the cemetery, that's as beautiful now almost as it used to be, ain't going to be for humans no more but only for business, and I don't want to lie there when my time is up. I say this to all of You, but especially to Pan Wróbel, who has a kind heart. Very sincerely, Erna Brakup, née Formella."

———

This letter may have prompted the town clerk to resign at the next opportunity—which occurred in mid-April. But as long as the current meeting is the substance of this record, he no doubt hoped, along with the priest of St. Peter's Church, Karau, and our couple, that after sulking a short while Brakup would be with us again in her cloche hat and felt boots. In any case, called to order by Vielbrand, we immediately came to order.

The progress report signed by Reschke and Piątkowska listed successes and voiced misgivings. It cited, with gratification, the founding of cemetery associations and the inauguration of cemeteries of reconciliation in the previously German cities of Breslau, Stettin, Landsberg an der Warthe, Küstrin, and Glogau. Difficulties were reported only from Posen. Bromberg sent a resounding no. "Nevertheless the idea has been sown, and the seed is sprouting on all sides. Openings can be expected in the near future in Stolp, Allenstein, Hirschberg, Bunzlau, and Gleiwitz . . ."

The report was greeted with applause. Marczak and Frau Dettlaff congratulated the couple. Since the number of applications from persons resettled from Silesia, East Prussia, and Pomerania had taken on a dimension that reduced the Danzig figures to medium size, Vielbrand and Marczak suggested the need for an additional supervisory board and proposed Warsaw as its headquarters. This would satisfy the Polish wish for central supervision.

In German-Polish accord, consistory councilor Karau and Father Bieroński warned against the dangers of centralization. And Reschke, along with Wróbel, was opposed to central supervision. This problem sparked

191

a long debate on the pros and cons of federalist state structures which heated up, finally subsided, and need not concern us here.

In time the spread of retirement communities, which the newspapers had at first denounced as no better than death-houses, was welcomed, all the more so when some of the homes initiated what could be interpreted as social welfare programs. Reports came in of soup kitchens for needy old people. It appeared as if the Germans were following the example of the former Polish minister for social services, though without dunning the poor with the so-called Kuroniówka tax—not for the Germans such bureaucracy.

The progress report was tedious in places. Attention began to flag. Bieróñski and Wróbel, even Karau, were as good as absent. On the agenda: drafting of new cemetery regulations; addressing the shortage of hotel rooms due to the steady increase in the number of mourners; the Orthodox Church in the former crematorium. The addition of the phrase "space-consolidating reburial" made the regulations longer, and at Piątkowska's urging they finally authorized anonymous burial. The Board decided to promote the construction of new hotels. In response to an appeal, Bieroñski, who had made room for an Armenian minority in a side chapel of St. Peter's, promised to do the same for the Orthodox minority. At the same time, he requested a contribution for the arch over the central nave of his church. Bieroñski got his contribution. Point after point was ticked off. The meeting went well, too well.

The introduction of a new project, however, caused alarm on the Polish side. Small wonder, since the couple had issued a warning against this section of the report: "The following motion is more than questionable, for it is hardly compatible with the principle of reconciliation. In our opinion it should be rejected."

It had to do with vacation bungalows and golf courses. On their visits to Gdańsk, the grandchildren and great-grandchildren of the deceased had come to know and appreciate not only the city with its many towers but also its flat and hilly environs. Some of these younger people, their wealth acquired through investment or by inheritance, gradually conceived the desire to spend their vacations in this region where grandparents or great-grandparents had found eternal peace through burial or reburial. The gentle, hilly country between Karthaus and Berendt appealed to them. They were enchanted with the region, and since the vacation spots of southern Europe were overrun and its coasts all ruined by obsessive building, they chose to relax or, as Reschke put it, "recharge" in the land of their ancestors, this lovely country where it was still possible to lead a quiet, simple life.

According to the report, the applicants promised to deal kindly with nature in building their bungalow colonies and laying out golf courses. There would be no repetition of the sins committed by builders on the Mediterranean coasts. In collaboration with Polish architects, whose blueprints were attached, they would develop the region caringly and only in places where agriculture had no future anyway; they would build environment-friendly golf courses, which, it went without saying, would be open to Polish members. God knows, they had no intention of making them exclusive. "On the contrary, they hope to extend the idea of reconciliation to spheres that are accessible to the living . . . "

A pilot project was appended. The first bungalow colony would hug the hilly, wooded lakeshore. The area

193

set aside for the golf course measured one hundred and eighty acres, included valleys and hills, and spared stands of trees. No tall buildings would be allowed on the lakeshore, only flat-roofed bungalows rising in terraces to a pointedly simple clubhouse.

The financial offer looked good to the Poles. Some two hundred prospective members were prepared to pay an advance of DM 30,000 for admission to the Bungagolf Club. The applicants assured that they would not ask for ownership of the land; in view of Polish reservations, they would be satisfied with a ninety-nine year lease, transferable to their heirs. Besides, all these ticklish questions of ownership would be rendered meaningless by European unity. And Poland, it seemed safe to assume, would want to be part of Europe.

The debate over this last point proceeded smoothly, as though rehearsed. The objections raised by Reschke and Piątkowska were at first shared, then put into perspective; Wróbel's unequivocal no was called hasty by the vice president of the National Bank, then changed to no but, and in the end modified to yes provided. The term of the Bungagolf lease should be shortened, the Cemetery Association should acquire a share in the capital stock, and job security should be given to Polish construction workers, gardeners, domestics, cooks, waiters . . .

The couple said nothing. In the midst of the discussion, which grew more and more detailed, Reschke got up and walked to one of the windows on the seventeenth floor of the Hevelius. He looked down on the city and let his eyes roam from right to left, as if to count the towers in the evening mist and check their order: the gable of the Big Mill; the tip of the Kiek in de Köck tower over the roof of St. Catherine's; the Do-

194

minican church behind the round roof of the covered market. The elongated Church of St. Bridget, with its vicarage, occupied the foreground. To the left, floating in the mist above the house gables, St. John's with its massive tower and delicate steeple stood dark. Far away, barely an intimation, St. Peter's in the suburbs. The slender Rathaus tower concealed by the hulk of St. Mary's topping all. In a small space, many towers. Inky clouds drifting overhead. And oh yes, down below, as though at the feet of the tall boxlike hotel, the small half-timbered house on the bank of the Radaune inviting him to barroom conversation.

When Reschke opened the window a crack, Piątkowska was standing beside him with a cigarette. Her smoke drifted away; the evening air smelled sweetly of gas. Later he wrote in his diary: "It seemed to me that the city was an illusion, and the only reality the exhaust-saturated air pouring in through the slightly open window. The longing for repose, for the ultimate repose last glimpsed in the crypt of Corpus Christi, rose up in me. But then it seemed that all the churches, the towers, the mill, the arsenal, and the covered market were possessed by an inner fire that would instantly blast the tall windows and the dormer windows . . . the whole city again in flame . . . firestorm in all the streets . . . the sky reddening . . . How good that Alexandra was beside me. She said: "Now they sell us piece by piece."

My classmate and I don't always agree. He wanted to see the warning against "German land grabbing" voiced in the Sejm nailed to the notice board here, but the outcry of a few members of that parliament was not made public until later—too late; while I was against mentioning the motion for burial in Danzig Bay, which was brought forward at the meeting before last and already noted by him. I now add: Although this motion was rejected in view of the wretched quality of the water along the coast, it later turned out that fishermen from Putzig and Heisternest were making extra money performing unauthorized burials at sea from their cutters. And it is further reported that from February on, charter planes flew in corpses for which a refrigerated compartment had to be built in the freight depot of the Gdańsk Rembiechowo Airport.

Details are missing; much was obscured or omitted altogether; the mess of paper my former classmate left me is marked by gaps. For instance, it is not clear precisely when a full-time planning manager became active on behalf of the Cemetery Association in a Düsseldorf office. Did Reschke appoint him? Or did the board of directors impose this young man on Reschke as a check? I don't know. I'm not Reschke.

It is certain that the new tasks put a strain on the couple. Casual telephone contact with the aristocratic secretary in Bochum and all-too innocent faxes via Interpress would no longer do. A planning manager became necessary with the start of reburials, if not sooner. And since the couple had argued against such an appointment, the Board, represented by the entrepreneur Vielbrand, took action; as long as Frau von Denkwitz was in Bochum, Reschke may have noticed nothing or suspected only a little.

All I know is that this young man, Dr. Torsten Timmstedt by name, had acquired management experience in a life insurance company. Age thirty-four, though himself not descended from refugees, he had seized upon the affairs of the homeland associations as a "genuine challenge" and outdid Reschke's rather

196

haphazard organizational talent with his professionalism. The last point in the progress report had been drafted in the Düsseldorf office; indeed, the daughter corporation Bungagolf was Timmstedt's ticket to membership in the GPCA. His arrival had appreciably rejuvenated the Cemetery Association. From the end of March on, according to Vielbrand, "a fresh wind was blowing."

Our still-executive couple accepted, even encouraged, this diminution of their power, for Reschke praised the customer service introduced by Timmstedt. "A discreet attentiveness including house calls had long been my intention, but I was tied down in Gdańsk . . ."

How true! That was his place. If he had grabbed the young manager's tasks, moved his desk to Düsseldorf, said yes to Bungagolf, and built up a countrywide customer service, it would have meant a parting of the ways—unthinkable. But by yielding and by giving up responsibility, the couple avoided the break. On the other hand, they must have given offense by acting as a couple. The gildress had moved a part of her professional activity into the kitchen of her three-room apartment, the professor conducted himself there as man of the house, and Jerzy Wróbel was a frequent visitor to Hundegasse 78/79. Certain members of the Board felt that this was going too far and would lead to malicious gossip.

Before the close of the session— "miscellaneous" was under discussion—Frau Johanna Dettlaff deplored failings on the part of the executive partners and was seconded by Karau when she moved to have the admonitory sentence "Private affairs and business must be kept separate" read into the record. It was Vielbrand, however, who brought up Brakup's dubious expense account.

These unpleasantnesses were aired after the couple left their secluded position at the window with the panoramic view and went back to the conference table. Alexandra was no longer smoking. Frau Dettlaff said that she was on the trail of certain "hidden reserves"—"As the wife of the manager of a district savings bank, I know whereof I speak"—but Marczak, who knew more than he thought wise to say, made light of this by characterizing Reschke's financial methods as "unorthodox but profitable." Wróbel argued that Brakup's slight irregularities should be forgotten and that the Board should, as he did, express their confidence in the executive couple. "We all know to whom we owe the idea of reconciliation and its implementation . . ."

Wróbel spoke softly, as though pleading for forbearance: he didn't know much about finance, but there was no evidence of wrongdoing because no money was missing; the money, on the contrary, had multiplied almost miraculously. He saw no reason to be small-minded. And Pan Marczak, who was so to speak at home with financial matters, said the same.

It was friend Wróbel who in the same soft voice brought alarming news to Hundegasse a few days later. Piątkowska had just applied a layer of mastic to the right wing of a kneeling late-Gothic angel and asked her Alexander to put water on for coffee when Wróbel arrived with news from Erna Brakup's sickbed.

Coffee and angel had to wait. Because Wróbel had been economizing on gasoline lately—and for weeks now not a word has been written about Reschke's car—they took the Nowy Port streetcar at the Brama Wyżynna stop and got out at Brzeźno. A wet, cold, blustery wind was blowing from the northwest. Rain squalls like whiplashes. The former fishing village now beach resort presented a picture of general decay. The new houses were deteriorating more quickly than the surviving old ones. Streets and sidewalks in similar condition. The visitors had to jump over puddles.

Wróbel led them to a side street. To the left, fishermen's shacks alternated with rotting woodsheds. The new interlocking boxlike structures that lined the right side also blocked off the street: it was a blind alley. In the other direction the street lost itself in sand dunes. A gap made by a narrow passage revealed the Baltic making little waves.

Among the half-timbered cottages with tarpaper roofs and front verandas was Erna Brakup's home. Lying under a fluffy eiderdown and in her hat, she sang out: "Come in, come in. I'm feeling a lot better. Be on my feet soon." Her felt boots were standing at the foot of the ancient bedstead with the chamberpot under it.

From then on she spoke only her rudimentary Polish, first with Wróbel, then with Piątkowska more sparingly; not a word to Reschke.

What Alexandra translated for her Alexander sounded like time run backward; only Erna Brakup's cough was in the present, because what she talked about took place in times of war or before wars. Her childhood, spent partly in the country and partly in the lower city, seems to have been most eventful. Time and again between Matern and Ramkau, cows calved; the teacher at the Weidengasse grade school kept breaking his cane; barns burned down, floods threatened; there was one less brother after the beginning of the First World War, and then, mournfully, she came to the flu-and-rutabaga winter of 1917.

Several times between her coughing fits she must have

mentioned potato bugs, because in his diary Reschke compares Brakup's childhood memories with his own: "Strange, that as early as the First World War the Colorado beetle should have appeared in such numbers. We were told it didn't cross the Rhine until the mid-thirties, and then spread as far as the Ukraine . . . ."

True. From the Polish campaign on, or at the latest from the French campaign on, we had to collect them in bottles, even in the rain, with numb fingers. Those disgusting yellow-and-black striped bugs. They said the British dropped tons of them from planes at night. At any rate we had to bring in at least three quart bottles full to the brim . . . Alex organized the collections . . . And Reschke and I . . . Anyway, regardless of the weather Brakup had to . . .

She was shaken by a hacking cough. The bedroom was also her living room. On the wall, across from the bed, hung a clock that had stopped. There was a gas stove in the glassed-in veranda—originally the panes had all been yellow and green, but a few had been replaced by milk glass. Piątkowska put water on to boil. With it she would fill a stoneware jug for use as a hot-water bottle and also brew a pot of herbal tea. Later the old woman dutifully drank it sip by sip.

Over the bed, more precisely, over the headboard, hung a multicolored picture of the Sacred Heart, its blood dripping into a golden cup, which matched the glowing heart-red brooch resting on Brakup's felt hat. Her broad face had grown perceptibly smaller. Wróbel held her right hand, which had emerged from the side of the eiderdown, its fingers reaching for his. She was breathing regularly now. A strong sour smell. Her visitors thought she had at last fallen asleep. They were already at the door when her old-time German reached

200

their ears. "What about the Board what I resigned from the other day? And what about the desert? The war still going on? You going so soon? All right. Then go."

Wróbel came back to Hundegasse with them only for a cup of coffee. There the late-Gothic angel was kneeling, his mastic priming on gesso still waiting for a layer of gold leaf. The angel, about three feet high, was kneeling on the kitchen table. While Reschke poured coffee, Piątkowska applied the extremely thin gold leaf and immediately tamped it with a soft camel's-hair brush. The men, forbidden to move the air, were sitting off to one side with their coffee cups.

At first they talked about Brakup—how long she was likely to last—then came to the board of directors. They took the members one by one, made entertaining comparisons between Bieroński and Karau, devoted a few words to the Bungagolf project, considered the possibility of a trip to Silesia together in the spring, as well as a visit to the latest reconciliation cemeteries. They thought of including Allenstein and Stolp, and even of making a last try in Bromberg. They praised the soup kitchens in some of the retirement communities, judged their activity—unlike the reburial program—to be sensible because it promoted reconciliation. But then, as though in passing, and while Piątkowska stroked the gold leaf on the angel's wing with her soft brush, Jerzy Wróbel let fall the word resignation. And at the very next Board meeting, he announced his resignation. He would not, could not, go on. As a Pole, he regretted having helped the new German land grabbers with his knowledge of the country and of the registry of deeds. As a patriot, he was therefore resigning. Unfortunately too late. He was ashamed of himself.

This happened at the start of the meeting. The Board took it in their stride. Our couple hesitated. Or for tactical reasons were they waiting for the Bungagolf project to be settled and point 3 on the agenda to be discussed? Point 3 dealt with explanatory inscriptions on historical buildings and with street signs in the Old and Right cities. Because this motion in all its particulars had been drafted by Wróbel, who left the conference room immediately after resigning, Father Bieroński took over. It was moved that side by side with their Polish designations, street signs and monuments display the traditional German names, as was already the case to the right of the portal of St. Bartholomew. There one could read, on a moss-green plaque ornamentally scalloped around the edges, what the church wished to be called in Polish, English, Russian, and German.

Wróbel had supported his motion by quoting from well-known political historians who had long wanted to see German cultural achievements in the western provinces of Poland recognized: "The time of suppressing, indeed of denying, is past. A pan-European view of culture demands a new openness . . ."

Pouncing on the word "Europe," consistory councilor Karau proposed the use of as many languages as possible on large attractive signs and deplored the absence of Swedish as well as French inscriptions.

The vice president of the National Bank disagreed. Few Scandinavians, he pointed out, had been seen during the main tourist season. American and French visitors were equally rare. Now at last it would be possible to dispense with Russian signs altogether. With this Father Bieroński could only agree. In conclusion Marian Marczak produced documents showing that to date over seventy percent of the foreign visitors had been German, a trend that seemed likely to continue.

Before the motions under point 3 of the agenda were put to a vote, Vielbrand asked the executive partners, who had been silent thus far, for their opinion. Since Wróbel's resignation and departure, our couple had been sitting there as though under a bell jar. Or had their thoughts taken flight, homeward to Alexandra's kitchen and the kneeling angel?

Reschke stood up to speak, which was unusual, and spoke for both. He saw no objection to bilingual signs, though he pleaded for inscriptions in four languages, including Russian. Respect for the cultural achievements of others must be regarded as an integral part of the reconciliation which Frau Piątkowska and he had been promoting for the past year. Since then the work of reconciliation had made a name for itself not only in Gdańsk but also in Silesia and Pomerania. More and more cemeteries had been opened for those coming home. Therefore, let us first and foremost give thanks to the many dead. It is from their silent help that the German-Polish Cemetery Association has drawn the strength it needed. Yet for some time now the idea has suffered. Worse, by adulterating it with a sordid striving for profit, we have stirred up an evil brew. It does not smell good, it stinks to high heaven . . .

At this point in his speech Reschke must have been shouting. In any case, I read him with reverberations: "Here and now the limit of the acceptable has been reached. We could live with the retirement communities, which after all, because of their convenient location, help the residents to prepare for death. This reburial business, however, precisely because it is flourishing, is thoroughly reprehensible if not obscene. And now land is to be taken. Money is to be made from the grandchildren's and great-grandchildren's only too well-known pursuit of pleasure. The whole business is adorned with the wordplay of reconciliation, as though golf courses were nothing more than enhanced cemeteries. No. I no longer recognize our idea. What was lost in the war is being retaken by economic power. True, it's being done peacefully. No tanks, no dive bombers. No dictator rules, only the free market. Am I right, Herr Vielbrand? Am I right, Pan Vice President of the National Bank? Money rules. Frau Piątkowska and I both regretfully must draw the line. We resign.''

I see that Reschke, though used to speaking extemporaneously as a professor, was exhausted when he sat down. It can only be conjectured how short or how long the silence was after his swan song. No mention is made of ironic applause, from Vielbrand for instance, but Alexandra's intervention is recorded in the diary: ''Contrary to our agreement, she took the floor and deplored—as I had before her—the failure of the Lithuanian component of the contract of incorporation. 'Bad condition of Soviet Union ruined whole thing,' she cried. Only thanks to my help, 'because Pan Aleksander always backed me up,' had she felt optimistic until recently. She asked to have the Lithuanian paragraph stricken from the contract of incorporation and the separate Wilno Reconciliation Cemetery account diverted to charitable purposes. 'There's plenty poor people.' Then she spoke softly, because toward the end of my speech I had spoken loudly, too loudly. She spoke sentence after sentence first in Polish, then in her lovable German, so I was able to understand her conclusion: 'Now I'm interested in Poland only. Not because

I'm nationalistic but because I'm afraid. Why afraid when I've never been coward? Pan Aleksander once said: We better watch out or Poland will be on German menu. I say what I see: Germans always hungry even when full. And that makes me afraid . . .' Then my Alexandra sat down and reached for her cigarettes and holder. She smoked with her eyes closed, ignoring Dettlaff, whose many bracelets jangled . . ."

"But my dear Frau Piątkowska, why this doom and gloom?" That was consistory councilor Karau.

Reschke claims to have heard Frau Johanna Dettlaff hissing under her breath: "You can still tell she was a red-hot Communist."

Then Vielbrand stood up. "We are all dismayed; we cannot but regard the resignation of Herr Reschke and Frau Piątkowska as a painful loss. But I must reject categorically all allegations of German greed. History, God knows, has taught us a lesson. For years we were forced to go in sackcloth and ashes. Our posture today is, if anything, too modest. No one need be afraid of us. I beg you therefore not to act with undue haste. I beg you, honored Frau Piątkowska, as well as our dear Herr Professor, to reconsider your decision. In the moving words of your anthem: 'Poland is not yet lost . . .' "

After that it gets farcical, or simply absurd, embarrassing. Friend Reschke, what devil possessed you, possessed our couple, to make you so sheepishly accept, after your vehement resignation, the "honorary chairmanship" that Vielbrand magically pulled out of his hat? Though that post was not provided for in the contract of incorporation, it was approved by the remaining members of the Board without a single dissenting voice, and offered to the two of them. Did the couple hope to rescue their idea from grasping interests? For this they lacked the mechanism. Apart from the honor, the honorary chairmen were given nothing. No right of appeal, no veto power. They could not sign or refuse to sign anything. No more say in financial matters. Reschke's "hidden reserves" were laid bare, his transactions brought to light.

No sooner had they resigned from their executive positions and taken their seats as honorary chairmen than Frau Johanna Dettlaff and Marian Marczak expressed their willingness to take their place. Immediately after changing chairs, the new executives asked Vielbrand to bring the board of directors, now full of holes, up to full strength, whereupon Vielbrand picked up the phone, reached four—exactly four—candidates waiting in their hotel rooms, and summoned them to the conference room, where they were welcomed, questioned, appointed, and confirmed. The two honorary chairmen may have been surprised to see that everything had been thought out in advance and went off smoothly, as if rehearsed.

One of the four freshly baked members was Torsten Timmstedt, whose planning activity in Düsseldorf was mentioned only in passing; all those present except for our couple seemed to be in the know. According to Reschke's notes, none of the new members was under thirty or over forty. The seats of the resigned Brakup and Wróbel and the now executive Marczak were taken by two young men born and raised in Gdańsk and a young woman who claimed to be of German extraction but barely understood the language of her parents. If Timmstedt, who took Frau Dettlaff's place on the Board, had acquired his business experience as manager of an insurance company, the professional experience of the two other young men was of a complementary nature: one was the director of an architectural firm which already had plans for Bungagolf on the drawing board, the other a member of the secretariat of the Bishop of Oliwa. The young woman of speechless German descent proved to be the owner of a private travel agency which was beginning to compete with the government Orbis agency. All the new members were of one mind: Efficiency is what counts.

Reschke, the fool, wrote in his diary: "Refreshing, how fairly the young people, once in positions of responsibility, set to work on the remaining motions. Just as I had suggested, they put through street signs in four languages, though substituting Swedish for Russian. Less to our liking was that all of them, Timmstedt in the lead, demanded a more expeditious pursuit of the reburial program. All our planning calculations, he said, show that the common graves will require constant attention. Considering the volume of prepaid orders received so far, not nearly enough second burials have been processed. The clientele—he actually used the word clientele!—are growing impatient at the unconscionably long waiting period. The office in Bochum is no longer equal to these and future tasks. Frau von Denkwitz shares this opinion. She is prepared to move to Düsseldorf with all the files and documents, but has requested a word of confirmation from the honorary chairman, whose trust she does not wish to lose . . ." What could Reschke do but nod?

Timmstedt then said that more cemetery land must be leased if the reburial program was to proceed smoothly. I don't know what decision the new Board reached. No sooner had Timmstedt revealed his plans and provided a buzzword by demanding a "covering of all bases" than Alexandra asked her Alexander to leave with her. She said, "Angel waiting, you know, for us in kitchen."

So it was not until much later that our couple learned that between the former sports center, which in the sixties had been transformed into the Baltic Opera House, and the area of the former United Cemeteries already under lease, an extensive tract, once the Maiwiese, also known as the Small Drillground, had now been made available to the Cemetery Association. Where the people had paraded and celebrated final victory in advance, where Reschke and I were in the crowd wearing the uniform of Hitler Cubs, where a rostrum with flags and trimmings had cast its Sunday morning shadow, there would soon be room for common graves in tight formation.

After the end of the war, a gauleiter, who for a time had given his name to the stadium behind the Cemetery of Reconciliation, was put on trial in this same sports center. In those days, when Reschke and I were still students at St. Peter's, then became Luftwaffe auxiliaries, ending up in the Labor Battalions—in those days, the crematorium above the United Cemeteries was still operating.

The three-foot kneeling angel on the newspaper-covered kitchen table. I must admit that Reschke describes his Alexandra's craft with love. He celebrates her tools as if they were ritual objects, and calls the gilder's cushion, on which she cuts the gold leaf into suitable squares, "her altar, handled like a palette, on which, with boxwood tweezers, she slowly, solemnly picks up extremely thin leaf before pressing it with a brush of soft camel's hair against the gesso sizing on the angel's ancient wood. A collapsible parchment screen protects the leaf on the gilder's cushion from drafts . . ."

Time and again Reschke points out that gilding can be done only with tightly closed doors and windows. He, a mere observer, who at the most reads or exchanges whispers with friend Wróbel, is forbidden to make any sweeping gesture; pages, finished, must be turned cautiously, as cautiously as she picks up the gold leaf and tamps it in place. Everything happens in slow motion. She never laughs while gilding. Sometimes classical music may supply the background to this kitchen idyll.

He omits nothing: her agate polishing stone, the various brushes with which the sizing is applied in eight successive layers, the chopped calfskin from which Alexandra, at the kitchen stove, prepares the glue, into which cinchona bark is later stirred. The art historian knows and doesn't mind telling us that the gilder's trade has been true to itself for four thousand years. "Already the Egyptians, by beating gold blow by blow, obtained hair-thin gold leaves, twenty-five of which, supported on paper and bound together, to this day make a booklet of gold leaf . . ."

Alexandra has been working with the last supplies from Dresden. "Is gold still from People-Owned Gold-Beating Works," she says.

The air-still kitchen, in which a kneeling late-Gothic angel acquired more and more gold, became the center of existence for those two, who had ceased to be anything more than honorary chairmen of the Cemetery Association. They seldom went out except to visit the sickbed of Erna Brakup, "who is sinking into memories that are becoming more and more childlike . . ."

A lot of coffee was consumed in the course of gilding. He called the angel "an anonymous, probably South

German if not Bohemian work." She said, "Is typical Cracow school." The humidity in the kitchen had to be repeatedly measured and maintained at an even level.

Little was said while gilding was in progress. Either he put on long-playing records, or they listened to a radio station that broadcast classical music from morning to night. Over it, the chimes from the Rathaus tower, striking the hour: "We will never let go the land from where our people came . . ."

The kneeling angel carved of linden wood was blowing a trumpet and could thus be associated with the Last Judgment. "Originally there were many of them, probably a full choir, every one of them gilded, with a blast of their trumpets waking the dead, opening tombs and charnel houses, and so fulfilling what I recently read on a memorial slab in the central nave of Holy Trinity: 'After pain and misery, in this tomb at rest I lie, until the day when I arise, summoned to eternal peace.' And it was Alexandra's angel who did the summoning . . ."

She had taken over the carved figure from another workshop. Intersections, plugs in the linden wood, sprayed and smoothed traces of woodworm bore witness to long handling. This angel kneeling on his left knee must have looked pathetic in his patched condition: a veteran of changing times. Even after the complicated application of eight glue-bound layers of gesso, much of his potential beauty was gone, though the gildress had not covered any of the subtleties of the late-Gothic drapery.

But as the kneeling angel acquired more and more gold, with both wings glistering golden, and as Alexandra applied the alloy of white gold and red gold in the mastic layer to the sizing and finally polished with the agate stone the layer of gold from the bell of the trumpet to the tips of his toes, the figure conceived by an anonymous hand was restored to life in all its beauty. The once morose expression of the blowing, long-haired angel, concealing more likely a young man than a maiden under the drapery, took on, as Reschke says, "the austere charm of early Riemenschneider angels . . ."

And yet, from an artistic point of view, he did not hold the resuscitated work in very high esteem: "Combined with other figurations, the angel might have been part of an altar, presumably with the Resurrection as the central motif. Amazing how the ruined piece has revived in Alexandra's hands. Time and again—just now, for instance, while polishing the upper parts— she promises herself and me: 'You'll see. Will be like new born.' "

Meanwhile spring had come. When Alexandra Piątkowska's kitchen was entirely inhabited by the gilded and highly polished angel of Resurrection, the town clerk Jerzy Wróbel brought the news of Erna Brakup's death.

But before the earth covers her, I must backtrack. Through April, or more precisely starting with (and in expectation of) April 8, all Poland was gripped by travel fever: from that date on, Poles were at last allowed to cross their western border without a visa, and to travel through Germany to France, Holland, and Italy, as long as they had enough zlotys to convert into a visible quantity of Western currency. Wishes wanted to be fulfilled, Polish troubles, for a few weeks or days, to be forgotten. But no sooner was the border crossed than hate shouted itself hoarse. Violence, set loose, struck, slogans from the vocabulary and the scenes of German-Polish history picture books were repeated in all their ugliness,

211

and all the fine phrases of the recent past were made worthless. One had to fear. Not welcomed, the Poles recovered from their travel fever, so it was not at all surprising that many who might have liked to be traveling westward turned up instead at Erna Brakup's funeral.

The ceremony was held in the chapel to one side of the Matarnia Cemetery. Jerzy Wróbel had had to promise her that: she didn't want to lie in the Cemetery of Reconciliation but in Matern, as it was formerly called. Young and old, they came in black. They didn't all fit into the chapel. In photos I see them clustering outside the door.

Frau Brakup lay in an open pinewood coffin. The service was slow, loud, and Catholic. She lay in her black woolen Sunday dress. Everybody sang enthusiastically and mournfully. No, she was not wearing her fur boots but laced bootees, and she had to leave her felt hat at home. How thinly her hair covered her shriveled little head. Two priests, one from Brzeźno, the other from Matarnia, celebrated the Requiem Mass. Someone— friend Wróbel perhaps—had removed from her hat the brooch, in the center of which glowed a bleeding-heart-red semiprecious stone, and fastened it to her high-necked dress just under her chin. The priests and servers in white and violet. Tulips and candles around the coffin. In her knotted fingers Erna Brakup held a rosary and the picture of a saint whom Reschke thinks he recognizes as the Black Madonna.

From him I know that during the Requiem Mass confessions were made and the host received. Since many unburdened themselves, the Mass went on for more than an hour. Reschke was neither a Catholic nor anything else, but suddenly Piątkowska, who had often told him how godlessly she had practiced her gilding trade, though endowing two dozen altars with new radiance, moved away from him in the pew, stood up, and waited in a long line outside one of the confessionals in which the priests were lending their ears. She disappeared into the confessional after the priest tapped the signal, reappeared in a state of deep introspection, stood in the center nave with all those who also had their confession behind them, waited humbly for the last sinners, then knelt among others in black at the communion rail, rested her head on it, pushed back her hat, received the host, returned with downcast eyes to the pew, went down on both knees, moved her lips, and taught her Alexander that in Poland a life of unbelief does not rule out Catholic reactions. He writes: "Without my asking her or urging her in any way, Alexandra said to me with a laugh on the way home: 'Now I can be godless again until next time.' "

All in all, Erna Brakup's funeral must have been a cheerful affair. The old woman's smile in her coffin with its brilliant white trimmings—a smile that I have on one of the photos and which in the words of the photographer is more a mocking grin than a smile of deliverance—spread to the mourners. Many of the old German inhabitants had come. They all had Erna Brakup stories to tell. When the mourners crowded around the coffin to take their leave, each and every one caressing her knotted fingers, Reschke heard a farewell mumbling untouched by sadness: "You're better off now," "You won't have to suffer no more," but also, "Thanks for everything, Erna," "Good luck," "See you soon, Erna."

The burial itself went quickly. Clayey soil up there. Seen from the cemetery hill, the Rembiechowo Airport was right next to the village. The airport building and freight depot could only be guessed at. No plane took off or landed during the burial.

As the closed coffin was carried out of the chapel and church banners with the likenesses of saints·unfurled, as the funeral procession—priests and servers in the lead, Wróbel right behind the coffin—formed into a black swarm and started on its way. S. Ch. Chatterjee pulled up at the cemetery gate in a taxi to add his wreath and ribbon to the funeral procession. He, too, was dressed in black, which made him seem no less foreign than usual.

Almost all those buried in Matarnia are Kashubians. Erna Brakup, née Formella, who lived to be ninety, found her place between Stefan Szulc and Rozalia Szwabe. Her ninetieth birthday had been celebrated on Hundegasse in January, when there was snow on the ground. A photo shows Wróbel and Brakup dancing.

When immediately after the burial Reschke greeted Chatterjee, the Bengali is reported to have said with a sad, evasive smile: "She was one of my best customers. Our friend especially liked to be driven to her favorite cemetery. Why is she buried here? Wasn't she German enough?"

Lately I have noticed episodes of confusion invading my classmate's papers more and more. Leaps in time are frequent. The handwriting remains unchanged, but the order of events changes in mid-sentence. Suddenly something that has just happened is set far back in the past. He introduces Chatterjee driving up to the cemetery in a taxi, then sees him removed in time; this he does with the backward look of an old man who is no longer Reschke but goes by the name of Reszkowski, as he did before the Germanizing of family names became common practice, and who years after the turn of the millennium dimly remembers Erna Brakup's funeral and Chatterjee's visit to the cemetery: ". . . but whenever I try to recollect that day and to my dismay realize that at that time I still felt obliged to abide by my father's decision of 1939 and cling to my Germanized name, my old friend Chatterjee appears to me, the first man to experiment with the now universally used rickshaw system . . ."

And Reschke as Reszkowski describes the present in retrospect, as follows: "Oh, how full of calamity the world looked then! Hunger and wars, countless dead, streams of refugees on their way, soon at the door . . . On every wall Mene tekel . . . Who at that time would have dared hope that life would ever be worth living again? Who would have dared believe that the city and surrounding countryside would ever again enjoy economic prosperity? True, everything in the meantime has fallen into Bengali hands, but they are not oppressive hands. Even Alexandra finds this commendable. Soon large-scale attempts will be made to take advantage of the altered climate: rice will be planted on the Island and soy beans grown in Kashubia. The new situation goes against the grain of the New Germans, whereas the old Poles seem to find Asian dominance acceptable, all the more so since Hinduism is not necessarily contrary to Catholic practice . . ."

I'm beginning to believe in his prognostications: "Not long ago a new altar was consecrated in Holy Trinity Church. Tuned to the same key, the Black Madonna of Wilno in her halo and Calcutta's mother goddess, black Kali with her red tongue, call to worship. Now even Alexandra has found her faith, and by her side I am becoming devout . . ."

215

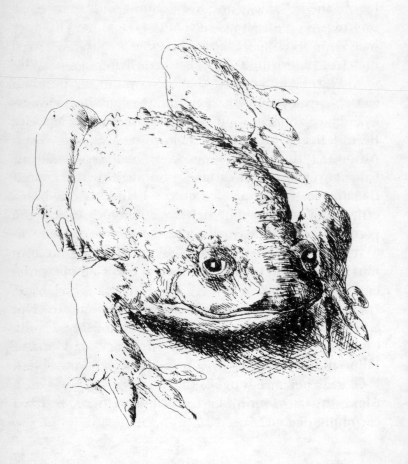

7

From the couch Alexander and Alexandra saw what the world had to offer. He looked on in bedroom slippers, she with cigarette holder, as tidal waves, raging fires, and fleeing Kurds provided, for the moment, food for newscasts in which image followed image in quick succession, each one blotting out everything previously seen from the couch. That was how the couple watched the Gulf War, whose dead no one wanted to count.

A small table laden with snacks went with the couch and the armchairs. When volcanic eruptions on Luzon Island buried under mud and ashes the burning oil wells, fleeing Kurds, victory proclamations, and rough estimates of the dead, the consequences of these now devalued events nevertheless were fertilized by the images that followed. Having noted all this in his calligraphic script, Reschke got up from the couch and, nibbling a pretzel, came to the conclusion: Nothing ever ends.

Against this belief, I enter a report from the autumn of 1944 into my record. We were escaping from the city of Danzig before it went up in flames. Discharged from the Reich Labor Battalion, we were put into uniform in army staging areas; he was trained as a radio operator, I as an armored infantryman, and we were both thrown into the final combat west of the Oder. And it was chance—hear this, Reschke—pure chance, nothing to do with higher dispensation, that we came through, that we survived, unharmed but for a few bruises, and got away to the West; while Alexandra's brother, age seventeen like us, was shot as a partisan the year before, and Reschke's brothers had been dead since the summer of '43—Maximilian, a tank driver, burned alive near Kursk, Eugen torn apart by a land mine near Tobruk; they ended, we did not.

These death reports were mixed in with a conversation that must now be recorded. Before Erna Brakup was buried with knotted fingers in the cemetery at Matarnia, the couple visited the fisherman's cottage for the last time. As soon as Wróbel brought word of the old woman's death to the kitchen and workshop, they, as on previous visits, took the streetcar to Brzeźno, past Saspe Cemetery, a route I've traveled over and over again in other stories. But neither the streetcar nor the farewell visit to the old woman, who had just been laid out, requires a leap in time; what does is a walk along the faintly rippling Baltic toward Jelitkowo, which in Reschke's diary drags on forever, since he returns to it repeatedly, first as an immediate event, then at a distance of seven years.

Key words tell me that in Erna Brakup's cottage the bedroom-living room as well as the veranda were jammed: no way to get through, not enough chairs. People crowding around the deathbed. Candles, flowers, the smell, and so forth. He writes. "On the veranda neighbors had gathered around a table, joined by Wróbel when a chair became free. I noticed three saucers half filled, then less than half filled, with hard candy, which those singing or praying sucked to keep in good voice. The perpetual rosary allowed endless prayer, which was interrupted from time to time by lamentation in song. Wróbel helped himself to hard candy. I

218

stood to one side. Our beloved Erna looked rather odd without her felt hat; she seemed to smile, but Alexandra thought, as I did, that her expression was more likely one of mockery. 'Because we're still honorary chairmen, though honor is gone, she's laughing at us a bit.' "

Without transition, the couple are next at the beach. Wróbel stayed with the hard candy, the supply of which was replenished as needed. They had probably walked across the dunes, past the old grade school. Reschke describes the Baltic as dull, gray, motionless, says nothing about the weather, mentions only briefly the fact that bathing has been prohibited on all the Bay beaches, and then goes on to the far too many swans on the water's edge, which he reviles as "the contaminated beneficiaries of the contaminated sea." "What an onslaught! Two swans may be beautiful, but a greedy, sated, yet still greedy horde of swans . . ."

I see the couple in changing perspective. As through a telescope held correctly, then held backward. Sometimes I'm in the lead, then I'm at their heels. I overtake them, see them come closer, grow larger, grow smaller: an unequal pair in motion. When shortly before Jelitkowo they turned around, they were still flanked by swans—talking to each other, she past him, he over her head.

This is how Reschke records their conversation: Erna Brakup's death, he says, laid bare the death of their brothers. Links between the Gulf War dead and the early loss of their brothers became evident. We felt we were in their company. "Because, I say, nothing, not even life, ends. Alexandra's brother who was shot and my burned, tattered brothers live on. Though buried somewhere and nowhere, they are still in us, unwilling to end, wanting rather to be lived, lived by us . . ."

After that, without announcing a leap in time, he has only pleasant things to report: "Who would have dared hope that these polluted waters would again be teeming with fish and again invite bathers in weather that continues mild? When Erna Brakup lay on her deathbed, who would ever have thought that summer tourism would revive? The Baltic Sea seemed dead forever. At that time, I too foresaw a dismal future, and my beloved Alexandra made fun of my tendency to read dire omens on walls, however solid: "Somebody who always sees Mene tekel on wall will live long and see that Mene tekel was wrong . . ."

Typical of Reschke that he shortened the time interval of his backward glance whenever he remembered his proposal of marriage uttered near Brösen. Immediately after the entry, "This afternoon, as we were walking on the filthy beach, I proposed to Alexandra," he sees himself happily married for seven years. "Time has not impaired our love. Though less frequently, we still embrace as we did that first time . . . When my proposal elicited her spontaneous yes, Alexandra must have known that we would grow old together happily, taking turns caring for each other, because of the accident and its consequences . . ." Then again he stirs up the sludge of memories . . . "Yet we had been rather depressed until shortly before our marriage. The thought of death as something to be shared lay in easy reach, and there were plenty of reasons for it. We tormented ourselves over that disgraceful honorary chairmanship. And then the weather. I remember, spring just refused to come. And then the trouble with the car, all that wretched, hateful suspicion. Small wonder that one day, soon after I proposed, we threw in the sponge, and by God not silently. Ah, the relief and the emptiness afterward. Gone was the vision. Now we were without an idea . . ."

In two of the diary entries the distant past and the recent past correspond. Reschke deals playfully with the light on Erna Brakup's veranda: "Just a moment ago, when I cast a glance at the endlessly praying then lamentingly-Catholically singing mourners, the three saucers filled with pink hard candy were what mattered to me, while the colored light filtered by the veranda glass mattered not at all; but now if I conjure up the scene, the predominantly yellow-green panes of glass transform the table and the people around it into an aquarium. Their praying and singing are soundless. Their mourning takes place underwater. They are all lamenting members of an underwater community at once near and far away . . ."

In another passage, the "many too many greedy swans in the shallow Baltic brew" are transformed for him after years of distance into a single greedy swan, "which then tried with its begging to upstage my proposal of marriage. How fortunate that Alexandra still remembers if not the swan at least my admittedly old-fashioned, stiff, and stilted proposal: 'Shall we, my dearest, become man and wife before the law as well?' I still remember her answer: 'Yes, yes, yes!' "

Having completed all the formalities, they were married May 30. In mid-May the couple for honorary reasons had to attend a meeting of the Board one more time. Frau Johanna Dettlaff and Marian Marczak reported on a meeting of the executive partners of all the cemetery associations that had mushroomed throughout western and northern Poland. It was reported that long-term leases had been successfully obtained every-

221

where. Soon there would be an even hundred cemeteries of reconciliation, and the turnover was increasing accordingly. At this meeting on the executive level, the question of establishing a central administration in Warsaw could not be avoided. Marczak stated that Cracow and Poznań as well as Gdańsk had been considered, but that after a heated quarrel the capital had won out. "That just happens to be a Polish tradition, which we Germans must respect," said Frau Dettlaff.

Consistory councilor Karau and Father Bieroński called the idea of a central administration "lunacy" and "absurdly bureaucratic." One excited, the other angry, they asked to be relieved of their positions and for others to be appointed to their seats on the Board.

Apart from the resignations, which were regretted, "the expanding area of the idea of reconciliation" provoked applause, especially as the "Spend the twilight of your life in the homeland in a retirement home" campaign, the "Reburial (or second burial) program," and the Bungagolf project were being emulated on all sides.

As a member of the board of directors, the Düsseldorf planning chief reported on the most recent achievements. A piece of lakeshore land suitable both for golf and bungalow colonies had been located in Kashubia, not far from Kartuzy. On signing the contract, the Cemetery Association had agreed to a lease of only sixty years, but with option to buy. Similar developments were reported from Olsztyn, where the first Bungagolf project was being planned in the Masurian lake region. From Elbląg came news that the so-called Vistula Slope was to be opened. Interest was also reported from Lower Silesia and the Pomeranian coast.

Reschke quotes Timmstedt: "In the long run nothing is more persuasive than profit . . . At long last the Poles are learning to figure in terms of European union, that is, to think . . . Land ownership is ceasing to be of primary importance. Of this and much more we can assure our honorary chairmen, who kindly consented to attend today, and to whom the German-Polish Cemetery Association owes such a large debt of gratitude."

Other urgent matters were taken up. The mass arrival of the bereaved, that permanent invasion of mourners, entailed risks: more and more often the conspicuously pregnant wives of the generation of grandchildren and great-grandchildren refused to be discouraged by the long trip. Before and after burials there were sudden confinements and premature births. Giving her report, Frau Johanna Dettlaff had this to say: "Gratifying as it is that Germans are again being born in our old homeland, we ought not to place an additional strain on the already overburdened hospital facilities of our Polish friends."

It was immediately resolved that a maternity clinic with delivery room be installed in a wing of the spacious retirement home on Pelonker Weg. "The medical equipment," said Frau Dettlaff, "must of course be up to Western standards, and I'm sure that Poland has plenty of doctors and midwives sufficiently qualified to bring our New Danzigers into the world."

Samples of four-language street signs and inscriptions for monuments were then displayed. Sketches which had the names and dates of historical events inscribed in parallel columns and identical type sizes were rejected. The German members of the Board felt that the Polish inscription at the top ought to be appreciably larger than the inscriptions in other languages. So much courtesy led to an exchange of compliments. Even the honorary chairmen participated cheerfully in this skirmish.

But it was not considered amusing when Alexandra Piątkowska suggested that in view of the latest development in the city's economy a fifth line might be called for, in Bengali. "It may come to that!" cried Vielbrand. "In Poland never!" Marczak assured them. Only Timmstedt took a relaxed view. "Why not? In a free society anything is possible."

In Reschke's diary Alexandra's question and Timmstedt's openmindedness are followed by a reference to the distant future. "These good people, Marczak in the lead, are in for a surprise: after briefly bearing the name of its founder, Burgomaster Daniel Gralath (whose escutcheon, incidentally, shows a lion shouldering two silver crutches), Grunwaldzka, once Grosse Allee then Hindenburgallee then Stalinallee, will finally bear the name of my Bengali business associate, to whom the whole world is indebted for the advancement of innercity rickshaw traffic . . ."

In the very next sentence, to be sure, which was written at a distance in time, as has now become frequent for Reschke, he corrects himself: "Because of Chatterjee's modesty and under pressure from the influential Bengali minority, Grunwaldzka has been named Rabindranath-Tagore-Allee. Nothing unusual, when Alexandra and I think how many streets, squares, cities, stadiums, and shipyards have in our lifetime discarded and renewed their names, after every about-face of history, as though there will never be an end to naming and renaming."

————

224

It should not be assumed that the meeting recorded here took place on the seventeenth floor of the Hotel Hevelius. The city magistrate had allotted the Cemetery Association a room in the nearby Old City Rathaus, with a heavy oak conference table and a dozen antique Danzig oak chairs, a perfect seventeenth-century setting.

There are photos of the meeting at the long table. Partners Dettlaff and Marczak preside executively at the head of the table, while at the foot of the table, by the door, sit our couple, the still-honorary chairmen. The Board members have taken their places on either side, but the German and Polish contingents no longer sit stiffly facing each other; a mixed seating arrangement has developed. As chairman, Vielbrand sits between the two new members; to his left, the young directress of the tourist agency, her hair demurely parted in Madonna style. I recognize Vielbrand by the rimless glasses and brush-cut hair often mentioned by Reschke. I can say with assurance that the tall seated gentleman, whose silvery wavy hair looks like a wig adapted to the period furniture, is consistory councilor Karau shortly after his resignation. The man pointedly bored and lolling in his chair has to be—you could tell even without his clerical garb—Father Bieroński, likewise resigned. As for the remaining members, I can't tell by their looks whether they are of the Polish or the German nation; relatively young, they show little personality but radiate abundant good nature, combined with an easygoing determination to achieve, which will benefit the treasury of the Cemetery Association. That fellow over there, youthful and vigorous, may be Torsten Timmstedt, attempting with the help of models no larger than matchboxes to familiarize the Board with the new coffin culture.

Through a magnifying glass I make out coffins egg-shaped, ziggurat-shaped, pyramid-shaped, and denatured-to-violin-case shaped, which Timmstedt as part of his customer service will carry in stock along with the traditional model which is tapered at the foot. With their postmodern inspiration they are intended to liberate the funeral business from unbending routine. Even Snow White's glass coffin is in the offing. Reschke has this to say on the subject: "Quite defensible, this artistic re-working of the classical coffin form, which has come to seem decadent and pretentious . . . But I had no difficulty approving Timmstedt's suggestion that coffins made of tropical woods such as teak, mahogany, and Brazilian rosewood should be prohibited . . ."

And the still vigorous lady and the casually elegant vice president, what did they have to say about the latest "earth furniture"? It is only the seating arrangement, the window behind them, that gives these two the appearance of a pair, whereas the honorary chairmen, though not yet married, strike one as a couple even photographed from behind high chairs and more surmised than seen.

The photos don't tell us much more. Uncomfortable and hard-edged as they may be, the sumptuously carved backs of the highly polished, solemnly dark-brown chairs create an illusion of Baroque solidity: the astronomer and master brewer Johann Hevelius, who once belonged to the Old City council and lived in nearby Pfefferstadt, might well take his place belatedly among the representatives of the German-Polish Cemetery Association to report on the phases of the moon or the cost of burying his recently deceased wife Catharina née Rebeschke . . .

My material is running out, but there's still a pile of notes at my elbow, full of leads that have not been followed. According to one note, Reschke intended to have a talk with Timmstedt about the new coffin culture, also to suggest the founding of a new necropolis near the formerly East Prussian city of Rastenburg, and furthermore to mount an exhibition designed to establish a historical bridge connecting "Etruscan sarcophagi, tombs, and ossuaries with the latest artistic creations . . ." Nothing came of it. Unless Timmstedt promoted exhibitions of this kind at a later date.

In another handsomely penned note, Alexandra is advised to collect documentation about her membership in the United Workers' Party, in order to have answers ready should she stand accused. There is no such documentation in my possession. Only this much is certain: she joined as a youthful believer and dropped out, disillusioned, at the age of fifty. At the World Youth Festival in Bucharest, she had praised Stalin, in a brief speech, as the liberator of Poland. Later came doubt, vacillation, playing the game, shame, silence, playing dead. "I was card-file corpse, as Germans say, long before 1968 when the anti-Semitic schweinerei started in Warsaw . . ."

In Reschke's diary this is accompanied with his sympathy: "She accuses herself, lists sins of omission, but insists that up to her official withdrawal—'I couldn't take martial law'—like a good Communist she kept hoping against hope. What consolation could I offer her? My own stupid stubbornness? The unshakable credulity of a Hitler Youth? We'll just have to live with it. We are still living with it. And then, to top it all, our idea failed . . ."

The following weekend they took a trip to Kashubia. True, Wróbel was at the wheel, but they were not riding in his Polski Fiat. Written on a slip of paper: "At last to the country in a new car."

It couldn't have been the weather that tempted them. If everything had come too early the year before, much too early—the rape, the toads—this spring everything came late, much too late. The fruit blossoms had suffered from night frost. Not only the farmers were complaining, the over-all mood was in keeping with the wet, cold May. Report followed report, each filled with disaster, and because nothing was right at home, the politicians took refuge in the vast perspectives of the European idea. Unified, the Germans were more disunited than ever, and free Poland surrendered to the tyrannical decrees of the Church. No sign of spontaneous revival. Even in the middle of May, no rape blossoms in sight.

When the three of them drove out into the country, the weather must have been changeable; now and then, the sun broke through. They drove to the Radaune Lakes, not far from Chmielno. Alexandra had prepared a picnic; this time no pickled Polish mushrooms or hard-boiled eggs. Forked out of cans were Greenland crabmeat and Norwegian smoked salmon; cheese from France, sliced mortadella and salami, Danish beer and Spanish olives. For everything was available now, even a fruit called kiwi from New Zealand, though expensive, too expensive.

The picnic was not to be. Before and after too brief

228

a burst of sunshine, showers poured water on their late lunch. Nevertheless, they stopped. As they walked down from the road to the low-lying lakeshore, it turned out that Alexandra was once again wearing unsuitable shoes. Along the reed-lined shore they found a small bay known to campers, as was clear from the charred, rain-wet remains of a campfire and a semicircle of stones of the kind often found at the edge of fields. "Some are as large as the boulders with simple inscriptions used in the Cemetery of Reconciliation, most recently over the common graves."

A dozen Boy Scouts may have rolled these boulders up to the campfire. Now the three used them as seats. Piątkowska lit a cigarette once, though there were no mosquitoes to give her an excuse. The picnic basket stayed in the car. All three sat silent on their boulders. Voices came from far over the lake, harsh, as though quarreling, then again silence. Wróbel skipped a few stones across the water, and sat down when no one wanted to join him. Again harsh voices in the distance. Then from across the road where they had left the new car, cows bellowing hoarsely, as they do just before slaughter. Silence again, all the more as there were no larks in the sky above the lake.

Reschke described the landscape for me, as though wishing to paint it in watercolor: the loosely planted mixed forest on the left, the fields descending to the lake, a flat-roofed wooden barn on a hill in the foreground, more forest, then more fields with clumps of trees in their midst. Not a boat, not a sail is mentioned, only two ducks swimming in opposite directions. "Rarely does a breeze ruffle the lake."

And then, after having neatly brushed everything in, including the old brown barn, he bestows on the lake a reflection that I can only reproduce in his words: "Though apart from the solitary barn the undulating country above the lake is bare of buildings, unvaried except for the alternation of field and forest, I read a different picture reflected in the smooth surface: the shore ringed not by shingle-brown but by the brick-red roofs of a bungalow colony, which hugs the hill in terraces that carefully conform to the contours of the land yet take possession; small parcels of forest and stands of trees yield to the will of the architect who drew the plans and the builder who carried them out, eliminating any obstruction to the box-on-box compactness of this colony, in which I see the mirror image of a settlement I know from the blueprints. This complex, crowned at the top by a clubhouse (though from my perspective at the bottom), this vast expanse spreading between and across gentle hills, adapted and greened for the game of golf, may strike you as in good taste and even well executed, since from my upside-down point of view this development shows concern for the landscape; and yet the longer I look, the more this reflection in the water fills me with a sorrow that grows, though by now gusts of wind have ruffled the surface of the lake and disturbed the picture. We must go now, Alexandra."

I don't know whether Reschke shared his view of the future—or rather vision—with Piątkowska and Wróbel; if he did, I doubt that they would have been able to see the image in the mirror which foreshadowed the Bungagolf builders' box-on-box activity. He alone could see it. You alone, Reschke, showed foresight. He alone was ahead of the times. But in resigning from their honorary chairmanship of the German-Polish Cemetery Association, Alexander and Alexandra resigned together.

They explained their resignation in writing. In addition, Reschke claims to have sent the Board a tape, in which both spoke, he at length, she in brief. This was done the next day, such was their hurry after they had made their decision.

At the time of their resignation, the Cemetery Association, whose board of directors met in the Old City Rathaus, already had offices of its own near the shipyard, occupying a floor of a highrise built under Gierek. One floor up, the rent was paid by the firm of Chatterjee & Co. Since an audit of all the accounts had shown how profitably Reschke had invested the diversified capital of the Cemetery Association, though unbeknownst to the Board—only Marczak knew but kept it to himself—and how he had put it, as it accrued, into the new assembly plants, thus linking rickshaw production with the interests of the Cemetery Association, it seemed only appropriate that the administrations of the expanding Association and of the firm aiming at the export market should have their offices one above the other in the same building.

There Reschke delivered the tape and also Alexandra's PC. In his explanation—and on the tape—he pointed out that this computer, linked with his home computer in Bochum, had served faithfully in realizing the idea of reconciliation. He even quipped: "It goes without saying that we are delivering our hard disk absolutely virus-free."

The taping was done at night. A first attempt, unsuccessful, was made on the lakeshore. "The weather was too unsettled. Not even suitable for a picnic. This spring everything comes too late. That, no doubt, is why no toads were heard . . ."

The second nocturnal attempt succeeded, thanks to some manipulation. "The toad song that we recorded last year among osier willows on the flat Island in the spring, a spring that started early, too early, proved helpful. At that time we recorded over a long period of time the melodious though profoundly melancholy calls of a few courting lowland toads, which we now took as the background for our spoken text or, rather, our valedictory message. We used the pauses between call and call, allowing nature to add emphasis to our admonitions."

I have copies of the written text only, but since Reschke's junk includes last year's toad calls, I can imagine the effect of this device on the assembled board of directors. The younger members probably reacted with no more than amused headshaking. Vielbrand, I am sure, tapped his forehead, and Frau Dettlaff may have called under her breath for a psychiatrist. Undoubtedly Marczak, with his taste for theatrics, enjoyed this offering. As for Timmstedt, I'm willing to believe that he regarded the whole thing as a successful collage.

Piątkowska's text, written and spoken in Polish, is brief; I've had it translated. Announcing her resignation, she says: "Since it is the duty of an honorary chairwoman to do honor, since the people she chairs should do her honor, and since in this Association I find no honor but only greed, I hereby terminate my membership."

Reschke's declaration is longer. Once again he projects his favorite subject, the Century of Expulsions, on a wide screen, beginning with the Armenians, omitting no refugees' exodus or forced resettlement, and finally bringing himself up to date with the expulsion of the Kurds. From the worldwide loss of homelands he then develops his and Alexandra's original idea, the homecoming of the dead, the idea of reconciliation, and cries out: "Two-and-a-half square meters of home soil are and remain a human right." He juxtaposes this right with the limited supply of cemeteries, goes on to question the quality of the soil contaminated by sewage, pesticides, and the excessive use of fertilizer, and now reflects, with the help of the foreshadowing sight experienced recently on the shore of a Kashubian lake, on the environmental consequences of the Bungagolf projects now in the planning stage, makes use of words such as "thieving," "abomination," "devil's work," paints a picture of ruthless land grabbing, says, "swan song, never again, a world lost," and then suddenly, without transition, looks back on the activities of the German-Polish Cemetery Association from a distance of ten years. "Now that I am forced to recognize that the leases taken out on cemetery land have in many places become titles of ownership, and worse, that the shores of the Masurian and Kashubian lakes, which used to mirror the clouds, have been overbuilt, made ugly, and laid waste by greed, I am assailed by doubt: Was our idea good and right? Even with right thinking and good intention, it led to evil. Today I know we failed, but I also see that some good has come of it. Right can come from wrong. Frugal Asia is setting the table for German gluttony. The Polish-Bengali symbiosis is blooming into marriage. It is proving to a nation of shopkeepers that titles of ownership are of limited value. It announces the predestined Asian future of Europe, free from nationalistic narrowness, no longer hemmed in by language boundaries, polyphonically religious, superrich in gods, and above all blessedly slowed down, softened by the new warm and wet climate . . ."

As I did with Alexandra's few words, I hear the song of the low-country toads accompanying these of the future. After each image, their melancholy song sets a caesura. Our couple could not have conceived of a more beautiful exit.

It was red-bellied toads, which have always been abundant in the low country of the Island. Ah, how frightened we children had been of the osier willows in the evening mist, ghosts coming ever closer. And then the alluring call of the males with their vocal bladders, who floated on the surface of the intricate system of drainage ditches. When the water temperature rose, the intervals between toad calls shortened. On a warm day in May a red-bellied toad, also known as a low-country or fire toad, could emit as many as forty calls a minute. If several were calling at once, their lament, echoing over the water, would swell to a single endlessly vibrant call.

I assume Reschke taped a chorus only as an overture, then took single low-country toads from the tapes. In this way he was able, between call and call, to highlight words such as "German" or "thieving" or "rights," or for that matter "homeless" or "nevermore." In no better way could the future Polish-Bengali symbiosis have been celebrated than with the help of the word "marriage" highlighted by toad song, a word, incidentally, that occurred more and more often in Reschke's diary as his wedding day approached.

But before I can put the couple in the registry office, something more must be said on the subject of Reschke's relation to automobiles. Since my classmate had occasionally made disparaging remarks about Mercedes drivers and scribbled contemptuous notes about the drivers of BMWs, and since I suspect a connection between his elegantly old-fashioned way of dressing and his taste in cars, I always imagined him driving archaic models on his trips between the Ruhr and Gdańsk, Gdańsk and Bochum; but when shortly before Erna Brakup's resignation I read in his diary, "My car stolen from unattended parking lot," I was sure that the car thieves, whose fences serve as middlemen all over Poland, would never have been tempted to steal and disguise a Skoda or any such ancient jalopy as a 1960 Peugeot 404; no, it would have to be something expensive and Western. Had Reschke tempted thieves with a Porsche? Someone advised me to saddle him with an Alfa Romeo; in the end I decided on a Swedish make, a Saab or Volvo.

In any event he had been without a car since the middle of March. As reported, the couple took the streetcar to visit Erna Brakup's sickbed. On longer trips they were driven by Jerzy Wróbel. And for the funeral at Matarnia they also used the Polski Fiat. Not until their drive to Kashubia to record toad calls—no toad called—did he introduce the "new car" in a note. Again no make is indicated, but it must have been an expensive model, since there was aggravation connected with its purchase.

Immediately after our couple's resignation from the honorary chairmanship, just as they were beginning to feel free, liberated, the board of directors was summoned to a special meeting. Because in her summons Frau Dettlaff had requested the presence of the former honorary chairmen, Reschke and Piątkowska had to submit to questioning about their finances in general and the financing of a new car in particular.

At first the tone was civil; Timmstedt praised the "imaginative and already profitable investments in the firm of Chatterjee & Co.," and Marczak wanted "no scandal." But then the interrogation began. Vielbrand and Dettlaff took turns attacking. There was no hard evidence, true, but plenty of grounds for suspicion. He, Reschke, since the start of the Gulf crisis had speculated on the fluctuations of the dollar; he, Reschke, had accepted special discounts from West German funeral companies without disclosing their amounts; he, Reschke, could not show from which account his new car, the car which must now be considered a private vehicle, had been financed—possibly from bequests?

Here Alexandra intervened: "Why not tell them your rickshaw man made you nice present?"

"That would be inappropriate."

"But if they treat you like thief?"

"Let them."

"But people stole old car from parking lot . . ."

"That's my business."

"All right, I tell them. Expensive car was given for his help in bicycle rickshaw production."

"Alexandra, please . . ."

"Why don't somebody laugh? Is funny, no?"

Timmstedt seems to have started the laughter, and Marczak gave it weight by seconding it. All the new members laughed as though infected. Finally even Vielbrand and Dettlaff discovered the funny side of Chatterjee's gift. Vielbrand was said to have "giggled at first, then burst into a loud, neighing guffaw." The best Dettlaff could manage was a "pinched smile," which suddenly turned to ice and put an end to the general merriment.

It was Alexandra's turn to be subjected to a barrage of questions. When nothing could be pinned on her but failure to make a sufficiently clear record of a donation for the Corpus Christi Church organ, Dettlaff got personal. She poked around in Piątkowska's past, quoting from a private file she had somehow got hold of. "You as a Communist of long standing," she thundered, "ought to know . . ." Or: "Even from a Communist one is entitled to expect . . ." She treated Alexandra's Party membership as a crime, even had Alexandra's 1953 hymn to Stalin at her fingertips, and with barbed vagueness conjured up "a disastrous connection between Stalinism and the Jews," "especially disastrous for Poland, am I right, Pan Marczak?" And Marczak nodded.

Piątkowska made no reply, but Reschke did. After presenting himself to the assembled board of directors as a former troop leader in the Hitler Youth, he asked Dettlaff what her rank had been in the League of German Girls; "You see how it is, my dear? Our generation ran with the hounds." Whereupon Johanna Dettlaff blushed to the roots of her silvery hair. And when Marian Marczak cast down his eyes and broke the general silence with "No one here is without a past," all acquiesced.

Reschke writes: "Even Gerhard Vielbrand was able to share this insight. He cried out, 'Enough discussion.' The young members of the Board, in any case, could not have cared less about the old stories. Timmstedt's mocking confession, 'To think that at the age of nineteen I was a Young Socialist, Statemonocap,' sparked more laughter, but the meeting ended on a sour note.

And Chatterjee's controversial gift? Well, it didn't bring us luck . . ."

No one was unmasked, the special meeting had no consequences, the couple remained unshorn, and Reschke's new car, a Volvo—yes, now I'm sure a Volvo— was in the attended parking lot between the theater and the Stockturm, across the way from the Arsenal, in mid-May, when the wedding provided an occasion for celebration.

However, they did not ride to the registry office in the product of a Swedish assembly line but in a bicycle rickshaw of Bengali-Polish make. This—what a surprise—was Alexandra's wish. She who had found "this Mr. Chatterjee" creepy, who had called the Bengali a "phony Englisher" and in her Catholic godlessness accused him of witchcraft and worse, "devilry—she, the gildress, absolutely insisted on riding to the Right City Rathaus in a rickshaw. "I want to drive up like queen, if not in carriage then in rickshaw."

It was probably just a whim, for Chatterjee and his cousins remained alien to her. Her standard pronouncement, which Reschke collected along with Piątkowska's other sayings, was: "I will never get used to so many Turks in Poland as soon as Russians gone." As often as he tried to explain the origin of the rickshaw manufacturer to his Alexandra—going so far as to spread the atlas out before her—she stuck to her rejection of the Turk, all Turks, in other words, all foreigners. She despised them all, even more than the Russians.

Piątkowska took a historic view of the matter. As a Pole, she tended to see everything in terms of the martyrdom of the Polish people. She usually went back to the battle of Liegnitz, in which a duke of the glorious house of Piast met his death while turning back the Mongols. After this first rescue of the West by Polish heroism, it was the turn of Jan Sobieski, the Polish king who defeated the Turks at the gates of Vienna. Once again the West could breathe easy. "Ever since that battle," said Alexandra, "all Turks are thirsting for revenge, and that goes for your Mr. Chatterjee too." Recently, she began to sniff out a plot. "Already see German gentlemen bringing their Turks with them to turn us into political coolies."

She often laughed after her historical snap judgments, as though implying by her laughter that it need not come to the worst. And yet she overcame her prejudice, for she liked the many sparklingly clean rickshaws with their melodious three-note bells that brought life into the Old and Right cities. "Air already much better," she cried.

In Reschke I read: "At last the time had come. A pity Chatterjee wasn't in town, or he would have taken us to the Rathaus himself. Even Alexandra was delighted with his wedding present, the delicate model of a bicycle rickshaw wrought in gold wire. Her childlike clapping after unpacking the miniature replica and discovering the two of us as dolls in the passenger seat of the golden rickshaw. 'Aren't we beautiful!' she cried. In time she and Chatterjee would surely have made friends. Unfortunately, just as we were exchanging rings, he had to take a quick trip to Paris and then on to Madrid, where the chaotic inner-city traffic awaited remedy by means of the bicycle rickshaw. One of his cousins pedaled us. And today, after so many years, when I remember that day in May . . ."

Of course their ride in the rickshaw was good for several photos, which I have before me in color. According to Reschke's labeling, it was the very latest model of the shipyard production. On the back of one photo, written in handsome script: "After a rigorous trial run, most recently outside Europe—in Rio—it can be said that the future belongs to this model."

The rickshaw carrying the bridal couple in the photos is adorned with flowers. No, no asters this time, tulips. "Peonies are late this year, like everything else." In a second rickshaw of the same model sit the witnesses Jerzy Wróbel and Helena, a gildress colleague of Alexandra's, who specializes more in calligraphy. The photos transmit neither sunshine nor showers. It must have been cool, because Alexandra is wearing a large woolen scarf over her suit. Nevertheless the couple are dressed for summer: he in a linen suit the color of sea sand and a straw hat with a narrow brim; she in a broad-rimmed violet hat and a snug tailored suit whose color Reschke described as "a warm Neapolitan yellow veering to gold."

From the house on Hundegasse—cocktails for friends and neighbors had been served on the front terrace— the two rickshaws pedaled down the street to the Riding Academy, past the National Bank and the Stockturm, then by way of the Coal Market and the Lumber Market to the Big Mill, from where they turned into familiar Old City territory—Kiek in de Köck, covered market, Dominican church. From there they passed through everyday market bustle, went down Wollwebergasse past the Arsenal, turned left into Langgasse, to the left of which, just before the Leningrad Cinema, still named after Leningrad, a gambling casino the width of two house fronts had been open only a few days. While above, deceptive imitations of Renaissance gables were rotting, below, Western glitter promised lasting riches. TRY YOUR LUCK! said a sign in English.

Langgasse as usual was crawling with tourists, who according to Reschke's note applauded when the flower-bedecked rickshaw with the bridal pair rolled slowly past in the direction of the Rathaus. Congratulations were shouted in Polish and German. One of a multitude of pigeons let something fall on the brim of his hat. "Brings luck, Aleksander. Brings luck!" cried the bride.

Actually, weddings were performed in the Rathaus only in exceptional cases, but Alexandra had succeeded in elevating this particular administrative act, and with it our couple, to the rank of an exceptional case. Over the years she had made a significant contribution to the interior of the late-Gothic edifice; past consoles, up the winding staircase, past Baroque drapery and luxuriant mirror frames—everywhere she was able to cry out: "This was done with gold leaf from my gilder's cushion."

About the actual ceremony Reschke writes only that it was performed "on the dot of eleven" in the Red Hall, in the presence of a wall-wide painting entitled *The Tribute Money,* in the center of which Jesus with a Biblical retinue stands in the Long Market, knowing that the Rathaus, where the couple are saying yes to each other, is behind him. An appropriate setting for an art historian who is getting married to a gildress. Not only the bridal couple but the witnesses as well believed themselves, so long as the ceremony was in progress, to be inside a treasure room of another time.

Because the sun suddenly broke through, pictures were taken, showing the newlyweds beside the Neptune Fountain and the Artushof, sometimes with, sometimes without, their witnesses. He in his beige linen suit, already wrinkled, she in her Neapolitan yellow suit, he in his narrow-brimmed straw hat, she shaded by an extravagantly overhanging brim—both look as if they were already traveling far away.

Then they walked across the Long Market into Ankerschmiedegasse. Everywhere street signs in several languages. Reschke had reserved a table for four in a restaurant nearby. No relatives had been invited, for our couple had notified neither his daughters nor her son; since the disastrous Christmas trip, I find no reference to family.

In the diary it is recorded in time-leaping retrospect: "We had perch filets in dill sauce followed by roast pork. Alexandra was in infectious high spirits. The girlish exuberance with which she—successfully, as I know today—was matchmaking between Wróbel and Helena, and her laughter of that day, both have remained true to themselves. If I remember rightly, she said, 'Why hasn't silly goose Alexandra been riding in rickshaw whole time!' "

No wonder Jerzy Wróbel and Alexandra's colleague were soon on easy terms. They laughed about the president of the Republic and his court at the Belvedere Palace in Warsaw. They talked about the impending visit of the Pope—Wróbel expected the Pope to have more influence on conditions in Poland than Piątkowska was willing to give the Vicar of God credit for. Then the discussion turned to S. Ch. Chatterjee. Speculations that the recently reported assassination of an Indian politician might have necessitated the Bengali's sudden departure gave way to other horrors. The eruptions of Mount Pinatubo. Not a word about the Cemetery Association until coffee was served.

Out of the blue, Wróbel suggested that someone should write a history of the Cemetery of Reconciliation, no matter in what language, not forgetting the history of the United Cemeteries of Sts. Catherine, Mary, Joseph, Bridget, etc., nor the brutal way in which they were leveled. In his black suit—rented, Reschke presumes—Wróbel grew solemn: Considering how much has been achieved in a single year, he said, it should be possible to write an account of the German-Polish Cemetery Association which would of necessity include a certain amount of criticism but should on the whole be positive. He said this even though for certain unpleasant reasons he had been obliged to resign. Such a history could place everything in a proper perspective. In Poland as well as Germany there would be no lack of interested readers. There was plenty of material. The one thing needed was a writer keen on detail.

Did the employee of the municipal land office see himself as the author? Or was he thinking of Reschke, whom he would be glad to assist with his knowledge of the registry of deeds?

Alexandra said: "We are much too deep in everything what happened and everything what went wrong."

Reschke said: "This kind of thing can be understood and thoroughly evaluated only from a distance in time."

Alexandra: "But history must be written now. Later will be too late. You must write it, Aleksander, how it all was."

Alexandra's colleague Helena was of the same opinion. But my former classmate had no wish to become an author. Piątkowska claimed that all she could write was love letters. Did Reschke, immediately after this conversation, start looking for someone with the writing itch; or did he, the moment Wróbel suggested a history, already have me in mind, his classmate filtered out of his childhood memories?

As though he had guessed the best way to snare me,

he wrote in the letter enclosed with all his junk: "You're the only one who can do it. You always enjoyed being more factual than the facts . . ."

In conclusion Jerzy Wróbel is said to have made a speech, from which only this much is communicated: "Our friend said little about the wedding, but parting with Olek and Ola made him say a good deal, and movingly, about the many things that grieved him . . ."

I, too, would be glad to take my leave now, and wish I could end my report at this point. Has everything, then, been said? How automatically the cemeteries of reconciliation fill up. The Germans return home as dead men and women. The future belongs to the bicycle rickshaw. Poland is not yet lost. Alexander and Alexandra are happily married. This ending would please me.

But the two of them went off on their honeymoon. Where to? Here is her answer: "If all Poles now can go where they like without visa, I finally want to see Naples."

They had planned to go by way of Slovenia and Trieste; instead, warned by the latest news reports, they took the classical route across Brenner Pass and straight down the boot to Rome. I know that the new car in which they drove south was a Volvo 440. No stops in eastern Germany. Of course they visited Assisi and Orvieto. The Volvo, like all Swedish cars, is believed to be especially stable. Soon after the wedding, and shortly before the Polish Pope visited Poland in stormy weather and kissed without a moment's delay the concrete runway over Polish soil, Alexander and Alexandra took off. There are photos only of their stays in Siena, Florence, and Rome, all alike, she no longer in a broad-rimmed hat but in a white kibbutz cap. Since he sent me his junk from Rome, I'm not sure whether they ever got to Naples. They probably left the Volvo in the hotel garage.

In pictures snapped by obliging tourists, the couple look happy, even in front of the Pantheon. He had wanted to visit this dome-shaped edifice. And in the middle of the rotunda, with a view of the hemisphere all the way to the circular opening at the top, their hearts, Reschke writes, swelled. Not Raphael's tomb but Hadrian's temple had made them light, lifted them up.

"Too many people of course, but no crowding. The noble magnitude of this idea-made-architecture dwarfs us humans, and yet an upward glance over the five tiers of coffered vault sets the spirit free; in the middle of this exhilarating space an elderly gentleman, obviously English, suddenly began to sing. His fine though slightly tremulous voice tested the dome, at first hesitantly, then boldly. He sang something by Purcell, and was applauded for it. Then a young Italian woman with a peasantlike charm sang with bravura, Verdi of course. She too was applauded. I hesitated a long while. Alexandra was plucking my sleeve, wanting to go. Then I stood under the dome, not to sing, I couldn't do that; no, I released a single toad call into the opening of the dome—short long long, short long long. Over and over. The dome of the Pantheon was as if built for toad calls, perhaps because its height and diameter are equal. My performance, Alexandra told me later, reduced the tourists all around to silence, even the Japanese. Not a camera clicked. But I was not the caller, it was the toad from deep within me . . . I stood there like the statue of a caller, my head tilted far back, my mouth open, my hat held to one side, and the toad call was lifted up from me, high up into the opening of the dome and beyond. Alexandra put it all in her own words: "People were all struck dumb and didn't even clap little."

Afterward they sat in a sidewalk café and wrote post-cards to nobody. Reschke's last entries reflect his condition, strained by time leaps: "Unfortunately many of the museums are closed. Since Alexandra is willing to visit 'three churches per day, tops,' where she would light asparagus-thin candles wherever possible, plenty of time is left for leisurely strolling and her beloved espresso. The Etruscan sarcophagi are always beautiful. With delight we both contemplate the wedded couples hewn in stone, lying on their sides, on the lids of stone coffins. In some of the couples we discover ourselves. What a privilege to lie like that! But Alexandra absolutely refuses to go near the catacombs. 'No more death and skeleton bones,' she exclaims. 'From now on we just live.' And so we live out our years. Interesting, how Rome has changed since our first visit. Even then we took a rickshaw for all our longer trips, across the Tiber to the Vatican. It was there, seven years ago, that she decided to stop puffing cigarettes and made her famous remark: 'Is funny. Pope in Poland, and me looking up at St. Peter's.' At that time the inner-city traffic, in spite of the rickshaws, was still dominated by cars, but today we can say: Rome has no fumes, no constant honking, only the melodious sound of the three-note bells. Friend Chatterjee has won—and we with him . . ."

In his covering letter, written on Roman hotel stationery, my classmate, apart from the date on the letter-head, dispensed with time leaps. Strictly factual, it gives a general outline of the submitted material and suggests that I write a history or report. "And please don't let yourself be carried away by certain events that sound like fiction; I know you prefer to tell stories . . ." And then he appeals to my memories of shared schooldays. "Surely you remember the war years when our whole class was ordered to the Kashubian fields. No matter how much it rained, no one was allowed to come in from the field until he had filled three liter bottles to the brim with potato bugs . . ."

Yes, Alex, I remember. You organized us. With you, we were successful. Your method of collecting was exemplary. We made a profit. And lazy dog that I was, always dreaming, you gave me a hand; often you even made me a present of my third bottle and helped top off my second. Those disgusting black-and-yellow striped bugs. It's true, I'm in your debt. That is the only reason I'm writing this report to the end. That's a fact. I tried to keep myself out of the story. I managed to skip the more romantic episodes. But did you absolutely have to go on that honeymoon, damn it?

At the end of his covering letter, he writes: "We're moving on tomorrow. Even though I warned her about conditions there, Naples remains Alexandra's long-cherished wish. I fear she will be disappointed. As soon as we get back, you will hear from me . . ."

That was the last I heard from him. The end, if there ever is an end, is documented. It happened on the way to Naples or on the way back. No, not in the Alban Hills. There's plenty of room between Rome and Naples.

Since it happened three days after their departure, I assume that Alexandra saw Naples, was shocked, and in a hurry to get back. On a winding stretch of road it must have thrown them off—but who is *it*? A sheer

247

drop of a hundred feet—even for a Volvo that's too much. Overturned several times. At the foot of the precipice, built on a rounded crest, there's a village, and just outside it, in an open field, encircled by a wall and planted with cypresses, a cemetery.

The police were helpful when I came to inquire and search. The priest, the mayor confirmed: the car a total wreck, the bodies charred. Nevertheless, the police report made it clear: it was a Volvo. Everything burned, even the papers in the glove compartment. Intact, because they had been thrown from the car when it turned over, and over, were a leather slipper and a crocheted string bag.

I won't give the name of the village in whose cemetery they lie right by the wall. I'm sure, as far as I can be sure, that Alexander and Alexandra lie there nameless. Only two wooden crosses mark their double grave. I won't have them reburied. They were against reburial. From that village cemetery there is a long view across the country. I thought I could see the sea. They are lying well there. There let them lie.